A girl could get used to this!

Bridget watched in awe as Darwin moved effortlessly from one saucepan to another. She closed her eyes and then pinched herself. If this wasn't real, she needed to wake up before things between her and Darwin went any further.

When Bridget opened her eyes again, Darwin was there, still moving as though he'd always belonged right there in her kitchen and in her life. As he pulled a tablespoon of simmering sauce to his lips, blowing lightly over the hot substance, Bridget closed her eyes for a second time, imagining what it might be like to have those lips blowing warm breath against her skin....

Books by Deborah Fletcher Mello

Kimani Romance

In the Light of Love
Always Means Forever

Kimani Arabesque

Forever and a Day
The Right Side of Love
A Love for All Time
Take Me to Heart

DEBORAH FLETCHER MELLO

is the author of seven romance novels. Her first novel, *Take Me to Heart,* earned her a 2004 Romance Slam Jam nomination for Best New Author. In 2005 she received Book of the Year and Favorite Heroine nominations for her novel *The Right Side of Love.*

For Deborah, writing is akin to breathing and she firmly believes that if she could not write she would cease to exist. Weaving a story that leaves her audience feeling full and complete, as if they've just enjoyed an incredible meal, is an ultimate thrill for her. Born and raised in Connecticut, she now calls Hillsborough, North Carolina, home, where she resides with her husband and son.

ALWAYS *Means* FOREVER

DEBORAH FLETCHER MELLO

KIMANI
ROMANCE

In memory of my son,
Allan Miquel Mello, Jr.,

Mere words cannot begin to express
how much you are missed.

Your spirit continues to move and inspire me,
And you will always be remembered with much love

KIMANI PRESS™

ISBN-13: 978-0-373-86021-0
ISBN-10:   0-373-86021-8

ALWAYS MEANS FOREVER

www.kimanipress.com

Printed in U.S.A.

Dear Reader,

This has been a roller-coaster ride filled with exceptional highs. I can't begin to tell you how much I love doing what I do. I know that this journey has been an incredible blessing and only possible because of a truly powerful and loving God.

I am extremely grateful to each and every one of you who has supported my writing by buying a book, borrowing a book, or sharing a book. Thank you for the kind words, the heartfelt expressions of love and those accolades for my many characters. As you have cheered each of them on, so have you cheered me on, as well. I can't begin to tell you how you all have nurtured my spirit.

I'd love to know what you think of Bridget and Darwin's story, so I hope you'll send me your comments at www.deborahmello.com or www.deborahmello.blogspot.com. Until the next time, take care and God bless.

With much love,

Deborah Fletcher Mello

Chapter 1

Bridget Hinton knew she had to be dreaming. Things like this never happened to her in real life, so the moment— and the man who stood above her—had to be a dream. It was such an erotic dream that she hoped she would never wake from it, or at least not until he, whoever he was, was finished doing what he was doing.

And what he was doing was massaging a slow, heated path up and down the length of her body. His long, firm, very experienced fingers were stroking every muscle until she was a weak puddle of female mush. He was triggering a reaction in every part of her to a point of no return. Teasing the curves of her breasts, he gently brushed the back of his hand against the lush tissue and her nipples blossomed full and hard. Her chest began to rise and fall faster than normal as she gasped for air. Bridget felt as if her flesh was straining for release against a satin night-gown that suddenly seemed to melt away from her body at will.

Sunlight shimmered above her, radiating from a clear, bright blue sky. She could hear the ripple of water coming from someplace close, and a warm breeze scented the air with the aroma of honeysuckle and tea roses. She took a deep inhale of fresh air and held her breath. She struggled to focus on the man who had her writhing in ecstasy, wanting to see his face. For a split second, the very handsome man bore a striking resemblance to majestic Laurence Fishburne in the movie *Othello*. A minute later he looked like a very sexy Djimon Hounsou, then the actor Dennis Haysbert. Bridget could feel herself smiling in her sleep. This was surely too good to be true!

Laurence-Djimon-Dennis was now naked, a solid six-foot-four-inch tower of rippling, Hershey's dark choco-late-toned muscle. His skin glistened with perspiration, light shimmering over the sinewy fibers. She examined every inch of him, her gaze caressing the broad wealth of his expansive chest, lingering on the firm, well-rounded globes of his behind that overfilled her small palms, and the thick length of male steel swaying blatantly between them.

He was palming both of her breasts beneath slightly rough hands, the contact against her skin moving her to moan. Her mouth parted just slightly as her tongue trailed slowly over the surface of her lips. As her dream lover eased himself above her, she could feel her body falling open, her legs parting eagerly. Her limbs felt light and buoyant, her body possessed as it moved in sync with his. The moment was suddenly electric, energy spinning her beyond her wildest dreams. And just as she could feel herself being consumed by the rise of heat, perspiration dancing against her skin, she woke up.

The clock radio on the nightstand beside her was buzzing harshly and Bridget was startled to find herself awake, and alone. It seemed as if it took forever for her mind to catch up with her body, the memories fading ever so slowly, and then she remembered that she was home, in her own bed, no man remotely close to making love to her.

A creeping dampness in her panties made her close her slim thighs tightly together. The dream had been too real, her body responding with a mind of its own. Turning to see what time it was, Bridget reached for the digital timepiece, depressing the alarm's off button. She squinted through the darkness at the pale green numbers on the clock. It was still early, not yet two o'clock in the morning. It dawned on her that she had set her alarm incorrectly, not paying attention before she'd turned over and had gone to sleep. She still had at least five hours of rest coming to her, and with any luck she could still take advantage of them.

A full bladder was suddenly calling her name and as she moved to get out of bed, pain bristled down the length of her right leg. Bridget swore, clutching the limb between her palms as she was suddenly reminded that her day had started badly and had only gotten worse with each passing hour, the wealth of it peaking on her return home.

She had literally tripped through the door of her town house, falling face-first across the threshold as the heel of her Ferragamo pump had lost a battle with the new doormat she'd purchased on discount from the Macy's department store in downtown Seattle. Pain had exploded from the center of her bruised kneecap, triggering a trail of hurt down the length of the limb, up her thigh and into her hip. Profanity had spilled over her lips as she'd cursed loudly, not caring that her next-door neighbor, Mrs. Eloise Gibson, had been watching from her own entranceway.

As she'd lain sprawled facedown against the foyer's tiled floor, Bridget couldn't help but think that her falling was an apropos ending for what had been a hellish day. Tears had burned hot against the back of her eyelids as she'd kicked off the overpriced shoes and pulled herself up and onto her feet. The old woman was still staring, her gray head and a wrinkled appendage waving for Bridget's attention.

"Are you okay, dear?" she'd asked.

Bridget had forced a smile on her face and had nodded her head. "Yes, ma'am. I'm fine, thank you. Just clumsy is all."

"Are you sure now? I can call somebody if you need me to."

"That's not necessary, Mrs. Gibson."

"Well, if you say so…"

"Thanks for everything, Mrs. Gibson. You have a nice evening," Bridget chimed as she'd moved too quickly to close her front door. As she'd secured the lock, she'd heaved a deep sigh and had cussed again. Reaching for her purse, she'd picked up the contents that had scattered across the floor and dropped them all onto the wooden bench that decorated the entranceway.

Wanting to cry, she'd let the first wave of hot tears flow over her cheeks, her palm rubbing gingerly against her bruised leg. Before the tears could flood into a full sob the telephone on the end table at her side rang, pulling at her attention.

Bridget had shaken her head as she'd pulled the receiver into her hand, noting the familiar number on the caller ID. "Hello?"

"You have some mail, dear!"

"Thank you, Mrs. Gibson."

"Just wanted you to know."

"Yes, ma'am."

As she hung up the telephone, Bridget heaved another deep sigh. She had grown weary of the old woman's timely reminders ages ago but had kept her annoyance to herself because Mrs. Gibson was better than any alarm system would ever be. Her watchful eye monitored all the comings and goings that occurred between her door and the entrances of the other occupants who resided in the small complex. And, for the most part, she was actually very sweet when she wanted to be.

Making her way to the rear of her home, Bridget had moved into the kitchen, searching her freezer for an ice pack to hold off the swelling. She had to be in court early the next morning and she didn't need a bum leg slowing her down. The telephone ringing for a second time served to further distract her.

"Hello?"

"Bridget, turn on your television!" a voice had screamed from the other end.

"What? Jeneva? Is that you?"

"Of course it's me. Turn on your television. Channel 76. Hurry!"

Bridget had reached for the remote and turned on the small, seven-inch monitor that was positioned beneath her oak cabinets. Her best friend's excitement filled her ears.

"Isn't he adorable! Look how cute he is! Hold on. I have to call Roshawn."

Jeneva's brother-in-law, Darwin Tolliver, beamed at Bridget from the television screen, the good-looking man promoting his new cooking show on the Homes and Food Network. He *had* been cute. Too cute, and Bridget had only been reminded that yet another man she'd been interested in hadn't been interested in her.

Jeneva came back on the line. "Roshawn's not home. I'll have to call her later. So, what's up with you?" she'd asked cheerily.

Bridget took a seat at the kitchen counter. "I lost my job."

"What?" Jeneva's voice was brimming with surprise. "What happened?"

"The partners are merging with another firm. It seems the new partners already have one intelligent, skilled, black female attorney on the roster and they don't feel they have a need for a second."

"Oh, sweetie! I'm so sorry," her best friend hummed into the receiver.

Bridget nodded. "They'll be transitioning our caseloads over and closing the doors in the next two to six weeks. I will actually be closing out my cases in the next few days so there's really little left for me to do. Then I'll officially be unemployed."

"That stinks. So, what do you plan to do?"

"I don't have a clue."

The two had talked for another hour and when she'd finally hung up the telephone, Bridget had been sufficiently depressed. As she'd sat there staring blankly at the television set, the station ran the commercial for a second time. When Darwin Tolliver crooned his slogan *"Let me show you how it's done!"* a chill had shimmered down her spine, straight into the pit of her stomach. What she wouldn't give to have Darwin Tolliver show her anything his heart desired, she'd thought, the words floating into the empty room as she spoke them out loud.

That had only been a few hours ago, and if the dream was any sign, she still had the effects of seeing Darwin on her brain. Her bladder was now screaming loudly and Bridget shook the clouds of memory from her head. She eased her body up onto her feet and limped into the bathroom. Just thinking about Darwin Tolliver again had made her stomach flutter. She'd had a crush on the man since forever. The two had met years ago when his twin brother, Mecan, and her friend Jeneva had fallen head over heels in love. Her infatuation for him had even caused a brief rift between her and her other best friend, Roshawn Bradsher, when she'd accused the woman's playful flirtations with him of being something much more. The two of them had worked through their differences and Bridget had been happy for her girl when Roshawn had gone on to meet and marry the love of her life, famed baseball star Angel Rios. Bridget was now godmother to their two children, three-year-old Dario and infant Belinda.

Between distance, bad timing and other relationships she and Darwin had never managed to hook up, though, and now here she was, still alone, unemployed, dreaming about men who would probably never cross her path. As she slid back beneath the warmth of her covers, Bridget shook her head for the umpteenth time. Things surely

didn't look like they were going to get any better anytime
soon, so she hoped her dream lover would still be hard,
wanting, and waiting for her when she finally fell back
to sleep.

Chapter 2

Darwin Tolliver couldn't help but think that there was something missing, and maybe whatever was missing was the reason he was so out of sorts. He looked around the enclosed office, observing the contemporary decor the television studio had paid far too much money to have installed. If the truth were to be told, the room really didn't give him any warm and fuzzy feelings to get excited about.

Everything from the walls to the carpet and half of the furniture was done in a striking shade of ice-blue. The other half of the furniture was either upholstered in black leather or painted in a high-gloss black lacquer. Polished chrome accents completed the sparse ensemble. The room was supposed to be cutting-edge stylish but as Darwin sat in the midst of it, studying every minute detail, he wished he could have told the interior designer they'd hired that it actually felt very cold and impersonal. He sighed, blowing a warm gust of breath past his full lips.

Reaching for the telephone, he dialed quickly then leaned back in the black leather executive's chair to wait for the line to be answered.

His twin brother's voice bellowed from the other end. "Hello?"

"Hey, Mecan. It's me."

"Yo, Darwin. What's up? How's the new gig?" Mecan Tolliver asked.

Darwin shrugged, his broad shoulders reaching up toward his earlobes. "Starting out well. The show premieres next week and the initial reactions to the promos have been great."

"I saw the commercial for the first time last night. You looked good, boy! You should have heard Jeneva on the phone calling her girls to check out the channel."

"Your wife is too sweet. Tell her I said hello and kiss my niece for me."

"Will do. Alexa's been mimicking you since she saw you on TV. '*Let me show you how it's done!*'" the man said, imitating his child's singsong voice. "It's too cute!" Mecan laughed, the wealth of it brimming over with pride for his five-year-old daughter. "So, for real, how are you doing? You sound a little down."

There was a brief pause and Darwin sat listening to the television set playing in the background on his brother's end. They'd been like two peas in a pod since day one. Mecan was the older by only five minutes and he was Darwin's best friend and closest confidant. Darwin wanted to tell his brother that something was making him feel as blue as the room he sat in, but he hadn't a clue how to express to his sibling what it was or why. Instead he shook the emotion away and changed the subject.

"Nah. All's well here. Just felt like checking in with you."

Mecan Tolliver nodded, his sixth sense kicking in. He shook his head slowly, oblivious to the fact that his brother could not see him through the phone line. "Sounds like there's more going on than you're saying. Why don't we make plans to have lunch tomorrow and you can tell me all about it. We haven't spent any time together in a good while."

"That sounds good," Darwin responded, a hint of gratitude seeping into his tone. "I could use some advice. Why don't you meet me at the Andaluca Restaurant."

"Where's that?"

"In the Mayflower Park Hotel down on Olive Way. A friend of mine is the chef there. I'd like to show him some love."

Mecan smiled into the receiver. "Why does that sound like you're checking up on your competition?"

Darwin chuckled. "Hey, my boy Wayne's one of the best chefs out here. There's no harm in checking out what he's up to."

His brother laughed with him. "If you say so. I'll see you tomorrow at one o'clock. Love you, bro."

"Right back at 'cha."

As the line went dead in his ear, Darwin suddenly felt even more out of sorts than he'd felt before he'd called. After hearing his brother's voice and his excitement as he talked about his family, Darwin realized he was lonely. Labeling the emotion only served to further frustrate him. Perhaps some female companionship could change his

mood, he thought, and hopefully help him move out of this
stupor he seemed to have fallen into. Taking a quick glance
at his wristwatch, he reached for his BlackBerry off the
desktop, sorted through the address index for a telephone
number, then pulled the phone receiver back into his hand
as he dialed. Three rings later a female's sultry voice
answered the call.

"Hey, beautiful. It's me. Got any plans for the night?"

There was something romantic about the atmosphere,
Darwin mused as he took a seat in one of the gray upholstered booths in the Andaluca Restaurant. The room had
an old-world feel to it with its rich fabrics, cherrywood
accents and the exquisite contemporary designs that decorated the walls. He'd arrived a few minutes early, nudging
his way past the blue-eyed hostess with the porcelain
veneer smile to say hello to the chef. His friend had been
guiding a staff of twelve almost effortlessly as they
prepped for the lunch crowd.

As he waited for his brother to arrive he studied the
menu, making mental notes about the food choices. The
selections were very European, fairly simplistic, with
generous offerings of grains, legumes, fruits, vegetables
and an incredible wine list. As Darwin mulled over the selections, it was only his brother's prompt arrival that kept
him from racing back to the kitchen to see if he could be
of any service.

The commotion at the door caught his eye, the young
woman leading Mecan to the table laughing warmly as the
two headed in his direction. Darwin could almost visual-
ize the events that had them chatting so comfortably. The
confused expression on her round face, her neck snapping

back and forth as she did a double take when Mecan had stepped through the door had probably been quite comical. It was a typical reaction when folks saw one and then the other, before realizing there were actually two of them. The young lady dropped a second menu on the table as she gestured toward the empty seat.

"Wow, talk about identical twins! I can't believe how much you two look alike," she exclaimed, her head waving from side to side. "Your brother scared me to death. One minute you were sitting here, then the next minute you were standing by my side. I didn't know what to think at first."

Darwin smiled. "Well, now that you see us together, you can see I'm the better-looking brother." He gave her a quick wink.

Mecan shook his head. "He's not shy, either." He extended his hand toward Darwin, who came to his feet to give him a quick greeting. The duo bumped shoulders in a one-armed embrace before dropping down into their respective seats. "So, how's it going, little brother?" Mecan asked.

Darwin nodded. "Can't complain, big brother."

"Your waitress will be right with you," the blonde said sweetly. "If I can be of any assistance please don't hesitate to let me know."

Darwin winked again. "Thank you."

The two men paused briefly to watch as she sashayed back to the front of the restaurant, both appreciating the overt side-to-side glide of her lean hips. Mecan shook his head as he turned back toward his brother. Making himself comfortable, he clasped his hands together in front of him, eyeing his look-alike curiously. "You don't look sick."

The other man chuckled. "What made you think I was sick?"

"There's something going on with you. I heard it in your voice last night."

Darwin grunted, a low growl rising from his midsection. Mecan noted his brother's avoidance, his eyes dancing around the room, hesitant to meet his.

"Yep. Something's up with you. Spill it."

Darwin heaved a deep sigh as he finally met Mecan's gaze. Just as he opened his mouth to speak, an attractive woman with a rich blue-black complexion moved to the table, a pen and pad in her hand. She smiled warmly, a brilliant row of pearl-white teeth greeting them.

"Hello. My name is Mina. I'm going to be your server today. Would you gentlemen like to start your meal with drinks and an appetizer?"

Darwin nodded, almost grateful for the interruption. "I think we'll start with a *charcuterie* plate, please."

"Very good, sir."

"And, for the entrées, my brother will have the crab tower salad, and I would like to try the North African risotto."

Mina nodded as she jotted their orders quickly. "Will that be all, sir?"

"No, why don't you bring us a bottle of that Bootleg Sauvignon Blanc. And, just to get it out of the way, for dessert we'll try the cheese sampler with the *bûche maître seguin*, the *fiore sardo* and the *tomino*, and two *pots du crème*."

"Yes, sir." Mina smiled sweetly as she gathered their menus, her gaze sweeping from one dark face to the other.

Mecan moved his head from side to side as the woman made her way to the rear of the restaurant and into the kitchen to place their orders. "You kill me! Have we ever gone out to eat together where I got to order my own food?"

Darwin shrugged, the two men laughing warmly together. "Old habits die hard. Just stop me next time."

"Don't worry about it. You must have been reading my mind, 'cause I really wanted to try the crab. Now, what the heck is all that other stuff you ordered? The *charcuterie* and that cheese thing?"

"Their *charcuterie* is just like an antipasto. It's a variety of salamis, pickled peppers, olives, and almonds. On the cheese platter, the *bûche maître seguin* is a goat's milk cheese served with a black fig jam, the other is sheep's milk cheese with paprika and almonds, and the *tomino* is a soft cow's milk cheese wrapped in Cullatello and served with fresh honey."

Mecan shook his head. "Do I dare ask what the cream pot is?"

His brother laughed. *"Pots du crème!* It's caramel and mocha custards with Valrhona chocolate and cinnamon."

Mecan adjusted his napkin into his lap. "Well, it sounds like I'll be eating well this afternoon."

"I told you I wanted to show the chef some love. You do that by ordering and eating well."

His brother leaned back against his cushioned seat. "Now, let's try this again. What's wrong with you?"

Darwin cut his eye toward his brother, then dropped his gaze back down to the table. "Nothing."

"Liar."

"Says you."

"Says anyone who knows you."

The two men locked eyes, Mecan raising his eyebrows

knowingly. "I know because it's not often that you ignore a beautiful woman trying to get your attention and you've ignored two of them."

"What two?"

Mecan shook his head. "I won't even talk about our hostess, but how could you miss the eyes our waitress was giving you?"

Darwin looked over to the woman at the bar, casting furtive looks in his direction as she stood in conversation with the hostess and the bartender. He shrugged again. "You're crazy. And how do you know they weren't looking at you?"

Mecan tossed him a look of annoyance. With his elbows propped against the edge of the table he spun the gold wedding band on his left hand between the thumb and forefinger of his other hand. "I think the fact that I wear a wedding band and you don't might have been the first clue."

His brother rolled his dark eyes and tossed the woman a second look. This time she smiled nervously, embarrassment flooding her face as she almost dropped the platter she'd been carrying.

Leaning forward, his fingers still entwined in front of him, Mecan's expression turned serious. "What's wrong? Don't tell me nothing. I can see it all over your face. Something's not right with you."

Holding his brother's gaze for a second time, Darwin suddenly felt like the younger brother. He leaned forward in his own seat and whispered as if the duo were conspiring together.

"Yeah, but I don't know what it is. It's like…" He paused, gathered his thoughts, then switched gears. "After

I talked to you last night, I went to visit an old friend. She and I kick it every so often."

"Kick it?"

"You know." Darwin rolled his eyes. "We have a sexual understanding."

"Is that what they're calling it these days?"

"You want to hear this or not?"

Mecan gestured for him to continue.

"Well, my girl set the mood right. Candlelight, a bottle of wine, some chocolate syrup…"

Mecan grimaced. "Too much information."

"Don't interrupt me."

"Sorry."

"We spent some time doing a little cuddling, a little tickling, then jumped in the Jacuzzi. Well, when the moment was just right…" there was a moment of hesitation as Darwin felt his cheeks flush with heat "…I couldn't perform." He let his last three words fall quickly from his mouth.

Mecan nodded, fighting not to let a smile cross his face, the muscles pulling against his resolve. Clearly, Darwin didn't find the problem to be a laughing matter. His brother's expression was too serious, a sudden wave of anxiety sweeping over the man. Mecan attempted to assuage his discomfort. "Well, that just happens every now and then," he finally managed to say, his smile not quite a smile as he struggled to keep a straight face.

"Has it ever happened to you?"

Mecan tossed a quick glance over his shoulder, then cast a gaze around the room. He opened his mouth to speak, then closed it again, words failing him.

"See. It doesn't just happen. And that's not all," Darwin said softly.

"You mean there's more?"

"I mean this isn't the first time. I haven't been able to get or keep an erection for weeks now," Darwin confessed, embarrassment painted in his expression.

"Have you seen a doctor?"

He nodded. "The official diagnosis for my problem is—" he paused, leaning in closer as his voice dropped another octave "—erectile dysfunction, and they can't find anything medically wrong to explain it. He thinks I should see a shrink, that maybe it's related to something emotional," he whispered.

"So, what are you waiting for?"

"I'm waiting for it to fix itself," Darwin whined, exasperation balancing his words.

Mina moved toward them with their bottle of wine and two glasses. On her heels another waitress was bringing the appetizers. Once they'd been served, she stepped back, pausing for just a brief moment. "Can I bring you anything else?" she asked politely.

Mecan shook his head. "No, thank you. I'm fine."

She smiled at Darwin again, the look she tossed him a clear invitation for something more. "And you, sir? Can I do anything else for you?" she asked, an air of seduction coating her tone.

Darwin forced himself to return the smile, his expression pained. "This is good for now, Mina. Thank you."

The young woman nodded as she moved to another station, tossing them both a quick look over her shoulder. Her expression was hopeful yet Darwin seemed oblivious.

"I don't know what to do, Mac," he said, his eyes skating over his brother's face.

Mecan took a deep breath. He could only imagine the

man's frustration. He had never played the field the way Darwin had, and the day he'd met his wife, Jeneva, he'd fallen hopelessly in love. He'd known almost instantly that no other woman would ever be able to make him feel the way Jeneva did. As he thought about his wife and their family and compared it to his brother's life, an idea suddenly crossed his mind. As if a lightbulb had gone off in his head, he smiled and nodded.

"You need to settle down. That's what you need."

"Excuse me?"

"You need to fall in love and commit to one woman. I'd bet my last dollar that would cure your problem almost instantly."

Darwin rolled his eyes skyward. "You're crazy."

"No, I'm very serious. That love stick of yours is probably just tired of being shuffled from one bed to another. And I think your heart is, as well. I'm certain if your heart's no longer in it, then you're sure to have problems."

Darwin pondered his brother's comments. He shook his head and the two men locked gazes. *Maybe,* he thought. Just maybe his big brother knew what he was talking about.

The words out of his mouth, though, were pure denial. "I truly doubt that the only cure I need is to settle down with one female happily-ever-after. That fairy-tale crap may have worked for you, but I'm not buying it."

Mecan shrugged, a wry grin returning to his face as the waitress approached with the first course of their meal. "Suit yourself, but don't say I didn't tell you so."

Chapter 3

When Darwin finally made his way back to his office, there was a stack of legal documents lying in a neat pile on top of his desk. At lunch, he and Mecan had quickly changed the subject from his sexual problems to news of family members and their own recent exploits. Although they'd enjoyed an exceptionally good meal, Darwin had actually been relieved when it was over. His brother's comments continued to haunt him, the idea having taken a firm hold in his consciousness.

He was desperate for an answer to his problem. The situation was really starting to wreak havoc on his personal life. Last night's fiasco had left him wounded, his ego sufficiently bruised as he'd crept from his friend's bed and out the front door as fast as he could run. The woman had professed to be understanding but her disappointment had been obvious. He could only imagine the tale she'd had to share with her friends once he was gone and she could get her hands on a telephone. Darwin cringed at the thought.

His new assistant, an intern named Rhonda Bishop, rushed into the office behind him, visibly flustered as she juggled a cup of hot coffee in one hand and more file folders in the other. She began talking at a rapid pace, words flying past her thin lips.

"Hi, Mr. Tolliver. Mrs. Scott asked me to give these to you. She said you need to have your personal attorney review them, then you need to sign where indicated and get them back to the legal department ASAP." The young woman took a deep inhale of air to catch her breath. "Did you enjoy your lunch, sir?" she finally asked, setting the mug of hot fluid down in front of him as he took a seat. She dropped the folders onto the other pile.

Darwin nodded, chuckling under his breath. "Lunch was very good. Did my esteemed producer leave any other instructions for me?"

Rhonda stared off into space, brushing a lock of red hair from in front of her eyes as she appeared to be searching her memory for a response. "Yes," she suddenly answered, excited that she hadn't forgotten something that was actually important. "Yes! She says she needs your final menus for the first week by end of business tomorrow. No exceptions."

Darwin nodded. "Attorney and menus. Sounds easy enough. Do you know any good attorneys?"

The young woman shrugged, a frown crossing her face. "I don't think so."

Darwin thought for a quick moment, then suddenly

smiled. "Don't worry about it. I actually happen to know a woman who's a very good lawyer." He reached for his BlackBerry and did a quick search for a telephone number. When he found it, the grin painting his face widened. Bridget Hinton would surely give him a hand, he mused, thoughts of the exquisite woman suddenly erasing the tension that had been holding him hostage since he'd seen his brother. *As least I hope she will help,* he thought.

Bridget was his sister-in-law's best friend. Darwin hadn't missed the fact that Jeneva had been trying to hook the two of them up since he could remember, but he'd not given in to her exploits willingly. He'd not been looking for a relationship and it had been clear to him from day one that Bridget was a woman who wasn't interested in being any man's "sexual understanding."

Bridget came to the table with high expectations, making it clear that a man had to match what she was putting down or step off. Her legal-eagle demeanor was cool and confident and she was clearly not a woman to be taken lightly. Darwin hadn't been ready or willing to test those waters and so he'd ignored the more flagrant overtures that his sibling and her friends had exhibited in their matchmaking efforts.

But there was something about the woman that had held his interest, despite his unwillingness to act on it. Something in her deep black eyes that he'd found intoxicating. It had something to do with the way she looked at him, the way she smiled when he came into the room. How her presence made him feel. Darwin felt a quiver of heat shift in his abdomen. He bit down against his bottom lip as memories of the woman skated through his mind.

Rhonda cleared her throat, the noise pulling him back

to the moment. "Is there anything else I can do for you, Mr. Tolliver?" she asked.

Darwin shook the clouds from his head, focusing his attention back on the young woman who stood staring at him curiously. "No, thank you. In fact, I think I'm going to get out of here early today. I want to work from home this afternoon. I have to get those menus together." He smiled.

"Yes, sir."

He watched as Rhonda made her way out of the room and back to her desk, then he reached for the telephone to make his call.

The ride home was too quiet for Darwin's comfort so he fiddled with the buttons on his radio for some song to amuse him. With one eye on the road and the other on the scan button, he finally decided on a classic R & B station that was spinning an old Motown tune. His brother was more of a Motown fan, the style reminiscent of their late father and their parents' Friday-night favorites. Darwin's tastes tended to lean more toward rock and roll and alternative rock. At the moment his favorite group was the Gorillaz and he was kicking himself for taking their latest CD out of the car and forgetting to put it back in when he'd cleaned the vehicle earlier that week.

After a few minutes Darwin decided Motown wasn't what he wanted at all and he switched the radio off, falling back into the silence that had annoyed him in the first place. He heaved a deep sigh, thoughts of Mecan's comments and the frustration over his medical condition once again playing havoc with his nerves. Images of Bridget tottered through his mind, as well, and he couldn't help but

wonder if his needing her services and the remembrance
of his attraction toward her was happening for a reason.
His brother's prediction seemed to be holding hands with
his fate, spinning him in the direction of a new destiny.

Darwin knew that if there was any one woman he could
see himself doing forever with, she would be a woman like
Bridget. Bridget reminded him of his mother, and what
man didn't want a woman like the one who'd given birth
to him and had loved him more than life itself? Frances
Tolliver had a strength and fortitude that was uncompro-
mising. She wore her emotions over her heart, loving deeply
and standing on the power of her convictions. His mother
was one tough cookie, with a chocolate heart of pure gold,
the ability to laugh in the face of unfathomable challenges
and a warm, gentle touch that instantly eased away any
hurt. His father had been blessed beyond reason to have a
woman like that at his side. Darwin could only begin to
wish for half that in a companion of his own, and Bridget
was a woman who came with an equally impressive list of
attributes. Plus, the woman had the body of a goddess.

As Darwin's thoughts lingered over each dip and curve
he could remember, he was reminded of his impotence, the
yearning in his mind not even igniting a flicker of warmth
through his groin. Reaching for the radio a second time he
found a station blasting Lynyrd Skynyrd's "Sweet Home
Alabama." As the music vibrated out of the speakers,
flooding the closed vehicle with a heavy bass, he thought
about what a sweet home could possibly entail. Darwin
suddenly found himself imagining the possibilities.

Bridget wasn't at all prepared when her doorbell rang.
Darwin Tolliver had called her out of the blue the day

before, asking for her assistance with some business contracts he didn't understand. She'd been surprised by his call, the sound of his voice reviving the more sensual thoughts she'd been having about him earlier that week, and the moment had unnerved her. There was something to be said for his timing, she mused, wondering if things really *did* happen for a reason.

She took one last glance in the foyer mirror to check her reflection, then reached for the door handle. As she pulled it open to find him standing confidently on the other side, she suddenly felt as if her knees would never stop quivering, threatening to send her straight to the floor. She was grateful for the linen slacks that shielded her shaking limbs from view.

Darwin Tolliver was one good-looking black man. Tall, like his brother Mecan, with the same blue-black complexion, brilliant white smile and dimpled cheeks, Darwin had a majestic presence. What woman could resist a man who carried himself like the emperor of his own private kingdom?

His Royal Highness greeted her warmly. "Bridget, I can't tell you how much this means to me," he said as he stepped over the threshold. He wrapped his arms around her torso and hugged her tightly as he kissed her cheek. "Are you sure it's not a problem?"

Bridget could feel herself melting beneath his touch. "It's not a problem at all," she answered. "And it's good to see you again."

Darwin nodded. "When was the last time we saw each other? Christmas?"

She shook her head. "Thanksgiving, I think. At Mac and Jeneva's. If I remember correctly, you were in Louisiana for Christmas."

"That's right. My sister did Christmas dinner." He screwed up his face as though the memory had brought back a bad taste.

Bridget chuckled. "Was it that awful?"

He laughed. "No, not really. But cooking isn't one of Paris's stronger attributes and she wouldn't let me help. We have to be nice, though, when she tries or Mama gets mad at us."

"How is Mama Frances?" Bridget asked, inquiring about his mother.

"She's doing very well. Still trying to keep Uncle Jake on the straight and narrow."

It suddenly dawned on Bridget that they were still standing in the foyer of her home. She shook her head. "How rude of me. Please, come in and make yourself comfortable."

"Thank you." Darwin smiled as she gestured toward the living room sofa. He took a seat, settling his large body against the cushioned perch. An awkward silence suddenly filled the space between them as Bridget dropped down against the wing chair across from him. Darwin stared down to the hardwood floor, searching his thoughts for something clever to say but words were fleeting. He suddenly felt silly, the moment reminiscent of grade school and after-school antics between the boys and the girls.

The rising uneasiness felt thick and heavy and both of them suddenly felt self-conscious. Bridget brushed her palms against her thighs, wiping at the dampness that had risen to her palms. This was the first time she and Darwin had ever been in a room alone together. She'd fantasized about this moment more times than she was willing to admit, but never had her dreams been as embarrassing and as uncomfortable as she was now feeling.

"So…" she started, her gaze skipping around the room as if she were afraid to rest her eyes on him.

Darwin smiled. "So…how have you been?"

Bridget smiled again, her hands twisting nervously in her lap. "As well as can be expected, I guess."

Quiet filled the space for a second time. Bridget was suddenly aware of his breathing, the slow inhale and exhale of his breath blending with the louder click of the grandfather clock in the hallway and the CD player that was playing softly in the other room. He sat with a large manila envelope between his palms, spinning the package over and over in his hands. She watched him as he looked around the room, slowly noting each detail of her decor. His gaze lingered ever so briefly on the large acrylic painting that hung just above her baby grand piano. His lips pulled up into the slightest smile and the gesture sent a shiver through the pit of her stomach and up her spine.

"That's beautiful," he said, his head bobbing up and down. "Is it an original or a reproduction?"

"An original. It was done by an artist named Joseph Holston."

"Very nice."

Bridget stared where he stared, reflecting on the abstract painting's cubist style. The image was of a couple embracing, and it had been one of her favorites from the moment she'd first laid eyes on it. She turned to stare back at him.

"Are those your contracts?" she asked, gesturing with her head to the mailer in his hands.

"Oh…yeah. These are them." He extended the

envelope toward her. "I really appreciate this, Bridget. In the past I've used my agent's attorney, but these needed to be reviewed in a hurry and I really wanted someone I trust to look them over for me. But if it's a bother or if I'm keeping you from anything, I'll understand."

She shook her head. "It's not a problem, really. I was just going to throw a chicken breast under the broiler and call it a night."

"You haven't eaten yet?"

"Not yet."

Darwin beamed, shifting forward in his seat. "I'll tell you what. Let me loose in your kitchen and I'll cook your dinner while you look at my contracts."

"That's not necessary—" she started.

"Really," he said, rising to his feet and heading boldly toward the back of her home. "I want to."

Bridget followed behind him. "Well, only if you promise to stay and eat with me."

The man smiled, winking an eye as he glanced back over his shoulder. "It's a deal."

"Now, I really don't have a whole lot to work with," she said. "I usually eat out."

Darwin chuckled as he took in the expanse of her immaculate kitchen. "It doesn't take much to eat well."

Taking a seat at the dining table, Bridget watched as he took command of her kitchen. Pulling open her cupboards, he gathered a row of spices onto the counter, then moved to lean into her refrigerator. The view of his backside and the tight pair of Levi's jeans he wore caused her body to heat with sudden wanting. Shaking the emotion, Bridget laid the documents onto the tabletop and began to read.

Darwin was grateful for the distraction. He'd not anticipated feeling this unnerved in Bridget's presence. He'd forgotten just how exquisite she was. Bridget bore a striking resemblance to the songstress Lauryn Hill. They shared the same rich, deep-chocolate complexion; charismatic smile framed by full, luscious lips and dark ebony eyes that shimmered with a hint of vulnerability. Her demeanor was controlled and confident and Darwin was willing to bet that Bridget didn't have a clue just how intimidating she could be to a man.

Bridget could bring a man to his knees with just the hint of a smile. And when she opened her mouth to speak, those around her were usually bowled over by her intellect, her beguiling sense of humor. And her laugh could make a whole room feel comfortable to be around her.

And damn, he thought as he laid four strips of chicken breast against a plastic cutting board, she smelled sweet, like a delicate concoction of vanilla and honey. As he'd wrapped his arms around her in greeting, it had taken every ounce of his control not to trail his tongue in the crevice of her neck to see if she tasted just as tantalizing. He heaved a deep sigh and Bridget looked up from her reading to meet his gaze with her own.

She smiled and his stomach did a quick flip. He smiled back, praying in the back of his mind that he didn't ruin this meal, his attention focused on everything but what he was cooking.

"You do that quite well," Bridget said, breaking the silence.

"Excuse me?"

She gestured in his direction. "Cooking. You *are* good at it. I've been watching how easily you've been moving around in my kitchen. It's almost like a ballet the way you've been dancing behind that counter. And whatever is in that pan smells incredible."

Darwin chuckled. "Girl, I don't do ballet. I'm more of a tap-dance, hip-hop kind of guy."

Bridget laughed with him. "Excuse me! Either way, you do your thing very well. You've got good moves."

"Well, it's easy when you've got a great kitchen to work in," he responded. "Are you sure you don't cook? Your kitchen is stocked way better than my own."

She shook her head. "Thank you, but no, it's more for show than anything else. I could probably burn water without any effort."

He nodded. "I guess I'll have to stop by more often and take advantage of this."

Bridget's eyes widened as he grinned in her direction. "Any…any time," she stammered, the prospect of Darwin returning for any reason raising her temperature.

The duo laughed, then almost simultaneously returned to what they were doing. Bridget grinned into the manila folder that lay open on the tabletop. Her body was on overdrive. She watched him out of the corner of her eye. Darwin was covering the chicken strips in flour, an egg wash, and then seasoned breadcrumbs before laying them into a pan of sizzling olive oil. The aromas wafting through the room had her insides bubbling with hunger, and the man himself had stirred a low flame through the rest of her.

A girl could get used to this, she thought as he moved effortlessly from one saucepan to another. She closed her eyes and then pinched herself, grasping just a bit of the flesh at her wrist between the thumb and forefinger of her other hand. If this wasn't real, she needed to wake up before it went any further. When she opened her eyes again, Darwin was still there, still moving as though he'd always belonged right there in her kitchen and her life. As he pulled a tablespoon of simmering sauce to his lips, blowing lightly over the hot substance, Bridget closed her eyes for a second time, imagining what it might be like to have those lips blowing warm breath against her skin.

Darwin's deep voice suddenly shook her from her reverie as he stepped in behind her, a large hand pressed easily against the center of her back. The tips of his fingers burned hot against the flesh beneath her silk blouse.

"I'm sorry. What did you say?" she asked, nervous energy quivering in her voice.

"No. I apologize," Darwin responded, smiling down at her. "I didn't mean to startle you. I just thought you might want to set the table. The food's almost ready."

Bridget stood up quickly, shifting away from the rise of heat that was spreading like a raging itch through her body. As if sensing her reaction, Darwin clenched his fingers into a tight fist and crossed both arms behind his back, staring sheepishly in her direction. The earlier awkwardness between them suddenly resurfaced with a vengeance.

Chapter 4

Roshawn and Jeneva were giggling hysterically into their telephone receivers. Bridget didn't find a thing funny about her situation and she said so.

"You two get right on my nerves. I called for some advice and instead you're making fun of me. I hate you both."

"Don't say hate. That's not nice," Jeneva responded.

"And it's very funny," Roshawn quipped. "You and Darwin have actually gone from making goo-goo eyes at each other to playing pocket pool. I personally think you're making great progress. Not!"

Jeneva laughed.

"Pocket pool?" Bridget questioned. "What's pocket pool?"

"You know how you play pool? That game with the long stick and the balls that you sink into the little holes?"

"Those of us with a little refinement call that billiards."

"Yeah, well, whatever you want to call the game, you two are playing it with both of your hands in your pockets instead of on each other. Unfortunately, that makes it kind of hard to sink his—"

"Don't even say it!" Bridget shook her head, fighting to suppress the smile pulling at her lips. "Roshawn, you are too nasty!"

"But she has a point," Jeneva interjected. "You like him and he likes you and for the life of me I can't figure out what's keeping you two from hooking up. It's been almost six years and the only kiss you've gotten has been on your cheek."

"And it wasn't the right cheek, either." Roshawn laughed. "I keep telling you he can't get there if you keep your clothes on."

"I'm convinced it's just not meant to be. He doesn't see me any differently from how he sees you, Jeneva."

"I wouldn't be so sure of that. Darwin is usually a lot smoother around women. Him being so nervous tells me he sees you quite differently."

"And he cooked for you. That has to count for something," Roshawn added. "So what else happened? Finish your story."

Bridget sighed. "Well, you would have thought I'd never set a dinner table before. I couldn't remember where my good silverware was. I knocked the water glasses over twice, dropped the wine bottle and forgot to light the candles."

"But was the food any good?" Jeneva asked.

"To die for. That man can cook his behind off. And he made dessert, too! It was the cutest little dish of wafer cookies, ice cream and sautéed peaches. He served it in a champagne glass."

"That's all well and good. But I want to know who had to wash all the dishes he dirtied?" Roshawn asked.

"We both did. He washed and I dried. Then he went home so I could finish reviewing his contracts."

"Did he kiss you good-night at least?" Roshawn inquired.

"No. In fact, he rushed out of here so fast I think I may have scared him."

The women laughed and Bridget could feel her face warming from embarrassment as she remembered how quickly Darwin had raced out of her home.

"But you get to see him again, right? To give him back his papers?"

Bridget nodded into the receiver. "Tomorrow. I'm taking them over to his studio in the morning."

"Well, wear something low-cut," Roshawn chimed. "Sounds like you need to step it up a notch."

Bridget heaved a deep sigh. Stepping it up a notch didn't begin to address what she needed to do, she thought. What she had never shared with Jeneva or Roshawn was that she'd resigned herself to never marrying, never having a man to spend the rest of her life with. Sure, she'd held out hope that her few flirtations would have netted her a companion, but Bridget had never been one to let wishful thinking take precedence over her common sense. Bridget was acutely aware of the many statistics that prophesied a black woman's chances of finding a mate, and they weren't favorable. The nearness of Darwin Tolliver suddenly had her rethinking her prior convictions and wondering whether or not love was actually a possibility for her. She shook the thought from her mind.

"I'm not wearing anything I wouldn't wear any other day of the week. If I can accept Darwin not being interested in me, then you two need to, as well."

Jeneva chuckled. "Who is she trying to convince?" she asked, her voice brimming with amusement. "Us or herself?"

Roshawn laughed with her. "Well, I know I haven't fallen for it. Sounds just like another excuse to me."

Bridget sucked in her breath. "I need new friends."

"New friends, a man and a job. Girlfriend, your need list is growing longer and longer," Roshawn said. "I need me a few things, too, so when you get yours let me know where you went shopping."

"Okay, we need to stop, Roshawn. Bridget didn't call us for a hard time."

"You got that right," Bridget said. "So stop being a cow and tell me what to do, heifer!"

"Oh, I got your heifer, heifer!"

Almost an hour later the three women were still talking nonsense over the telephone. And as Roshawn regaled them with a story about her life in Arizona, Bridget couldn't help but wonder what Darwin might have been doing right then.

A nondescript noise woke him from a sound sleep. For only a quick moment he was dazed and disoriented, his vision still blurred from the deep slumber he'd been wrapped in. Then he remembered that he'd been dreaming, floating blissfully on clouds of visual pleasure.

He'd been dreaming about Bridget. The two of them had been cooking up more than chicken and vegetables in her kitchen. In fact, Bridget had been dessert, the icing on his cake, and he'd been licking every square inch of her spoon. Unfortunately, just when he'd needed his own utensil to function, it didn't and he'd woken up thoroughly frustrated.

As he lay sprawled across the surface of his king-size bed, he imagined he could still feel her body pressed warmly against his. He even thought he could still smell the delicate scent of her perfume teasing his senses. He inhaled deeply, savoring the moment as he reached a hand down to cup the limp bulge of flesh between his legs. Even in the throes of sleep his body was failing him, not even a quiver or a twitch to boost his manhood.

Darwin slammed a fist against the padded mattress top and swore. Loudly. The profanity pierced through the dark and the silence that filled the space around him. The harshness of it frightened the snow-white Maltese that lay sound asleep at his bedside. The small animal jumped with a low growl, then barked, a series of high-pitched yips crying for some attention. Darwin blew a gust of warm breath past his lips.

"Hush, Biscuit. Stop that noise."

The tiny bundle of puppy energy stood up on her hind legs, a tiny paw scratching the air for his attention. With one hand he swept all six pounds of fluff up to his side, gently stroking the animal's head as she struggled to lick his hand and his face.

"No kisses, you. Stop that! Stop, Biscuit!" he said, his pleas a half-hearted attempt at a reprimand.

Ignoring him, Biscuit jumped about, then finally settled down against a pillow on the other side of the bed.

Great, Darwin thought, palming his crotch for a second time before pulling both of his arms up and over his head.

Here I am, dreaming of a female in my bed, and the one actually here has four legs and a tail.

As if reading his mind, Biscuit barked again, then settled her head back down against the pillow, her dark eyes eyeing him curiously.

"Don't you get comfortable," Darwin said out loud. "Your bed is on the floor, dog."

Biscuit tilted her head ever so slightly.

Darwin sighed. Bridget had been on his mind since he'd raced out of her home. Although he'd gotten the impression that she wouldn't have minded him staying longer, his nerves wouldn't allow it. The woman had had him trembling in his seat as they'd enjoyed dinner and dessert. By the time the meal was finished and the dishes washed, he was a walking time bomb set to explode.

It was one thing to be in a loving relationship with a woman and then become impotent, but it had to be something else altogether to be impotent walking into the relationship. He couldn't imagine any woman wanting only half a man. He wasn't about to set himself up for that kind of disappointment and embarrassment. It was best that he just leave any thoughts of him and Bridget alone. "It couldn't possibly work, could it, Biscuit?" he said softly. He tossed a quick glance over to the animal beside him. His pet barely opened her eyes, quickly resuming her soft snores. Darwin shook his head. Even his dog couldn't be bothered with the traumas of his love life.

Chapter 5

The downtown production studio where Darwin's show was being taped was just minutes from the Space Needle in the Seattle Center. It was a new, digital, state-of-the-art facility, and as Bridget eased her Cadillac CTS into an empty parking space, she couldn't help but be impressed.

A stint in family court had worn on her last nerves that morning. One father's continuous refusal to pay support for his four children by three different mothers had been more than enough to set her on edge. When the fool had actually accused her of conspiring against him to make points with the prosecutor, she'd been ready to quit on the spot. She'd had enough of representing clients who clearly knew they were wrong and expected her to just overlook their more glaring faults to help them get over on someone else. When the judge entire ride over insisting to herself that she would not let Darwin have any effect on her and here she was, standing like soft butter before him.

A tall woman with a mane of auburn hair that skimmed the crest of her buttocks suddenly pulled at Darwin's elbow. The voice was deep and thick like molasses as she purred the man's name.

"Darwin. That was absolutely perfect. If you do that every time we are sure to have a hit on our hands." The woman's gaze moved from Darwin to Bridget. She extended a limp hand. "Hello, I'm Ella Scott, Darwin's producer and the associate station manager here."

Bridget returned the greeting. "Bridget Hinton. Mr. Tolliver's attorney."

The woman smiled, seemingly content with Bridget's response. "It's very nice to meet you. Have you been in practice long?" Ella asked.

"A while now."

"So, you're from Seattle originally?"

"Born and raised. You?"

"I'm fairly new to the area. I was born and raised in a very small town a few hours from here."

"I love small towns. Is it one I know?"

"Coulee City?"

Bridget nodded. "That's near Colville and the Indian Reservation, correct?"

"Yes."

"It's a lovely community."

Ella shrugged, then resumed her conversation with Darwin. "Darwin, I have some suggestions that we should discuss later. But I loved the show. Just loved it."

"Thank you, Ella. I appreciate that."

"Well, if you two will excuse me, I'm going to see if I can sneak me a little taste of that meal you prepared before the crew eats it all up. We can meet at three o'clock, Darwin," she said, not bothering to wait for a response. "It was nice meeting you, Ms. Hinton."

They watched as Ella rushed off in the other direction. Darwin pressed a palm against Bridget's elbow. "Let's go to my office," he said, leading her back toward the maze of offices.

As they entered his personal space, he closed the door behind them, gesturing for her to take a seat on a plush leather sofa that lined one of the walls. Darwin pulled up a chair directly in front of her, leaning forward with his elbows against his thighs, his hands clasped together in front of him. For a brief moment he sat staring at her, oblivious to the time that ticked too quickly away.

He'd noticed her the moment she'd walked into the studio. His heart had skipped one beat, and then a second, and he had barely been able to pull his baked dish from the oven without dropping it. It felt like puppy love and he was enjoying every minute of it. He hadn't felt anything like this since high school and the homecoming queen, Cassandra Tripp, who'd been his date to the senior prom.

Bridget wore a sharkskin denim blazer with a chic white blouse beneath it and dark slacks. Her hair was pulled back into a slick ponytail that hung just below her shoulders. As always, he was taken aback by her bright eyes, the slight dimple in her full cheeks and the most intoxicating mouth he imagined any woman ever possessing. As he sat staring he could see the flush that suddenly flamed her face.

Bridget eyed him curiously. "Are you okay? You're staring."

Darwin could feel himself blush. "Sorry. I…" he stammered, searching for the words to ease the moment.

Bridget shook her head. "There's nothing caught in my teeth, is there?"

Darwin laughed. "No. Your teeth are perfect. Absolutely beautiful, in fact. The prettiest smile I've ever seen."

Bridget rolled her eyes, smirking.

"Don't pay me any attention. I get stupid around beautiful women." He chuckled.

"Then I'm scared," she responded coyly. "From what I hear you've made being around beautiful women a personal mission."

"Has my brother been talking out of turn again?"

She shrugged and then they both burst out laughing. Bridget shifted the conversation. "Do you want to talk about your contracts?"

Darwin shook his head. "Not really. Were there any problems?"

"Just a few items I think need to be clarified."

"I'll tell you what. Call the attorney here, do that lawyer thing you guys do, and when it's fixed where you like it, I'll sign."

"Don't you want to know what the issues are?"

"No. I trust your judgment. I know you'll take care of me."

"What makes you so sure?"

Darwin leaned in closer, his hand falling against her knee. "Well, we're almost family, aren't we? Sort of like kissing cousins or something."

She eyed him warily. "Kissing cousins? I don't think so."

A smug smirk crossed his face. "Okay, we'll leave out the cousins part, but the kissing…"

"Like you kissed my best friend?"

Darwin was only slightly taken aback by the comment. He cleared his throat before responding. "For the record, your friend kissed me. I did not kiss her."

"That's not what it looked like. In fact, it looked like the two of you were getting quite cozy with one another."

Darwin shook his head, his smile still full and wide. "Am I in trouble? Because I don't think I should be. Your friend was flirting with me. It was absolutely shameless!" he said, his tone teasing. "And it happened how many years ago? Don't I get a reprieve for good behavior or something?"

She studied him carefully, noting the gleam of mischief that flickered in his eyes. "That depends."

"On what?"

"On whether or not you plan to go around kissing my best friend again."

His head moved from side to side. "Never. But I do hope I get to kiss you. I really would like to kiss you. Someday. Someday soon, maybe?"

Bridget eyed him with amusement. "Darwin Tolliver, are you flirting with me?" she asked playfully.

A wide grin filled his face again. "I'm trying. I hope you don't mind."

Bridget placed her hand over his and gently moved it from her leg back to his own lap. His touch had been burning, sending a shiver up and down the length of her spine.

"You don't need to tease me, Darwin Tolliver. Like you said, we're almost family, so you can trust that I'll represent your interests. Besides, I thought we considered each other friends."

"But I can't flirt?"

"That depends."

"On?"

"On whether or not you're planning to cook dinner for me again."

"Is that all?"

"That's a lot for some men."

"Maybe, but it's not a big deal for me at all."

"Then we have a deal?"

Darwin nodded. "Tonight. At my place. Dinner's at seven."

Bridget rose to her feet. "I'll be there," she said, moving swiftly toward the door. She smiled. "Thank you," she said softly.

Confusion swept over his expression. "For what?"

"I was afraid that you might still be uncomfortable around me. We had a few awkward moments last night. It had me worried."

Darwin chuckled, his head bobbing up and down. "I thought it was just me. Glad to know I wasn't alone."

"Let's not let it happen again, either."

"No problem. And by the way…" Darwin paused for just a brief second. "I really wasn't interested in kissing your friend. I just didn't want to hurt her feelings."

"I know. That heifer can be shameless sometimes," Bridget said with a sly wink. "See you later."

As she moved to make her exit, Darwin called out her name.

"Yes?"

"Don't you want to know where I live?"

Seconds after Bridget was out the door with directions to his home tucked into her purse, Darwin was kicking himself. *What in the world was I thinking?* he thought, dropping his head into his hands and his rear end into a chair. *This can't possibly go anywhere.*

But he hadn't been able to stop himself. The woman had been irresistible and all he'd been able to think about was spending more time with her. Reaching for the telephone, he pushed the seven digits to his brother's cell phone and waited anxiously for the man to pick up on the other end.

Bridget sat motionless in her car, her forehead pressed against the steering wheel. She wasn't quite sure what had just happened between her and Darwin, and although she was excited on one hand, she was scared to death on the other. Leaning back against the leather seat, she took a deep breath, wishing for the influx of oxygen to slow her rapid heartbeat.

There had been more comfort between them than discomfort. It had felt strangely familiar in one second and very odd in the next. She was curious to know more about Darwin, to share more of herself with him, and the prospect of doing so actually had her terrified. Taking another deep breath, Bridget started the ignition and headed in the direction of home.

Mecan was laughing into the receiver. "What's wrong, playa? I've never known you to let a woman run you scared. You losing your touch?"

"Don't joke. This isn't funny."

Mecan continued to chuckle. "You need to relax. Bridget is an incredible woman. You two have had a crush on each other since you first met. Enjoy it. This may be just what you need."

"Maybe, but I hope it's not a mistake. I'd hate to ruin a good friendship."

Mecan shook his head. "You two need to get to know each other before you can truly be friends. You haven't allowed yourself to do that yet. But just let it happen. I know it'll work out for you."

Darwin nodded as if his brother could see him. His gaze floated to the view outside. "How did you know with Jeneva, Mac? How did you know she was the one and only woman you could see yourself being with?"

The older brother took a deep breath, reflecting back on his courtship with his wife. Their relationship had blossomed over their mutual concern for Jeneva's son. Young Quincy had been born with some mental and physical challenges that had tested the strength and fortitude of his single mother. As director of the residential care facility Jeneva had moved the boy into, Mecan had helped the struggling teenager maneuver his way to adulthood.

Jeneva had been the most exquisite woman Mecan had ever met, and while her beauty began on the outside, it was all-consuming on the inside. She'd had spirit and fire and one of the biggest hearts of any woman he'd ever dated. It had taken an extended road trip to Atlanta, Georgia, and then back to Seattle to solidify the bond between them. From that moment on they'd been inseparable, every facet of their lives revolving around their love for each other and their two children.

Blowing the gust of air out slowly, Mecan answered his brother's question. "I think Jeneva said it best. We were both just standing on the right side of love and we both knew there was no other place we could ever imagine ourselves being. It's something you feel inside you,

Darwin. It's something that moves you to get up each and every day, excited about the future. When it happens you won't be able to explain it to anyone with mere words. They'll be able to see it in everything you do or don't do. And you'll see it on her face and she'll see it on yours."

Darwin nodded. "Bridget's special, Mac. I just don't want to mess this up."

Jeneva Tolliver sat with her legs crossed on Bridget's queen-size bed. Alexa, her five-year-old daughter, sat beside her, and the two of them were watching Bridget flit back and forth from her closet to the bed. Clothes were being pulled off their hangers and tossed madly about as Bridget struggled with what to wear on her date. *Her date.* The thought sent a sudden wave of panic straight through her and she dropped down against the bedside, her gaze resting on Jeneva.

"Are you all right?" her best friend asked.

She shook her head, tears burning hot against the back of her eyelids. "I shouldn't be doing this," she managed to sputter, swiping at her face with the back of her hand.

Jeneva smiled, reaching a warm palm out to caress Bridget's shoulder. "Yes, you should. I promise you. It's going to be just fine."

"Why you cryin'?" Alexa asked, little-girl concern painting her expression. "Why Auntie Bridget cryin', Mama? She hurt?"

Jeneva smiled, leaning to kiss her child's forehead. "Auntie Bridget is happy. She and Uncle Darwin are going on a date."

The child's gaze moved from her mother to her godmother. "You not supposed to cry when you go on a date.

Quincy didn't cry when he went on his date," the child said, referring to her twenty-one-year-old brother.

Jeneva rolled her eyes skyward. "Quincy didn't go on a date."

"Yes, he did. Daddy said."

Bridget laughed. "When did Mr. Quincy go on a date?"

Jeneva winced. "It wasn't a date. They just had a dance at the school and he met one of his friends there."

"Her name's Tasha and Quincy says she special like him," Alexa interjected.

Jeneva pointed an index finger at her friend. "Don't you say one word," she hissed softly.

Bridget laughed for a second time. "Well, he is of age, Jeneva. You knew it was bound to happen sooner or later."

"You sound like my husband."

"I bet she's a sweet girl."

Jeneva shrugged her shoulders. "She is sweet but she has as many developmental issues as Quincy has."

Alexa interrupted. "Are you gone kiss Uncle Darwin? Daddy says when you go on a date with your boyfriend you get a kiss."

Jeneva's look was incredulous. "I know your father did not say anything like that, girlie! When did he say that?"

"Quincy asked him if he could kiss Tasha and Daddy said that if Tasha gave her permission that he could give her a kiss on the cheek at the end of the date. Daddy said!" the child pronounced before turning back to her godmother. "You gone kiss Uncle Darwin on the cheek, Auntie Bridget?"

Jeneva shook her head. "You wait until I get my hands on that man!" she exclaimed.

The two women burst out laughing.

Alexa's hands flew to her hips. "Well?"

Catching her breath, Bridget reached over to give the child a quick tickle. Alexa giggled, falling over onto her side between the two adults.

"I don't know, girlie. But if I do I'll make sure to tell you."

Alexa stood up on the mattress, reaching to wrap her arms around her mother's neck. "Uncle Darwin is my man," she said, her precocious tone rising with enthusiasm.

"You don't have a man, Alexa Tolliver. You're too grown with your fresh self. And Uncle Darwin is your uncle. He can't be your man."

"Yes, he can."

"No, he can't."

The little girl pouted, moving from her mother's neck to Bridget's. She pulled her small fingers through Bridget's hair. "I'm gone wear a pink dress on my dates, Auntie Bridget. You should wear a pink one, too."

Bridget giggled. "Girlie, you've got good taste. Come on," she said, rising from the bedside and extending her hand in the child's direction. "Come help me pick out the perfect shoes."

Minutes later with shoes and dress in hand and little Alexa distracted in front of the television set, Bridget sat back against the bed. She leaned her head against Jeneva's shoulder as her friend draped a comforting arm around her shoulders.

"I'm too old for this, Jay."

The other woman laughed. "No, you're not. Thirty-eight is hardly old. Things happen for a reason and obviously this is your time. Stop worrying about it and go have some fun."

"But…"

"But nothing," Jeneva interrupted. "Darwin is a great guy! You like him and he likes you. You won't know how far the relationship will go until both of you actually go through the motions of moving it someplace. So, go get pretty and just think about having a good time."

Bridget nodded. "Were you this nervous with Mecan?"

"You remember how anxious I was," Jeneva said with a light chuckle. "If you and Roshawn hadn't been there to help me get ready I'd probably still be trying to figure out what to wear."

"You did look good."

"It was the scarf."

The two women laughed.

"Okay," Bridget said, moving to peer into the other room to check that Alexa was still planted in front of the cartoon station. She sat back down, drawing her legs up beneath her buttocks.

"What about sex?" she whispered. "I mean…you know…" She paused, taking a deep breath.

Jeneva smiled, shifting herself back against a pillow. "When you know it's right there won't be anything to worry about. You'll know exactly what to do, and how to do it, and it will be the most amazing experience. Just trust your instincts."

"But it's been so long."

"It hasn't been fourteen years. I had a fourteen-year dry spell to make up for, remember?"

"Maybe, but the last time I was with a man was what? A year ago? And you remember how badly that turned out. That brother fumbled like it was his first time. I barely got a wham and a bam before it was all over. Instead of thanking me he should have been apologizing and begging for my forgiveness. That's the last time I bother with anyone from the D.A.'s office."

Both women suddenly burst out laughing at the memory. Jeneva clutched her chest, tears swelling in her eyes. "Okay…okay…" she sputtered as she sucked in air. "Okay, you have a point there."

Bridget wiped her own eyes, tears of laughter misting her cheeks. "Exactly. What if it's that bad?"

"It won't be. It's Darwin and he's related to Mecan, and my Mac…well, you get the idea," she said with a wide grin.

Bridget rolled her eyes.

"It's not Darwin I'm worried about. What if I do something to turn him off? I might take my clothes off and he sees that I have cellulite on my thighs, or my breasts are too small, or…"

"Give it a rest!" Jeneva exclaimed, throwing her hands into the air. "Darwin *likes* you. If and when you two ever get naked with each other he will *love* everything about you. Trust that. Now go get dressed or you're going to be late. And hurry up so I can see you before I have to take the girl home so her daddy can spoil her some before her bedtime."

Bridget heaved another deep sigh and reached for her dress. "If you say so."

As she headed toward the adjoining bathroom she turned back toward her friend and smiled. "Thanks, Jay. I don't know what I would do without you."

Chapter 6

Bridget maneuvered her car through downtown Seattle toward the district of Madronas where Darwin lived. His directions were precise, right down to the mileage. She took the left and right turns onto Aurora and Denny Way, crossing over to Boren and Pike Streets until she pulled in front of his condominium unit.

The buildings were new Craftsman-styled townhomes with lots of curb appeal. The neighborhood was immaculate and decidedly upscale. There was an abundance of neighbor-friendly activity in the area and Bridget noted the couples and families out for an evening's stroll or headed toward the quaint shopping district.

Easing out of her car, she hesitated for just a quick minute, pausing to adjust the back of her mint-green, A-line shift neatly against the length of her body. Her nerves had kicked into high gear somewhere around the intersection of 15th Avenue and Union Street. She felt nauseous, her stomach twisting in one hundred different directions. Good sense told her she was being foolish, but in that moment, anxiety was prevailing.

She hesitated one last time just before pushing the doorbell with a freshly manicured index finger. Darwin and the cutest Maltese puppy greeted her. Both seemed overly excited to see her and the minute Darwin smiled, her name floating over his lips, she felt at ease.

"Bridget, welcome," the man gushed, the small dog squirming anxiously in his arms. "Come on in." Darwin leaned to press a quick kiss on her cheek and Bridget suddenly thought about Alexa.

"Thank you. Who is this?" she asked, reaching to take the animal out of his grip. Pulling the bundle of fur to her chest, she hugged it easily, the dog's exuberance igniting her own.

"That's my guard dog. Her name's Biscuit."

"Hi, Biscuit. Aren't you too cute!"

Biscuit yipped, delighted by the attention.

"I didn't know if you liked pets or not. I was just about to lock her in my bedroom."

"Don't you dare! I love dogs. If I had the time to care for them I'd have two or three myself. I'm not partial to cats though," she said, making a face.

Darwin found the gesture amusing and he chuckled, leading her into a tastefully decorated family room that was situated adjacent to an open kitchen area. Taking a quick glance around the space, Bridget was impressed with the custom cherry cabinets, stainless steel appliances and solid granite counters. Shiny, copper-bottomed pots hung from an intricate rack on the ceiling. They gleamed beneath the warm lighting, looking as if they'd never been used. The rich color of the Brazilian cherry floors also made a nice impression, and Darwin's tastes were very simple, an eclectic mix of artifacts from his travels around the world.

Her eye was drawn to the painting over his fireplace and as she stood staring at it, the puppy cuddling comfortably against her chest, she could only shake her head.

"Why didn't you tell me you collected Holston? That's a wonderful piece!" she exclaimed, turning to stare at the man.

Darwin shrugged. "I wanted to surprise you. In fact, I actually tried to buy the one you have in your living room. You beat me to it. I ended up getting the one that's in my bedroom instead. I'll give you a tour later on so you can see it."

She nodded as he gestured toward a plush recliner in the corner of the room. Just as Bridget moved to take a seat he stopped her. "That's Biscuit's favorite spot. Just drop her there."

Bridget laughed. "Okay," she said as she placed the dog on top of a pillow and watched as she settled herself comfortably down.

Darwin gave her a quick wink. "You can't get comfortable yet. We have a meal to make. So, as soon as you wash your hands we can get started. I'm hungry."

Bridget looked surprised, her mouth open slightly as she stood staring at him. "What happened to you cooking me dinner?"

The man's warm laughter made her smile, a wide grin filling her face.

"I am cooking. You're just going to help." He pointed

to the sink. "There's plenty of soap in that dispenser," he quipped, moving to wash his own hands.

As Bridget moved to his side, he continued talking. "When you're cooking, it's important to pay attention to basics such as hand-washing, proper storage temperatures and cleanliness. Food safety is critical. You don't want to risk making anyone sick."

"Really," Bridget said with an eye roll, tossing him an annoyed look.

Darwin grinned down at her, the heat from his broad body spreading to her own. Shutting off the water, he pulled her hands into his, gently wiping away the dampness with a cotton towel. Bridget's gaze met his as he brushed the soft fabric across her palms. "Most definitely," he said, his voice dropping a half octave.

"So," Bridget said, her voice cracking slightly as she moved to withdraw her hands from his, sidestepping her sudden wanting. "What are we cooking?"

Darwin chuckled. "Salad. You cut the tomatoes and I'll prep the lettuce."

"You're kidding, right?"

"Why would I kid? Are you afraid to make salad?"

Bridget raised her eyebrows. "No. I can make salad."

"Good. We need a nice leafy vegetable to go with the beef short ribs and the corn bread."

"I'm not cooking the ribs and the corn bread, I hope?"

"Oh, heck, no! Didn't you tell me you could burn water?"

Bridget swatted a hand in his direction. "You're not funny, Darwin. You're not funny at all."

The two laughed, chatting easily together as they put the finishing touches on the meal. Their conversation flowed like water, the joy of Bridget's laugh warming his spirit. As they sat down to dinner he discovered they had much in common. Bridget was a jazz buff, her knowledge as proficient as his. They admired and collected the same visual artists, and she was an avid football fan, the Seattle Seahawks her favorite team. The mutual interest could make for some interesting Monday-night football games, he mused.

Bridget grinned as if thinking the same thing. She broke off a small piece of her cornbread and dipped it into a line of brown gravy that covered her plate. Lifting the delicacy to her mouth she ate it with gusto, even pausing to lick the tips of her fingers. She hummed softly and Darwin grinned back.

"I'm glad you're enjoying the meal," he said, chuckling warmly.

"It's very good," she responded, laughter shimmering in her eyes. "I guess you can tell I do like to eat."

"I like a woman who attacks her plate with such enthusiasm."

Bridget laughed. "I don't play when it comes to my food so you tease all you want, Darwin Tolliver. Your cute comments don't faze me in the least."

"What!" the man responded, feigning ignorance. "I was being serious. I wasn't teasing."

Bridget rolled her eyes as she lifted a glass of lemonade to her lips, sipping a taste of the ice-cold drink. She shook her head. "So, when did you know you wanted to be a chef?"

"I was twelve and my father had taken me and Mac to a barbecue competition in New Orleans. There was this old man there who was just working this old, beat-up grill he'd manufactured out of a metal barrel. We were standing in the crowd watching him and out of the blue he invited me and Mac to come taste test his chicken and steaks." Darwin shrugged, his broad shoulders jutting skyward as he continued. "I was hooked from that moment on. I wanted to cook and feed people and enjoy the expressions on their faces when they'd been satisfied with a good meal."

Bridget smiled. "What was the first thing you ever cooked?"

Darwin laughed. "It was a dish called Chicken of Seven Seasonings. I got the recipe from this old cookbook my mother had and thought I'd surprise the family by making dinner."

"Were they surprised?"

"That's putting it mildly. The meal was so bad that my father actually got up from the table, tossed his plate out into the yard to the dog and walked out of the house."

"That's awful!" Bridget exclaimed, her eyes widening.

The man shook his head. "Actually, the food was that bad. The dog wouldn't even eat it," he said with a hearty laugh.

Bridget shook her head, laughing with him.

"So why did you become an attorney?"

"My father. From the day I was born he would introduce me to people as his daughter, 'the future attorney.' He wanted me to be a lawyer and I wanted to please him."

Darwin eyed her warily. "Now, Bridget, you don't seem like the type of woman who does something simply because a man wants her to. Even if he is your father."

"No," she said, her mouth bending into a slight smile. "I'm not. But my daddy could be a very convincing man.

He wanted to be a lawyer and it just never happened for him so he made it happen for me. I saw his love for the law and I eventually fell in love with it, as well."

"And you like what you do? Practicing law makes you happy?" Darwin asked.

Bridget nodded. "Extremely," she said, her gaze meeting his.

He was finding it difficult to take his eyes off of her. As she talked, her enthusiasm for her subjects radiated from her eyes, the dark orbs gleaming brightly. She asked a lot of questions about him, his career, his love of good food and his family. Her interest seemed to come from someplace genuine and the gesture filled his spirit.

He was interested in her, excited for the opportunity to discuss her career, her lifelong friendship with the two women who all referred to themselves as the Dynamic Divas and her family. And she made him laugh, her keen sense of humor a nice match to his own. They were joking about his dog as he began to fill the dishwasher with dirty dishes.

"So, why didn't you get yourself a manly dog?" Bridget asked. "Something with a large bite?"

"What are you trying to say? Biscuit's a manly dog!"

She laughed.

"I can't believe you're making fun of my animal. Keep it up and I'll make her bite you. Then you'll see how manly she is."

"I'm so scared!"

"Get her, Biscuit!" Darwin chimed, pointing in Bridget's direction. "Get her, girl!"

Biscuit looked from one to the other then laid her head back down against the cushioned seat.

Bridget burst out laughing again. "That sure is one dangerous dog!"

"She's afraid if she bites you, she'll catch something. I can't fault her."

"I beg your pardon!" Bridget exclaimed, her hands falling to her lean hips. "Oh, no, you didn't!"

Darwin bumped his shoulder and arm against hers, teasing her side with his hip. "Oh, yes, I did."

Bridget reached into the sink and flicked a palm full of water at him. Reaching for the sink's sprayer, Darwin aimed it in her direction, laughing heartily as he prepared to shoot.

Giggling, Bridget ducked in defense. "Don't you dare," she said with a wry laugh, her hands posed defensively in front of her.

Reaching for her, Darwin pulled her body toward his, the two pretending to wrestle against each other. Biscuit barked excitedly from her seat, wanting to join in the fun. With a quick twist, Bridget claimed the sprayer and pumped the handle. Darwin jumped as cold water hit him squarely in the face and chest.

"Oops!" Bridget laughed.

Darwin sputtered, swiping at the moisture with the back of his hand. "You're going to get it now," he cried as Bridget dropped the sprayer back into the sink and raced into the family room. She positioned herself at one end of the chenille sofa, placing the upholstered unit between them.

They were playing like schoolkids racing in circles around the room. Darwin paused at the other end of the sofa, mischief painting his expression.

"What's the matter?" Bridget asked, breathing heavily. "Can't you catch me?"

"Oh, I will catch you!" Darwin exclaimed.

The moment was interrupted by the ringing telephone. The duo stood eyeing each other, both refusing to move as it rang a second and third time.

"Aren't you going to answer that?" Bridget asked. "It might be important."

Darwin grinned. "I have voice mail," he responded, lunging toward her.

Bridget jumped out of his reach. The answering machine clicked twice then Darwin's seductive voice filled the room. "I'm not in. Leave me a message and I'll call you back." The machine beeped and a woman's voice replaced his.

"Mr. Tolliver, this is Yvonne from Dr. Page's office. Your sample of Viagra is ready for pickup, but the doctor would like to schedule an appointment to speak with you first. We'll be back in the office tomorrow after eight o'clock, if you would please give us a call. Thank you."

The answering machine clicked off, the sound of the tape rewinding suddenly piercing through the quiet. Even Biscuit could sense the quick change in atmosphere, a blanket of embarrassment clouding the room.

"Well," Darwin said, clearing his throat. "If this isn't an awkward date moment, I don't know what is," he said, turning back into the kitchen.

Bridget was at a loss for words as she followed behind him.

Darwin met her gaze as he returned back to the sink and the last of the dishes. His humiliation was acute and if it were at all physically possible he would have dug a deep hole in the center of the room and buried himself beneath it.

They continued to stare at each other as she eased into

the room, moving to stand by his side. Reaching for the dishcloth, Bridget swiped the last bit of moisture from a freshly washed pot resting on the dryer rack. Darwin heaved a deep sigh.

"I guess I should have answered that call," he said, finally breaking the silence.

Bridget smiled. "Sounds like you've got a personal problem," she said smugly, humor brimming in her tone.

"Oh, so you've got jokes now."

She shrugged. "It's always been my experience that when something like this happens, if you can laugh about it, then you won't be inclined to cry about it."

Darwin leaned back against the sink, crossing his arms over his chest. "Well, now that you know my most embarrassing moment, what was yours?"

A moment of reflection crossed her face. Her smile widened to a full grin as she leaned against the countertop beside him. "I had just passed the bar exam and it was my first week with Hartley, Liebermann and Stone. All the attorneys were in our weekly review meeting and I was making a presentation on a new case I'd been assigned.

"I really thought I had things under control. New suit, Roshawn had done my hair the night before and I was working it. Well, I'm doing my thing and all of a sudden one of my new microbraids falls onto the conference table. Then another, and another, and before I realize it I have a trail of yaki hair following me around the room.

"One of the partners reaches down, picks one up, examines it, and says, 'Miss Hinton, I think you're shedding. Please see if you can get a handle on that problem before you have to go before Judge Baines. He's bald as a cucumber and might think you're poking fun at him.' I was so embarrassed!"

Darwin laughed. "So, we will really laugh about this in a few years?"

"I thought we were laughing about it now."

The man smiled, reaching to draw a warm palm against her arm. "Thank you."

"Besides," Bridget added, "you probably don't remember, but this isn't nearly as bad as when you and I first met and I tripped into the room, right into your mother's lap. That was my second most embarrassing moment."

Darwin closed his eyes, a faint smile pulling at his full lips. "But I do remember the first time I saw you," he said softly, his voice just a hair shy of a whisper. "You were wearing a pair of those capri pants. They had a drawstring waist and your hands were pushed deep into the pockets. They were green, army green, and the shirt you wore was a pale floral print. It had these thin straps and one of them had fallen off your shoulder. I remember that I wanted to touch you. I was thinking that all I had to do was push that strap back onto your shoulder and that could be my excuse to touch you. I remember thinking that you were the most beautiful woman I had ever seen." He opened his eyes and stared into hers. "Should I continue?" he asked, an air of seduction rising in his tone.

Bridget hadn't expected the comment and she stood staring at him, her mouth parted ever so slightly as a look of awe washed over her expression. A wave of something she couldn't quite name twisted slowly in the pit of her stomach. Her voice caught in her throat as she tried to speak. She inhaled deeply, then tried for a second time. "You have a good memory."

Darwin grinned. "Only about the things that are important to me."

The man continued to stare at her and the room suddenly felt as if it were spinning in slow motion. Darwin swallowed every inch of her with his eyes, his gaze stroking each curve and dip of her body. He could see her quiver and he stepped in closer, wrapping his arms around her waist and pulling her tightly to him. Once she was in his arms he couldn't begin to imagine the moment that he would have to let her go.

Bridget slid her palms over his biceps, the muscles solid beneath her touch. Her hands looked small against his arms and she felt safe and secure with them wrapped so tightly around her. She hugged her own arms around his neck and pulled him closer, lifting her mouth to his.

The kiss was tender, a sweet brushing of his mouth to hers. Neither moved, both lingering in the beauty of that first touch, the sensual glide of a duet they were starting to dance. Darwin deepened the embrace, drawing her even closer as he pressed his body anxiously against hers, his lips moving with more intensity against her mouth.

"If you want me to stop, just say so," he murmured, his warm breath caressing her flesh.

Bridget responded by pulling him back to her. As his tongue slowly caressed her top lip and then her bottom, she opened her mouth and began to nuzzle his tongue with her own. Although only a moment had passed, Bridget imagined that she could spend an eternity feeling Darwin's sweet mouth tied to hers. She was trembling and it was only Darwin's solid frame and the wealth of his arms wrapped so tightly around her that kept her from dropping to the floor. When he finally lifted his mouth from hers she would have done almost anything to have kept him close to her.

Darwin sighed, a low gust of air easing past his lips. He pressed his mouth against her cheek, gently kissing the soft flesh, then leaned his forehead against hers. "That was very nice," he whispered.

Bridget nodded, her palms skating lightly across his back. "*Very* nice," she responded, her head bobbing ever so slightly. Taking a quick step back, she needed to ease away from the rising heat that was swirling like brush fire over them. She smiled shyly. "I think I should be going," she said.

Darwin returned the smile, his own filling his dark face. "Do you have to?"

"I think it's a good idea."

"Will you come back?"

"Will you invite me?"

His grin widened. "What are you doing tomorrow?"

Chapter 7

Ella Scott was knee-deep in conversation. So intent on the exchange she was having she was oblivious to all else around her.

"Look, this is exactly what this station needs. We've been taping for weeks now. We need to stir things up some, draw some attention to our lineup. We've been airing long enough now to really go full-throttle. We've played up his nice-guy image, and it's working nicely for us. But we need to do more. The man has a reputation for being quite a ladies' man. Let's use that." She paused, listening intently to the party on the other end before she continued. "He's a cook, for crying out loud, and as far as I'm concerned, if it backfires, he's expendable. We can find a dozen pretty faces to show us how to fry eggs so I really wouldn't worry about Darwin Tolliver. Besides, you never know, although his ratings are good and rising nicely, a little negative publicity might actually be the fuel we need to generate more interest." She paused a second time. "Bad publicity is better than no publicity. The public likes a little scandal. They'll eat it up. You just be ready to take the pictures. I'll take care of the rest."

The knock on the office door interrupted the exchange.

"I have to go. You just do what I'm paying you for. Goodbye."

As she slammed the receiver back onto its hook, Darwin pushed his way inside, gesturing to see if he should come back later.

"Darwin! Please, come in. I was just on the phone with one of our investors. They are so thrilled with your show that the man couldn't stop raving about you!" Ella smiled as she pointed to the chair in front of her oak desk. There was no hint of the lie that had just fallen past her lips.

Darwin took a seat in the cushioned chair. "I'm glad everyone is pleased," he said.

Ella's smile widened. "We're all more than pleased. We're absolutely delirious."

The telephone on the desk rang for attention. Ella gestured with her index finger for Darwin to hold on while she answered the call. "Ella Scott."

Darwin clasped his hands together in front of him, his elbows propped against the chair's arms. He sat watching as she commanded the conversation she was having.

Ella was an attractive woman with porcelain features, a complexion that hinted of some mixed breeding and dark, ebony eyes that shadowed a mysterious air. Had it been another time or another place, he might have entertained thoughts of the two of them, but at this stage in his life he was hardly interested. He was convinced that Ella was not an easy woman for any man to handle. There was a significant part of her personality that was cold as ice, with walls made of thick, crystallized water around her spirit. Darwin found her propensity for control to be a large turn-off, and everything the woman did seemed overtly contrived and oddly calculating.

Darwin had no doubts that the network's decision to pick up the show and hire him had been all her doing but he didn't have a clue about her motivations. What he was certain of was his own intention to show Ella and everyone else that the sum and total success of the *Cooking with Darwin Tolliver* show would be all his doing.

Ella's grin beamed in his direction as she hung up the receiver, disconnecting her call. "Now, where were we? Oh, yes. The numbers have been exceptionally good for a new show and the advertisers are very happy. At this rate you'll be in syndication in no time."

"My agent and I would both like to see that happen," Darwin said with a light chuckle.

"Where are we with those additional contracts?"

"Signed, sealed and delivered."

"Wonderful. So everything met with your approval?"

"Nothing my attorney couldn't resolve with yours."

The woman nodded, her smile fading ever so slightly. She reached for the calendar on her desk. "I have a promotional function to attend this evening with our sponsors. I think you should be there. Can you be ready at seven?"

Darwin was only slightly taken aback. "Tonight? I actually had plans…."

She interrupted him, her tone bordering on demanding. "This is very important for your career, Darwin. I'm sure it won't be a problem if you cancel. I'll pick you up at your place. It's black tie so you'll need a tuxedo. Should I have my secretary arrange for one?"

Darwin shook his head, reeling in his growing annoyance. "That's not necessary. I own a tuxedo. If this is necessary then I'll be ready."

"It is. Trust me. I am as anxious for you and the show to do well as you are. Regrettably, the work sometimes has to interfere with our personal lives."

Darwin rose from his seat. "I'll see you at seven, Ella. I need to go get ready to tape."

Ella watched as he exited the room, displeasure pulling at his expression. She smiled, her plans falling into place easier than she'd anticipated.

The star-studded event at the Fairmont Olympic Hotel was a cornucopia of local television, news and radio personalities, plus the requisite political leaders and Chamber of Commerce members. Ella and Darwin arrived fashionably late, Ella looping her arm through his as they made their way into the ballroom.

"Let me introduce you around," she said, smiling brightly, "and talk up the show. Let everyone get to know the real Darwin Tolliver."

Darwin put on his game face as she escorted him around the room. It took no time at all before he'd shaken more hands and posed for more promotional shots than he would have cared to. The entire time Darwin wished he were at home, with Bridget. They'd both been disappointed when he'd had to cancel their plans, but she'd been understanding, promising to have breakfast with him the next morning.

As he stood in conversation with a member of the Seattle city council, a representative from the governor's office and a visiting professor from the University of Washington, it was a struggle to stay focused. His mind was drifting back to the previous evening, Ella's current aggressive demeanor and his own personal issues. He was totally distracted when Ella moved back to his side to introduce him to infamous personality Ava St. John.

Ava's flamboyant reputation preceded her. The woman had come into notoriety on the heels of a government sex scandal that had her allegedly trading favors with some of the most noted men in politics and the media. Her tell-all exposé, a twenty-six-chapter page-turner that had actually hit the *New York Times* bestseller's list three weeks running, was still being heavily promoted by her publicists. Ava was trying to transition careers, looking to be the next name and face in feature films.

There was no denying her beauty and Darwin imagined it took very little for her to charm any man right out of his pants. She was what he and his boys would have called a "cocktail babe," sugar-sweet with just a little of this and a touch of that. She had features that were not quite European, a tad Native American, and her coloring was a rich, warm, dark cinnamon brown. Her face was almost square with large onyx eyes and long, thick, lush lashes. Tresses in a rich shade of sun-streaked honey-brown hung in soft waves past her shoulders. As Darwin eyed her, he had to admit the many photographs he'd seen didn't begin to do her justice. When she opened her mouth to speak, the deep, smoky alto voice was beguiling, the influx of raw sexuality permeating everything around her.

"It's a pleasure to meet you," Darwin said, politely extending his hand in greeting. He suddenly found his hand lost in the woman's firm grip, both of her palms caressing his fingers.

Ava purred. "Hmm. I'm sure the pleasure will be all mine. How do you do, Mr. Tolliver."

"Please, call me Darwin."

"Darwin," she said, rolling the syllables of his name over her tongue. "I hear you're the man of the hour. Our newest celebrity du jour?"

Darwin chuckled, finally extracting his hand from her grip. "Is that what you hear?"

The woman smiled, seduction washing over her expression. She leaned her body closer to his, one palm falling against his chest as the other snaked around his waist.

"You'd be surprised what I've heard about you."

Darwin laughed, tossing his head back. He gave her a quick wink. "I doubt it."

Ava laughed with him, turning to the others who stood watching them. "Ella, gentlemen, if you will excuse us. I'm going to steal Mr. Tolliver away for just a brief moment," she said. She turned back to Darwin. "Is there someplace a girl can get a glass of champagne?"

Darwin nodded. "I'm sure we can find one," he said as he gestured toward the others. "Excuse us, please."

The two headed in the direction of the open bar. As they moved out of earshot, Darwin stepped away from the woman's grasp, moving her to drop her hands back to her sides.

"Do I bother you, Darwin?"

"No. Not at all. I just wouldn't want people to get the wrong impression."

"And what impression might that be?"

He met her gaze with his own but said nothing, the look saying more than words would have been able to.

"Don't you like Ava?" she asked, referring to herself in the third person.

He raised his eyebrows ever so slightly. "I don't know you. And if I don't know you, I can't say what I do or don't like."

She purred again. "Hmm. Why does that sound like a challenge?"

"Trust me. It isn't."

"Have you read my book, Darwin?"

"No. I haven't. Have you seen my show, Ava?"

This time she laughed. "No."

"Then I guess you and I are on the same page. I'm not your type and you aren't mine."

"I'm offended," she said as she took a quick sip from the glass that had been handed to her. She gave him a wry pout.

"I doubt that."

Ava tapped the length of her manicured fingers against his chest as she leaned to press a moist kiss against his cheek. Resting her own cheek next to his she whispered softly into his ear. "This has been quite entertaining, but I actually have *important* people to meet."

He nodded as she stepped back.

"I'll see you later, darling," she said, blowing him a quick kiss as the waitstaff stood watching them.

Darwin watched as she slithered away, the form-fitting dress she wore clinging to her body like wet paint. Taking a quick glance around the room he realized that as many in the room were watching him as her. And the one person whose stare he found most disconcerting had a cell phone pressed to her ear, Ella's gaze as enigmatic as his encounter with Ava St. John.

Jeneva Tolliver stood in the doorway of her daughter's bedroom, her arms crossed evenly over her chest. Alexa was sound asleep, the faint hiss of a stuffed nose disrupting the quiet in the room. Watching her child sleep had become a nightly ritual, the habit formed the day of her birth. Jeneva watched over Alexa, whispering a nightly prayer skyward, just as she had done for her son, Quincy, when he had been that age.

Mecan stepped in behind her, wrapping his own arms tightly around her torso as he leaned in to kiss her cheek. "Is she okay?" he whispered, his mouth blowing warm breath against her ear.

She nodded, leaning her weight against his broad chest. "She's just fine. I thought she might be catching a cold so I gave her a baby aspirin before I put her to bed. She fell asleep the minute her head hit the pillow. You wore her out today."

The man grinned, a wide smile filling his face. "She couldn't be half as tired as I am. I had a hard time keeping up."

Jeneva shook her head, a low chuckle spilling past her lips. Reaching for the doorknob, she pulled it closed, leaving it open just a fraction in case the child came creeping for attention in the middle of the night. Clasping her husband's hand, she followed as he led her down the short length of hallway to the master bedroom and her own bed. Dropping down against the mattress she kicked off her bedroom slippers and slipped beneath the covers, rolling to press the length of her body against his as he lay down on the other side.

"Did you talk to Darwin?" Jeneva asked, settling into her husband's arms as he pulled her close, adjusting the cotton sheet and blanket around her shoulders.

"About what?"

"His date, silly. How did it go with him and Bridget?"

"Didn't you talk to her?"

Jeneva shook her head no. "She must have gotten in very late last night because she didn't call me and she hasn't returned any of my calls today. So what did Darwin say?"

Mecan shrugged. "Nothing. I haven't spoken to him yet, but I'm sure they had a very nice time."

"Maybe they spent the night together," Jeneva mused.

Thoughts of his brother's medical problem trickled across his mind. "I doubt it."

"Why? You know how much they like each other. It's about time they tried to work something out."

"Don't you think they should take things slow?"

"Bridget deserves some happiness in her life. I think they would make each other very happy and things with those two can't get much slower."

"We'll just have to wait and see what happens."

Jeneva leaned up on her forearms to stare down at him. "What aren't you telling me? Why are you being so doubtful?"

The man shrugged, his gaze skirting away from his wife's face. "I wasn't being doubtful. I was being cautious. You know how my brother is. He might not be ready for a monogamous relationship and I wouldn't want to see Bridget or Darwin get hurt."

There was a lengthy pause as Jeneva continued to stare at him. "Are you sure there isn't something else that you're not telling me about? Darwin isn't playing Bridget, is he?"

Mecan pulled her back down against his chest. "Darwin knows better than to play with Bridget's emotions. You know him. He wouldn't do anything to purposely hurt her. Now, forget about those two and let's get some rest."

Jeneva tossed him a coy glance, easing the length of her body up and over his body. She straddled his waist, leaning to press her mouth to his. "Just how tired are you, Mr. Tolliver?" she said, seduction painting her tone. She rotated her pelvis slowly against his.

Mecan laughed, his large hands slipping beneath her nightgown. One palm gripped her waist as the other snaked up to mold his fingers against her breast.

"I think I can be persuaded to stay awake just a little longer," he whispered.

"Good," Jeneva whispered back. "Consider yourself persuaded."

Darwin was grateful for the end of the evening. Taking a quick glance at his watch, he was ready for some quiet, to be away from the gathering of people prodding him for information and pulling for his attention. Ella stood in conversation with one of the station's more generous benefactors. She gestured for him to go ahead without her, promising not to be too long.

Above him, a full moon was watching. He paused to stare back at it, the brilliance of light flooding over the dark landscape. He found himself wishing that with the next full moon, Bridget might be standing with him, his arms wrapped protectively around her as they really gave the terrestrial globe something to see.

The driver greeted him, gesturing with the cap perched atop his bald head. "Did you have a nice evening, sir?"

"Yes, thank you, but I'm glad it's over," Darwin said with a light chuckle.

"I can imagine, sir," the man said, giving him a sly wink as he reached for the rear door handle and opened it for Darwin to enter.

Darwin was taken aback as he stepped into the limousine. He stopped short, his gaze locked on the view in front of him. Ava lay across the leather seat in all her glory, her clothes strewn on the vehicle's floor. Breasts the size of large grapefruit were sitting at full attention. Bare legs were splayed open, the view meant to be inviting. Her smile was a mile wide as she beckoned him to her. He moved as if to back out of the car just as someone pushed in behind him and before he could catch himself he tripped, falling with a loud thud against the naked woman.

Ava laughed, pulling him by the lapels of his jacket as she wrapped her legs tightly around his back, thrusting her pelvis against his. She kissed him, her mouth lunging for his. Darwin could feel his entire body tensing as he pressed his lips tightly together. The commotion at the car's door caused them both to turn at the same time and before he realized what was happening a photographer in the entrance was snapping photos, the camera's flash blinding his view.

"Do you have any comment, Mr. Tolliver?" someone else shouted as Darwin scrambled to free himself from Ava's grasp. He sputtered foolishly.

"How about you, Ava?"

Ava chuckled. "I guess Mr. Tolliver got caught with his hands in Ava's cookie jar!" she chimed as if she were commenting on the weather.

Ella jumped into the limousine and slammed the door closed. Within seconds the vehicle was pulling away from the front of the hotel and down the street.

"What the hell were you doing?" Darwin fumed as Ava gathered her belongings, slipping her dress back over her head.

"Oh, don't be such a baby," the woman said, rolling her eyes in his direction. "A girl just likes to have a little fun now and then."

"At someone else's expense?"

"Darwin, calm down," Ella said. She looked from one to the other. "If I'd known you two had plans I would have found my own way home."

Darwin hissed. "We didn't have plans," he said between clenched teeth.

"We could have had a good time," Ava interjected, "but you wouldn't play."

"Did you know that photographer?" Darwin asked, directing his question at Ella.

The woman shrugged her narrow shoulders. "Paparazzi. One of Ava's fans, I imagine."

Ava giggled. "I wouldn't worry if I were you, stud. Ava will be the center of attention. I doubt anyone will even remember your name after tomorrow."

Darwin scowled, pulling at his necktie as he loosened his collar. He ignored her. "Ella, is there anything the station can do to get those photos?"

She fanned her hand at him. "Darwin, stop worrying.

I'm sure nothing at all will come of this and if it does, we'll take care of it. Don't you worry."

"Well, I am worried and I'm a little surprised that you aren't."

He could feel Ella bristle, her eyes narrowing as she turned to stare at him. Although her tone was even and controlled as she spoke, there was a hint of animosity punctuating each word. "Although I can appreciate your discomfort, Darwin, I'm sure our making an issue about this will only serve to cast negative attention on you, the show and the station. It has been my experience that if we leave well enough alone it rarely comes back to bite us in the behind later on.

"Now, the driver is going to drop you back at your home. I'll make sure we get Ms. St. John to wherever she needs to be taken, and tomorrow we'll all forget this unfortunate situation ever happened. So, like I said before, don't you worry."

Ava burst out laughing, pulling her index finger into her mouth as she uncrossed and crossed her legs, all her glory seeming to laugh with her. Darwin looked from one woman to the other and shook his head as he settled back against the seat. *Sure,* he thought to himself, *that's easy for you to say*.

Chapter 8

Bridget had hoped Darwin would call her and when he didn't she'd gone to bed only slightly depressed. He'd sounded genuinely disappointed that he wouldn't be able to see her, a business event for the television station usurping their plans. He'd been contrite, apologizing profusely, and it had been his idea for them to meet for breakfast instead, before their respective days got started.

She'd been up before dawn. Her excitement had been consuming and not even the forty-five minutes on her stationary bicycle had been of any help. She was also anxious, uncertain of where the relationship was actually going or if there was even a relationship to speak of.

Although it felt like the two of them had known each other since forever, she had to wonder *why now?* Why was Darwin suddenly interested in her now? And not before?

She wondered whether or not his interest was genuine or if she were just another notch in what she knew to be a very lengthy belt. As she contemplated the possible answers, her mind rapidly assessing every possible scenario, she couldn't help but question her own motives.

Darwin had been on her wish list since the first time she'd laid eyes on him. Although they'd joked and teased and flirted whenever they were in each other's company, she'd always hesitated at the prospect of pushing for more from him. Now, here she was not only ready to push, but to pull, pinch, pick, paw and, most importantly, pray for this man to want her in his life as much as she wanted him.

Gathering her purse, her briefcase and her keys, she checked her makeup and the fit of her navy-blue suit before exiting out the door. As she slid into the driver's seat of her car, still thinking about Darwin, she couldn't help but reflect on their last dinner and that telephone call from his doctor's office.

Viagra. She had made light of it because his discomfort and embarrassment had been too obvious. It was clear that he wasn't ready to discuss the reason for its necessity and quite frankly it hadn't been any of her business. But she did want him to know that she didn't care one way or the other. Whatever his medical condition she would be more than supportive because somewhere, somehow, he'd gotten right up under her skin.

She was thoroughly enjoying their time together. They'd found a level of comfort with one another that couldn't be denied and she liked what that felt like. She liked that he made her smile, that he laughed and didn't take himself, or her, too seriously. When he looked at her, his dark eyes piercing her own, she loved seeing her reflection in his eyes.

Bridget sighed impatiently. A morning accident had traffic at a complete standstill. Bridget had barely driven a quarter of a mile and she'd been driving for almost thirty minutes. The driver of a Mercedes ML350 SUV in front of her had actually exited his vehicle and was pacing like a caged animal back and forth. She watched as he took quick drags off one cigarette and then a second. A news bulletin on the 710 KIRO radio station announced a six-car pileup with casualties and delays.

She shook her head from side to side, tossing a quick glance to the digital clock on the dashboard. Realizing she was going to be stuck for a while, she turned off the car's engine. Fuel prices were too high to waste running the engine unnecessarily. Others around her had done the same thing, everyone sitting back in their seats to enjoy the early morning weather while they waited it out.

Reaching for her cell phone, Bridget pushed a speed dial number and listened as it rang on the other end. Darwin's voice mail picked up the call and she left him a message that she was stuck in traffic and would definitely be late. Disconnecting the line, she dialed a second number and waited.

"Hello?"

"Hey, Roshawn. It's me."

"Hi, Bridget. What's wrong?"

"Nothing. Why would you ask that?"

"Because it's only seven-thirty in the morning and you never call this early."

"I'm sorry. I wasn't even thinking."

"Where are you?"

"Stuck in traffic on Interstate 5. I'm headed to breakfast with Darwin and I'm about to be late."

"Hmm. That sounds interesting."

"It could be if I can ever get there. So, how are you? I didn't wake you, did I?"

"Girlfriend, please! Belinda woke up crying at five-thirty. By the time I could get her back to sleep Dario was wide-awake and watching cartoons in my bed. He and I were just sitting here eating Cheerios out of the box."

Bridget chuckled. "Motherhood is obviously suiting you nicely."

"It does, but I hate when Angel's on the road. He does this much better than I do."

Her friend smiled into the receiver. "So, how's my godchild? Is she enjoying her new job?"

"I think so. My daughter is so grown now. I told you she got her own apartment, didn't I? Her daddy about had a fit when she moved out."

"Chen still wishes he could put a chastity belt on her," Bridget said with a quick laugh.

Roshawn nodded on the other end. "I don't know what he worries for. Ming has grown up to be an incredible young woman. I am so proud of her."

"You should be. She took right after you."

"My china doll did, didn't she!"

"Well, I'm not going to keep you. I just felt like hearing your voice."

"No, you didn't. You called about that man. What's Darwin doing that's got you on edge?"

"Is it that obvious?"

"I just know you that well."

Bridget tossed a quick glance around her. Traffic still hadn't budged an inch. "I guess I'm just trying to figure out if this could be the real thing or if I've just wanted it for so long that I'm trying to talk myself into something that's not really there."

"How does Darwin feel about it?"

"I'm not sure. I think he's feeling me but you never know. He could just be tired of me making a fool of myself over him so he's tossing me a few sympathy dates."

"Girl, don't make me reach through this phone and slap some sense into you! I know you know better than that."

Bridget went silent. Roshawn continued speaking.

"I know you do. And I know that if this is feeling like the real thing to you, then it is. Darwin wouldn't waste your time and you wouldn't waste your time. Stop tripping. Besides, it's about time you got yourself a real man so you can cut that vibrator of yours loose."

"I like my vibrator."

"I'm surprised you ain't worn out the batteries on that thing."

"I retired that one. I have a new one now with dual action."

Roshawn roared with laughter. "I swear, Bridget. One day you're going to electrocute your fool self!"

"It's battery powered."

"I don't care what it is. Go play with a real one. I will call Darwin myself if I have to."

"Don't you even think about it!" Bridget exclaimed, putting nothing past her best friend. "You're such a cow!"

"Who are you calling a cow, heifer!"

Around her, engines were restarting, the man in front of her jumping back into his car. Bridget wiped a fleck of moisture from her eye.

"Look, I've got to go. We're finally moving again."

"I really am happy for you, Bridget. You know that, don't you?"

"I do. And I love you, too, Roshawn. Kiss the kids and tell Angel hello."

"I will, and plan on coming to see me soon. I really miss you and Jeneva."

"We miss you, too. I have to run. I'll call you later."

"Bye!"

Darwin flipped his cell phone closed, pocketing the appliance in the leather holder attached to the belt on his waist. After hearing the message that Bridget was stuck in traffic and would be delayed, he'd called Rhonda and had her clear his morning schedule. After last night's fiasco he was in no mood to sit in any meeting with Ella.

He'd gone over and over every detail of the previous evening's activities and after some thoughtful consideration, he was convinced he'd been set up. Instinct told him he'd only been an unwitting pawn in some twisted scheme the two women had concocted. Why they'd chosen him and his life to play games with, though, was beyond his immediate comprehension.

He took a quick glance around him, suddenly aware that he'd been standing in the entrance of Espresso Vivace Roasteria, staring out into space as if he were lost. He nodded politely as a hostess directed him to a corner table set for two.

The café's decor and ambience hinted at a subtle sophistication. Darwin was a big fan of their elaborate lattes and cappuccinos with the intricate marbled foam swirls the Vivace servers were famous for creating. Their pastry bar was decadent and the croissants melted like sweet butter in your mouth. He hoped Bridget would be impressed, as well as pleased that the café's location, sitting just off Broadway, the main drag through Capitol Hill, would get her to her eleven o'clock appointment without either of them feeling rushed.

So distracted, his mind racing a mile a minute, Darwin didn't notice the couple sitting directly across from him, the woman whispering to her companion as she gestured toward a newspaper in her hand. The man looked at him, the paper, and back to him, his head bobbing up and down against a thick neck. The robust woman watched excitedly as the man rose from his seat, the periodical in hand, to make his way over to Darwin's side.

"Excuse me, sorry to bother you, guy, but are you Darwin Tolliver? That cooking show host?" he asked, taking a quick glance to the woman staring intently.

Looking up, Darwin smiled, a faint bending of his lips. "Yes, I am. May I help you?"

The man extended his hand, a full grin filling his ruddy cheeks. "My name's Harvey and that's my wife, Jill." He pointed at the woman, who waved excitedly. "Jill loves to watch that cooking show that you have. She tried to make those dumplings you did once but hers didn't turn out so well."

Darwin continued smiling, nodding ever so slightly. "Well, thank you. I appreciate your wife's support."

"We were wondering if you would sign this article for us. Jill saw it on the newsstand this morning and just had to have it." The man gestured with the journal in his hand, then laid it on the table in front of Darwin.

The photographic image staring back up at Darwin caught him off guard. Pulling the paper closer, he scanned the bolded caption and the article. What little there was of his good mood suddenly nosedived. He opened his mouth to speak, then closed it, words suddenly lost.

The morning edition of the *International Examiner* had gone all out with its cover story, including color photos and quotes from sources claiming to have the full scoop about him and that woman. Darwin stared at the provocative image of himself lost between Ava St. John's legs. The expression across the woman's face looked as if she were lost in the throes of an erotic moment. Not one graphic caption of his surprise and disgust could be found.

The man named Harvey disrupted his thoughts. "I have a pen right here if you need one."

"It's not necessary," Darwin muttered. He passed the newspaper back to the man as he reached into the breast pocket of his blazer for a business card and a ballpoint pen. He scribbled his name across the back and handed it to the man.

"Call my office. If you and your wife would like a tour of the studio I'd be delighted to show you around and arrange for you to be at a taping of one of my shows."

The man nodded his head. "Thanks, but aren't you going to sign my newspaper?"

Darwin shook his head no. "Tell Jill she shouldn't believe everything she reads. There is nothing going on with me and that woman and I can't autograph that picture as if there were. In fact..." he said, reaching into his pocket for his wallet. He pulled a ten-dollar bill from the leather billfold and passed it to the man.

"If you don't mind, I'd like to buy this copy from you. This should cover your troubles."

Without a thought the man snatched the money from his hand and pushed it deep into the front pocket of his denim jeans. "No problem. Jill can buy herself an-other one."

"Thanks," Darwin said, folding the paper in half and laying it beside him on the cushioned bench.

Harvey stood staring at him. "Too bad," he said as he cast a quick glance toward his wife. "Ava St. John is one fine piece of booty. I'd sure do her if I had the opportu-nity. And it sure looks like you did."

Darwin watched as Harvey returned to Jill's side, both of them tossing him a look before they paid their bill and exited the restaurant. Darwin heaved a deep sigh. Ella had told him not to worry. He should have known then that he was standing in the bull's-eye of a barracuda out to do him harm. A clenched fist dropped to the newspaper beside him.

Once again he was lost in his thoughts. He hadn't seen Bridget enter the café, gliding to his side. Her hand drop-ping to his shoulder startled him and he jumped, knocking his small glass of orange juice across the table's top. He tossed a paper napkin down to stall the flow as Bridget stepped back to avoid the splatter against her blue suit.

"Bridget, you scared me."

"Sorry about that. Are you all right?"

Darwin met her gaze, his halfhearted attempt at a smile hardly masking his obvious distress. "No, I'm not."

A waitress rushed to intervene, swiping at the table with a damp cloth. As Bridget finally took a seat, the woman took an order for a replacement juice, a white chocolate mocha latte, a double espresso with whipped cream and two buttered croissants.

Bridget waited until the young woman was out of earshot before she spoke. She reached a manicured hand across the table and gently caressed the back of his hand. "Do you want to talk about it?"

Darwin drew his gaze across her face. Concern painted her expression, her eyes searching his for answers. They sat in silence as he mulled over his options. Then he answered.

As Darwin relayed the events of the previous evening he could feel his rising anger threatening to consume him. The details were seemingly bizarre, even to him, and when he hypothesized that it had been done on purpose, Ella instigating the entire scenario, even he found himself not totally convinced. He needed Bridget to believe him though, wanted her to see details of his conspiracy theory that he himself might have overlooked. But when he was through, it was her attorney's face that stared back at him, her expression and mood devoid of any emotion.

"Where's this article?" she asked softly, the tone to her voice oddly disconcerting.

He passed her the newspaper, his face flushed with heat as she opened it to the front page and stared down at the pictures, quickly scanning the article.

"Is this the only news release that you're aware of?"

He nodded. "This is the only one I've seen. I don't know if there are any others, but isn't this enough?"

"Enough for what?"

Darwin tossed his hands in the air. "I don't know what. But it has to be enough for something! I can't just ignore this, Bridget," he said emphatically.

Bridget swallowed, carefully choosing her words. "I can understand that something like this can be upsetting, Darwin, but I have to question if you making an issue out of it won't do you more harm than good. Have you even discussed it yet with Ella? Or the studio?"

"Not yet."

They were interrupted as breakfast was placed against the table, the waitress grinning broadly. "Can I get you anything else?" she asked.

"No, thank you," Darwin answered, reaching for his mug of hot brew.

"Everything is just fine," Bridget said politely, watching as the woman turned and headed in the opposite direction.

Across the table Darwin was pouting, wearing his frustration like a neon banner. He pushed his plate to the center of the table, his appetite having disappeared with his mood.

"Darwin, you're upset. I think when you calm down this won't feel as bad as it feels right now. You just—"

Darwin interrupted her. "What? Relax? Ignore it? Pretend it didn't happen? I can't do that. I'm angry. They both played me and I don't understand why you can't see that."

Bridget tossed the tabloid back onto the table in front of him. Her index finger tapped harshly against the image of him in Ava's embrace. "What I see is you having a good time with a woman notorious for her persuasive talents with a long list of eligible bachelors and allegedly with a few men who were married. What I see are multiple shots of you and a woman who appears to be your date enjoying yourselves at a dinner party last night. In fact, you're actually smiling in this photo, and in this one, and in that one the woman is whispering in your ear. It doesn't appear that you're in any distress or that you aren't actively participating. Now, maybe you were set up. Maybe it was planned, but there is nothing here that indicates you weren't enjoying every minute of it. Seeing is believing, Darwin, and a picture is worth a thousand words."

For the first time Bridget's voice had risen an octave, her tone harsher than she'd wanted it to be. Her words were cutting, her own emotions spinning out of control. Jealousy coated every syllable out of her mouth, anger washing over each consonant and vowel.

Darwin stared at her. His mood shifted into a pit of hostility. "I really don't care what it looks like. I told you what it was and more importantly, what it wasn't. But I didn't expect you to believe me. I'm just a client anyway, right, Counselor? There was nothing else between us so why should you?"

Bridget bit against her bottom lip. She sucked in a lungful of oxygen, blowing it slowly out. Then she spoke. "Clients typically pay for my services. I don't remember seeing a check with your name on it," she responded, regretting the words before they were out of her mouth, but thoroughly annoyed by his tone and attitude.

Darwin stood up abruptly. Reaching into his pocket for his checkbook, he scribbled across the paper quickly, tearing it out of the book. He dropped it into Bridget's lap and then tossed a handful of bills onto the table to cover the cost of the meal. "I think that should cover the expenses for your services, Ms. Hinton. You can mail my statement," he said, refusing to meet her stare. And then he turned an about-face, striding heavily out of the restaurant and as far from Bridget as he could run.

Darwin pulled his car out of its parking spot and gunned the engine as he tore down the road. Two miles later, as he sped past a state trooper already writing one ticket, he realized he was only asking for trouble he didn't need. Switching lanes, he depressed the brake, slowing down until he was conforming to the speed limit.

It wasn't nine-thirty in the morning yet and already his entire day seemed to be spinning out of control. He had no reason to be angry with Bridget and even less reason to have stormed out on her the way he had. He understood she had to look at things with an objective eye. But he had wanted to be coddled, to be told he wasn't being irrational, and when she hadn't appeased him, he'd thrown a tantrum. *I'm sure that made quite an impression,* Darwin thought to himself as he made a right turn off the exit ramp.

Eventually he would have to apologize but he wasn't ready to make amends anytime soon. His ego had been fractured and at that moment wallowing in self-pity felt just fine. He shook his head, wishing he could kick himself for being so rash. He didn't know why it was so important to him that Bridget believe him, but it was. He'd seen how her jaw had tightened, the sparkle dimming noticeably from her eyes as she'd stared at those photos. She had tried not to show it but she'd been disappointed and hurt. He could hear in her voice that it had made her angry and there he was at the core of all that emotion.

As he pulled into the studio's parking garage, guiding his car into his reserved space, he thought about calling her. He sat staring at his cell phone for some time trying to find the right words. Too embarrassed, he changed his mind and headed inside.

Rhonda jumped to her feet, rushing behind him as he made his way into his office. "Good morning, Mr. Tolliver.

Ms. Scott says she needs to see you right away," the young woman gushed.

"Good morning, Rhonda. Were there any calls?"

Rhonda's eyes widened. "The phone hasn't stopped ringing! The press, all the affiliates, everyone wants a comment about you and Ava St. John. Ms. Scott said to refer them all to her office."

Darwin could feel the tension bristle across his shoulders and up the length of his neck.

Rhonda continued. "*The Morning Show* said they want to schedule you for an interview and…"

Darwin held up his hand, stalling Rhonda's words.

"Thank you, Rhonda. I'll deal with it all later."

She nodded. "Yes, sir." Rhonda stood staring at him, twisting her hands together nervously as a question pressing against her conscience begged to be asked.

Darwin tossed her a look of annoyance, his eyes rolling skyward. "What is it, Rhonda?" he asked curtly.

"Is it true about what they're saying?"

"Is what true?"

"About you and that Ava woman?"

Darwin sighed.

"Everybody's whispering about it."

He shook his head. "No. It's not true."

Rhonda smiled, a wide grin filling her youthful face. "Oh, I'm so glad. I don't like her at all."

Darwin smiled back. "She's not a favorite of mine, either, Rhonda. Now, let's get some work done today. I'm headed over to Ella's office. You need to check that all the ingredients for today's menu are ready, please."

She gave him a quick salute. "Yes, sir. I'm on it."

He winked, a smile replacing his earlier frown. "I'm

sorry if I snapped at you earlier. I didn't mean to. This Ava mess just has me a little unnerved."

"I understand." Rhonda smiled back. "I'm sure it's going to be okay, Mr. Tolliver."

They exited the office together, Rhonda stopping at her own desk as Darwin sauntered down the narrow length of hallway to meet with Ella. He tapped lightly against the closed door before pushing it open and moving inside. Across the room, Ella stood staring out the window, a smug expression gracing her face. She turned, meeting his gaze with a full smile, as he crossed over to sit in the upholstered chair in front of her desk.

She greeted him cheerfully. "Darwin, I thought you'd gone into hiding."

"Why? I didn't do anything I need to hide from."

"Of course you didn't. It's just ugly how the tabloids and media are making such a fuss over last night's debacle."

"Really, I wasn't aware that anyone was making a fuss," Darwin responded, hoping for some sort of reaction.

Ella nodded. "It seems that photos of you and Ava are popping up in all the tabloids. And every gossip segment on national news has had a comment. In fact, it seems you even made page six of the *New York Post*. Like I said, it's just ugly," she said, gesturing with a palm pressed to her heart.

"It's very ugly, Ella. Lies usually are."

"I'm sure it will all die down soon enough. I wouldn't let it bother me if I were you."

"But you're not me and I am worried. We're talking about my reputation here." Darwin's voice cracked with rising anger.

Ella's eyes narrowed. "Darwin, negative publicity isn't

pleasant, but it's still publicity. The public is interested in you. They want to know more. You should capitalize on that. Swing it to your advantage. You're a celebrity now, and celebrities deal with this stuff all the time. In the long run, it can only help you, the show and the studio."

Darwin struggled to contain his emotions. "How do you figure that, Ella?"

A wide grin filled the woman's face, deepening the heavy creases that lined her eyes and forehead. "The affiliates are asking about you. National news stations want to know more. If you play your cards right there's no telling where this could take the show. I can just see us now," she exclaimed, her eyes glazing with enthusiasm.

"Us?" Darwin tilted his head ever so slightly, leaning forward in his seat.

"We're all in this together, Darwin. National distribution of your show will be of benefit to you, me, the studio. Our whole team could get a boost from the attention. This could just be the beginning of something bigger and better for all of us."

Darwin shook his head, chuckling under his breath. His gaze met Ella's for a second time. "So, what is it you suggest I do now?"

"We're going to get you in front of the cameras. Let you talk up the show. Everyone is champing at the bit for an interview. We can get them started first thing tomorrow."

"And if the only thing they want to talk about is Ava St. John, then what?"

Ella tossed up her hands. "Then talk about her. Heaven knows she's talking about you."

Darwin glanced down to his watch. "I'll give it some thought," he said as he eased his way back toward the door.

"I hate to cut this meeting short, but I have to run an errand before I have to tape this afternoon."

Ella continued to grin, thoroughly pleased with herself. "Don't you worry, Darwin! Everything is going to work out just fine."

Darwin forced a grin back. He mumbled under his breath as he exited the room, his teeth clenched tightly. "You just don't know, Ella. You just don't know."

Bridget sat stone-faced, refusing to make her exit until she was certain Darwin was a good distance ahead of her. She'd been sitting for so long that the waitress had brought her a second cup of coffee without asking, tapping her lightly against the shoulder as if she understood.

To say that breakfast had gone badly was putting it mildly. Her emotions had gotten away from her and if there were some way for her to roll back the clock to do it all differently, she would do it in a heartbeat. Seeing Darwin in such a compromising position and learning that it had happened just last night when she'd been wishing for his attention had cut like a knife through soft butter. Even if he hadn't gone to the event with Ava St. John, they had obviously spent time together. Bridget knew she had no right to be envious but the emotion had been all-consuming, sweeping right through her.

The *International Examiner* was still sitting open on the tabletop. Picking it up, Bridget read the article word by word once and then a second time, looking for one paragraph, or a single sentence, that would support Darwin's claims. Most of the story centered on Ava St. John's string of sexual trysts, which supposedly now included WKTV's newest rising star. There was a paragraph or two that nicely expounded Darwin's credentials. Barely a column away, though, it cast Darwin as some sort of notorious playboy, wining and dining the likes of Ava St. John as if that were an accomplishment any man would be proud of.

The photos were all crystal-clear and in full color. Two quarter-page images showed the woman wrapped around him like a silk smoking jacket. In one, his head was tossed back in a deep laugh. In the other he was grinning widely, clearly amused. The journalistic coup, of course, was the graphic pictorial of a very naked Ava with her long legs wrapped tightly around Darwin's back, rapture her expression of choice. You couldn't see Darwin's expression, the partial view of his face pressed into Ava's neck, so there was no discerning whether he was enjoying the moment or not. The image left much to the imagination if one were so inclined. But it was, after all, just a tabloid, Bridget mused, and if it wasn't for Darwin's reaction she would probably be inclined to give it very little thought.

Bridget folded the paper closed and slid it into her leather attaché. With most of her cases, training had taught her to examine the facts the way a jury would see them and most saw things at face value. To heck with what could have been, should have been, or really didn't happen. But experience had taught her that if you truly believed in your client's innocence, you fought tooth and nail to confirm it. Darwin felt he had a case. Bridget wasn't so sure.

She had her work cut out for herself, she decided as she sipped the last of her coffee. If Darwin had been set up for the sake of a publicity stunt, she would have to figure out why and prove it one way or another. And if it turned out he was lying, then neither one of them needed to waste any more of their time.

and the lie that proved just okay that sounded And if it sound a too cut it right and kill limp the romantici very part of the cour

Chapter 9

Bridget packed the last of her personal items into a corrugated box that sat on top of the polished oak desk. As she took one last look around the now empty space that had once been her office, melancholy tugged at her emotions.

The man standing in the doorway watching her offered a sympathetic smile, folding his arms across his thin chest. "We're going to miss you, Bridget. You were a real asset to this firm."

Bridget chuckled. "Obviously not enough to keep me," she said, leaning easily against the desk's edge.

His smile was suddenly nervous, color flushing his buttermilk complexion a vibrant shade of red. Joshua Bayer, one of the senior partners, shifted his weight from one foot to the other. "You never were one to mince words, were you?" he responded, nodding his bald head slightly.

"Mincing words makes for bad business. You taught me that, Josh."

He smiled again. "So, have you made any plans? You know you'll get a glowing review from us no matter where you decide to go."

"I appreciate that. And, actually, I have made plans. I've decided to start my own practice."

Joshua looked surprised, masking it quickly.

"Are you sure about that? It won't leave you much time for a personal life."

Bridget laughed loudly. "That's the least of my worries. But yes, I am sure. In fact, I received a retainer from my first client this morning," she said, patting her blazer pocket where Darwin's check was tucked away.

He nodded, hesitating briefly before speaking. He took a step toward her. "I hope I'm not out of line here, Bridget, but I was hoping since we're no longer business associates that you might consider having dinner with me one night. I'd really like to get to know you on a social level." The man rocked back and forth on the heels of his leather shoes.

With her eyebrows raised in surprise, Bridget stared at him, her voice catching in her throat.

Josh laughed, an anxious giggle meant to mask his nervousness. "At a loss for words, huh? I think this is a first for both of us."

Bridget smiled, working to regain her composure. "Your timing really bites," she said with a soft chuckle.

"So, is that a no?"

She nodded. "I'm sorry but I have to pass. I'm involved with someone."

This time Josh looked surprised. "Really? I wasn't aware you were dating anyone."

"It's fairly new. He and I have been friends for a while and now we're exploring our possibilities."

"Wow! You've been keeping it very secret. I haven't heard one of the paralegals or any of the secretaries gossiping about you."

This time Bridget laughed. "I told you the relationship was very new."

He scoffed. "Oh, please. These she-devils can sniff out news about your personal life before you know it's even happened."

"She-devils! You wait until I tell them what you said."

The duo laughed warmly together. Josh moved to lean against the desk beside her. Bridget cut her eyes in his direction but said nothing. When Josh sighed for the third time, blowing a loud swell of air past his thin lips, she laughed again, clearly amused. He dropped a clammy palm against the back of her hand.

"Can I at least call you every now and then to say hello and ask how things are going?"

"I don't think that will be a problem."

"And if you and this new guy don't work out then maybe you might reconsider and let me take you out?"

She shrugged, her slim shoulders jutting skyward. "You never know."

Josh leaned and kissed her cheek, allowing his lips to linger for just a brief moment. "I will miss you, Attorney Hinton. You've been a thrill to work with and I've appreciated your friendship very much. Let's stay in touch. Please?"

Bridget dropped her other hand against the back of his. "Don't get too soft on me, Joshua. I don't know if I can handle it."

"See, there's a lot about me that you don't know about. I'm really just a cuddly teddy bear."

Bridget chuckled. "A teddy bear with the heart of a viper."

"Only in the courtroom." He grinned. "Really though, if you need anything, just call. And, if the opportunity arises, I'll see if I can't help spin some business in your direction." He pulled his hand from beneath hers and moved back to the doorway. "If I ever need an attorney to represent me, I hope I can call you."

"Please do. And, Josh…" Bridget paused.

"Yes?"

"Thank you."

Tossing her a quick wave, Josh made his way out of the room and down the hallway. Bridget stood watching him until he was well out of sight, disappearing behind a closed door. Shaking her head, she retrieved the last of her possessions, flicked off the light and headed out the door toward home.

Bridget was pensive for the entire ride, her mind reflecting on everything she needed to accomplish. The idea of starting her own law practice had been one she'd been toying with for some time. As she'd weighed all her options she'd not been able to find one viable reason to keep herself from building her own successful practice. Her own law firm. Bridget couldn't help smiling at the prospect.

She'd noted the look of skepticism that had crossed Joshua Bayer's face. Although Joshua had been more supportive of her career than could have been imagined, there had been those rare occasions when he had doubted her abilities. And, whether he had voiced his concerns out loud or not, she had always seen his reservations on his face. The two had successfully managed to balance a professional relationship with a casual friendship, but she had never once given any thought to seeing the man on a romantic level.

As she contemplated their conversation, Bridget knew dating Joshua wasn't something she would ever give any serious thought to. The doubt on his face would always be a barrier between them and that was one wall she wasn't interested in butting her head against.

Thoughts of Darwin resurfaced. Whatever was happening between the two of them needed to be defined. She needed to know what he was feeling, if anything at all. Her crush was blossoming into something more. It was a full sensation of wanting and yearning that had to do with more than that casual tickle of electricity that ran rampant from her womanhood when she thought about him. It was more than his exciting her, or her being intrigued by the possibility of any romantic liaisons. Darwin's presence in her life had revived her spirit, had given her hope, and she felt energized when they were together. It was a sensation she hoped could last her a lifetime.

Making her way into her home, she dropped the box down onto the bench and eased her way into the kitchen. The little green light on her answering machine was blinking rapidly for her attention. Depressing the play button, she kicked off her shoes as the tape rewound and began to play.

"Bridget, hey, it's Darwin. Look, I was an ass and I'm sorry. I wanted to call and talk to you, but I'm too embarrassed to say this in person yet. But I will. I just wanted you to know that I was a fool. And I know it. And I'm sorry. I hope you'll forgive me. I'll call you later."

The machine beeped.

"It's me again. I just called your office and they said you'd left already and you're not answering your cell phone. Look, if you're not too mad at me, I would really like to see you later. Then I can apologize properly. Think about it and I'll try to give you a call later. Okay? Okay. Thanks, Bridget. Later."

Beep.

Bridget found herself grinning foolishly. A third and final message began to play.

"I am probably making a complete and total fool of myself but I really don't want what happened to spoil things between us. I…well…I…" The man paused, taking a deep inhale of air before he continued. "I think you and I are good together and I probably should have just shut my mouth and kissed you this morning and none of this would ever have happened. I really missed that I didn't kiss you. God, I hope you're still speaking to me. I—" The machine clicked off, cutting off the last of his message.

Just as Bridget spun around toward the bedroom to go and change her clothes, the telephone rang. She turned back and pulled the receiver into her palm.

"Hello?"

There was a brief pause.

"Hello?"

"Bridget, I'm sorry. I wasn't expecting you to pick up. Hi."

"Hi, Darwin."

"Did you get my messages?"

"I did."

On the other end, Darwin was fidgeting nervously, strumming the fingers of his free hand against his pant leg.

"If I have to beg for your forgiveness, I will. I'll get down on my hands and knees, if necessary."

Bridget laughed. "It's not, but I appreciate the offer."

"I really do apologize. I just—"

"I understand. You were frustrated," Bridget said, interrupting him. "But don't let it happen again or you and I are going to be really bad friends."

Darwin smiled into the receiver. "I promise."

Bridget slid to the floor, her back pressed against the cool surface of her stainless steel refrigerator as she pulled her knees up and into her chest, her heels tucked against her buttocks. "So, are you feeling any better about what happened last night?"

Darwin shook his head. "Not really, but I'm trying not to be irrational. I had a meeting with Ella this morning and her attitude just annoys me."

"How so?"

"She's just too nonchalant about the whole thing. I still think that something's not kosher with her and Ava."

"You didn't accuse her of anything, did you?"

"No, but don't you think I should have at least asked her if she was involved?"

"No, I don't. Even if she is, I doubt highly that she would have admitted anything. For now, you just need to keep your guard up and don't let on that you suspect her of anything, at least not until we can figure out why she did it and prove it."

"We?"

"You really didn't think I wouldn't help you, did you?"

"I don't know what I was thinking, to be honest with you. I was just reacting and we both know how badly that turned out."

"Yes, we do."

There was a brief moment of silence.

"Bridget, would you do me a favor?"

"What's that?"

"Open your front door, 'cause your neighbor is starting to make me nervous."

Bridget laughed, rising from her seat to make her way to the front door. She pulled it open, surprised to find Darwin standing sheepishly on the other side. Behind him, Mrs. Gibson was standing in her own doorway, eyeing him suspiciously.

She tossed her hand into the air and waved at the old woman. "Hi, Mrs. Gibson!"

"Hello, dear. Is everything okay?"

"Yes, ma'am. Everything is just fine," Bridget said as she grabbed Darwin's hand and pulled him inside. "You have a good day now!" she called out before shutting the door behind them.

Away from prying stares, Darwin pulled her into his arms and stared into her eyes. The dark pools were swirling with emotion and Darwin sensed that she was feeling as vulnerable as he was.

"I'm sorry," he said softly, his voice barely a loud whisper. "I should never have behaved that way. And it will never happen again. Can you forgive me?"

Bridget smiled, her gaze still entwined with his and she nodded, her head bobbing ever so easily. "You're forgiven."

Darwin continued to meet her stare, his hands pressed beneath her suit jacket, his fingers gently caressing the line of her back, above her silk blouse. He watched as her dark eyelashes fluttered against her skin, a blush of color rising to warm her cheeks. He pulled her even closer, melding his body tightly against hers. Raising his hand to her face, he cradled her cheek in his palm, rubbing his thumb over the skin as he traced the line of her high cheekbones.

Slowly, he lowered his face to hers, pressing his mouth to her forehead. He kissed the soft flesh lightly, inching a slow path down the side of her face, over her earlobe, down her jawline, and back to her mouth where he covered her lips with his own.

Bridget stood completely lost in the moment. As his mouth moved like silk against hers she realized she'd not taken a breath since he'd stepped into the room. She was floating, her body reacting with a mind of its own. In that short span of time, she realized that her life had changed, that nothing would ever again be the same. The realization was amazing, and frightening, and so deliciously exciting that it was all she could do to contain herself.

Darwin sensed it, as well, and he said so. "I don't know what's happening with us but I don't ever want it to stop," he said, pulling his mouth away from hers.

Bridget rested her head against his chest. "I have to tell you, Darwin, I've been fantasizing about us for a long time now. If this is a dream, I don't ever want to wake up," she said.

Darwin laughed, the rustle of his chest vibrating warmly against the side of her face. He pulled his fingers through the length of her hair, inhaling the sweet scent of coconut oil that moisturized each strand.

"I'll admit to a fantasy or two myself. But I knew I wasn't ready for a relationship with anyone. Not back then."

"And now?" Bridget asked, stepping out of the embrace.

Darwin smiled. "I don't think I have much choice. This feels right."

"Oh, you have a choice, Darwin. You have all the free will in the world. You have as much control over what happens between us as I do."

Darwin clasped her hand beneath his, pulling her along as he moved into her living room to the oversize chenille sofa. They sat down facing each other. Darwin pressed both of her hands between his. He kissed her fingers, then both of her palms, entwining his fingers between hers. He heaved a deep sigh, his expression strained.

"Bridget, I'm just going to say this and I hope it comes out right. Since that first time we met there hasn't been one time that you haven't been in the back of my thoughts. I've found myself thinking about you when I've least expected it. So when I say it's like I have no choice, it's because I don't.

"It hit me this morning as I was speeding down the highway that if I lost you before we had a real chance to build something between us, I wouldn't know what to do with myself."

Darwin studied her face, searching her expression for acknowledgment and approval, looking deep into her eyes to see if she was feeling the same way. When she smiled, there was hope brimming at the edge of her stare, her eyes glistening with warmth.

"You were speeding?"

Darwin nodded. "Like a madman. And the only thing I really wanted to do was turn around and come back to you."

"So, why didn't you?"

"I don't make it a habit of embarrassing myself on

purpose and you have to admit, I made a fool of myself. But I had to see you and that's why I'm here now."

He shifted his body closer to hers, wrapping his arms around her torso. "I just needed to hold you to make sure we were still cool with each other."

Bridget nodded, pressing her lips to his. "I think we're just fine."

She could feel his thigh move against hers. He let it rest there and the heat from his body seeped into hers. Darwin could feel his chest tighten, his breath coming in shorter gasps as he fought to maintain his composure. Bridget leaned even closer, the whole of her body falling against his as they leaned back against the cushioned seat.

He felt her lips searching his, her breath mixing with his. His hands were moving of their own volition and Bridget imagined they were memorizing every dimple and curve of her body. Her skin burned hot beneath her silk blouse and the dark blue Elie Tahari skirt. She pressed both of her palms to his chest, allowing her own fingers to gently caress the rock-hard muscles as she began her own inspection. When one palm fell against the waistband of his slacks and the other against his upper thigh, Darwin grabbed her wrists and broke the connection. They were both panting, sucking in oxygen as if they'd been denied. The room was spinning with heat, the temperature having risen to an unreasonable level.

"I need to get back to the office," he said, still gasping for air, "before we get into something we don't have time for."

Bridget nodded her head, perspiration beading in the valley of cleavage beneath her lace bra.

"If you say so."

He grinned. "I can cook here tonight or at my place. Your choice."

"I'll come to you. I have a few errands to run this afternoon so I'll be out and about anyway."

Rising onto his feet, Darwin pulled her up beside him, wrapping his arms around her one last time. He tasted her lips once more before moving to the door.

Standing in the doorway, he said nothing, only staring intently at her as she stood staring back. His smile was a mile wide, warming his face with joy. Easing out the entrance, he closed the door behind him and headed back to work.

Dropping back to the sofa, Bridget pressed her knees tightly together. The man had left her weak, her limbs quivering for release. The sensations were almost too much to handle and she knew the dinner hour couldn't come soon enough.

As Darwin made his way through downtown Seattle, back toward the studio and his office, he could feel a rise of anxiety pulling at his already strained nerves. The brief moment with Bridget had gone two steps beyond a flirtatious kiss and cuddle session. In fact, had the timing been different, Darwin imagined that there would have only been one reason that would have kept the two of them from taking the moment as far as it could go.

He heaved a deep sigh. He bit down on his bottom lip, chewing against the flesh nervously. Heat had exploded through his bloodstream, but nothing had rained South, not one spark or current of electricity had ignited a quiver of an erection, his flesh lying limp and staid. That alone would surely have spoiled the moment.

It had begun to rain, the sky darkening in deep, dark, gray striations. Thick, heavy, moisture-filled clouds had rolled in with a cooling breeze and had finally let go, water spilling down over the landscape with a vengeance. The weather seemed to be setting the tone for the rest of his day and as Darwin raced through the studio's employee entrance, he was no longer feeling the buoyant joy he'd left behind with Bridget.

Chapter 10

Ella had sat in her car watching Darwin as he'd exited the building, gotten into his own vehicle, and had pulled off into midday traffic. Once he was out of sight, she started the ignition and drove off in the opposite direction.

Minutes later she gave a quick wave to the guard monitoring the brick entrance of a gated community as she drove into an enclave of very expensive, upscale, luxury homes. She pulled up in front of a large Tudor-style estate, parking her Jeep Cherokee behind a sleek, Mercedes-Benz SLR McLaren. The four-hundred-thousand-dollar automobile, as well as the million-dollar house, had been a gift to its owner from one of her numerous male friends. As she walked past the vehicle, Ella resisted the urge to swipe the keys in her hand against the car's side.

She entered the home through a side door, not bothering to knock before she pushed her way inside. Ava St. John greeted her from the kitchen counter as she sat picking over a salad of mixed baby greens and raw vegetables.

"And why do you look like the cat who ate the canary?" Ava inquired, eyeing the other woman curiously.

Ella cut an eye in her direction as she pulled open the door of the stainless steel refrigerator. She reached inside for a can of Sprite soda, popped open the top and took a swig of the carbonated beverage. It trickled a bubbly path down her throat, moistening her dry mouth. She leaned against the counter, reaching to pick a baby carrot from Ava's plate.

Then she responded. "It was too easy, little sister. Now all I have to do is sit back and reap the rewards. The owners are thrilled with how I'm handling our Darwin Tolliver problem."

"And just how are you handling Mr. Tolliver?"

"I'm telling him what he wants to hear. Unfortunately for him, I also have to tell the powers in charge something else altogether, but in the end, I'll be president of my own division."

Ava leaned forward on her elbows. "And you really believe Darwin is just going to sit back and take whatever you throw at him?"

"The man's a fool. Handling him is the least of my concerns."

"I wouldn't underestimate Darwin if I were you. I told you before it's the nice guys who always prove to be more problematic."

Ella rolled her eyes. "You just do what I ask you to do, please. I'll take care of everything else."

"Well, I've told you before, don't waste your time with boys on the bottom of the totem pole. To get to the top you have to work the men at the top. Darwin is small fish and small fish usually net you small results."

Ella scowled. "You really think you know everything, don't you?"

Ava shook her head and shrugged her shoulders. "I'm the star that I am, sister dear, because to work a man for all he's worth you have to know his weaknesses to be able to exploit those weaknesses to your advantage. What I know is that you don't know anything about Darwin Tolliver and that is going to be your downfall."

Ella glared at her sibling. "Don't you wish."

Ava pushed her plate aside as she rose from her seat, heading into the other room. "No," she said, her voice softening, "actually I don't wish such a thing, Ella. I don't wish anything like that on you at all."

Ella watched as her sister disappeared out of sight, moving to place a telephone call. She could hear her in the distance, a low, seductive voice teasing and taunting some poor fool. Slamming out the back door, Ella stopped to kick Ava's tire before heading back to her job.

Driving back to the office, she chewed on her sister's comments. They were only half sisters, same mother, different fathers, and the sibling rivalry raged rampant through Ella's spirit. Ava had always been prettier, smarter, thinner, more cunning, worldlier, and she let Ella know it at every opportunity. Ella believed Ava relished each and every opportunity she had to show her up. There was no disputing they had love for each other—their mother had insisted on it—but there was absolutely nothing about the other that either liked. Ella had resented Ava from day one, the baby girl her mother and stepfather had doted on.

Ava's father had been perfect. The ideal husband and adoring parent any woman would have been lucky to have. He'd spoiled Ava endlessly and though he'd been extraordinarily kind and loving with Ella, she'd always been acutely sensitive to the fact that she wasn't his child by blood.

Ella's father had been every woman's worst nightmare, an abusive, uncaring cad who'd made her mother cry more times than anyone cared to count. He'd disappeared when Ella had been five years old and though she could count on one hand with fingers left over the number of times he'd ever come to visit her, she still mourned the loss of him as if it had happened just yesterday. As she pulled into her reserved parking space, Ella was even more determined to get what she wanted. She was desperate to prove Ava wrong.

It had taken Bridget less than an hour to get her hands on copies of all the daily tabloids. The lead story in five out of six of them was about Ava St. John and her illicit tryst with her new boy toy, Darwin Tolliver. To add insult to injury, a rival television station was touting an upcoming, exclusive interview with Ava, photos of the two of them flashing across the television screen.

Bridget pressed the off button on her remote control, striding into her home office to her computer on the desktop. Logging on to the Internet, she made her way to a search engine and typed in Ava St. John's name. Bridget could only shake her head at the 199,000 entries that were found.

She headed first to the official Web site of Ava St. John. The site was page upon page of color images of Ava in free-flowing gowns or scant articles of clothing that were more sequins and glitter than actual fabric. There was promotion for her tell-all book with a tour section for fans to find out where she would be speaking. The gallery area was a who's who of celebrity stardom posed adoringly alongside the woman. Newly added was a press image of Ava and Darwin smiling into a camera.

Bridget read Ava's personal statement with interest, the woman proclaiming herself to be an authentic goddess above all other women. To hear Ava tell it, her way was the way to a New World where women were in full control and men mere stepping stones to be walked on. Bridget found the rhetoric to be akin to walking knee-deep in Ava's delusions of grandeur. As she reached the end of Ava's bio page, one line of information caught her full attention. Ava St. John had been born and raised in Coulee City, Washington, just like Ella Scott.

Ava sank into a large pool of hot water and rose-scented bath bubbles. Closing her eyes, she settled her naked body back against the bath pillow, allowing the rush of warm steam to seep into her pores.

It felt good to finally relax, she thought, to disconnect away from the stress and strain that had become her daily life. Soaking in a hot tub at four o'clock in the afternoon was only slightly out of character for Ava, but since Ella's plea for her help the month before, she was finding it necessary to make full use of any free moment she had to unwind.

Ella was six years older and Ava couldn't remember a

time in her life when she'd not been working to gain her big sister's approval. No matter what Ella had ever asked of her, Ava had complied, hopeful for just one glint of acceptance in Ella's eyes.

This time, though, Ava sensed they'd gone too far with the wrong man. Ava had never been above getting whatever she could from a suitor and more times than not they had all gotten the best of Ava in return, but Darwin Tolliver hadn't been one of Ava's usual conquests. In fact, Ava hadn't conquered Darwin at all and from their very brief exchange, she knew that she never would. Being so sure of that fact was why her blood pressure was skating on high.

Reading the male sex had always been her specialty and she had read Darwin like a good book. Ella hadn't wanted to listen to her concerns, though, believing she had the situation under control. But Ava knew better. Ava knew when it came to a man's soul, no woman but the one who had his heart could ever control anything else about him.

Ava sighed, filling her palms with warm water and allowing it to flow slowly through her fingers and back into the tub. She needed to figure a way out of this mess before it got any worse. She loved her sister dearly and though she was no stranger to controversy, she couldn't afford to let this fiasco come back to bite her on the behind.

An hour later Ava was dressed for another night on the town. She was having dinner with an old friend, a man who'd proven himself useful when she'd least expected it. If she'd had a choice, she would have preferred to just crawl into her bed with the new Deborah Fletcher Mello novel she'd picked up at the bookstore. But she needed to ensure that if her friend's services were ever needed down the road that the few hours of her attention he'd receive tonight would be credit against any future favors she might need.

Bridget had closed down the law library, the staff locking the doors behind her as she'd left. Her research had gone better than expected and she was excited to get to Darwin to tell him what she had planned.

As she followed the traffic into downtown Seattle, she mulled over the information she'd discovered about Ava and how she might be able to use that to their benefit. Ava's history was interesting to say the least, but there was something vulnerable, almost fragile about the woman's persona that seemed way out of character for the image she portrayed.

Darwin was standing on his front stoop, peering into his mailbox when she pulled into the driveway. Biscuit was sniffing the grass at the bottom of the steps, her tail wagging, excited to be out in the fresh air. The dog yipped as Bridget approached, racing down the walkway to greet her.

Bridget swept the puppy up in her arms and hugged it to her chest, scratching the fur behind the animal's ears. "Hi, Biscuit," she chimed as she climbed the two steps up to where Darwin stood. "Hi, you," she said with a wide grin.

Darwin grinned back, leaning in to kiss her mouth before greeting her. "Hey, sweetheart. You are right on time. I was just starting to miss you."

Bridget was slightly taken aback by the gesture. There was a comfort and familiarity that Bridget had never experienced before. Her gaze met his and held it, allowing the emotion to caress both their spirits. Darwin's smile was all-consuming and then he wrapped an easy arm around her waist as he guided her inside.

"How did your day go?" Bridget asked, dropping Biscuit down onto her special chair.

Darwin shrugged, his smile fading noticeably. "Taping was great, but then anytime I'm cooking, I feel better. Ella was still acting like I shouldn't have a care in the world, but I still have a bad feeling about that woman. I don't know, Bridget, I just keep getting the feeling like she's trying to play me for a fool."

Bridget nodded her understanding, leaning against the counter as Darwin dropped a pan of fresh pasta into a pot of boiling water. A concoction of red gravy simmered in a large saucepan, a melange of fresh Roma tomatoes, sweet onions, shiitake mushrooms, olives and cloves of garlic scenting the air. The aroma was intoxicating and Bridget took a deep inhale of air, the warmth of it filling her lungs. A pang of hunger suddenly cramped her stomach and she realized she'd not eaten anything since that buttered croissant at breakfast.

As if reading her mind, Darwin gestured toward the dining table. "The food is almost done. If you'll set the table, I'll get the garlic bread in the oven and we should be ready to eat in just a few minutes."

Bridget moved around the table laying out the plates and silverware resting on top. "How would you feel about bringing a civil lawsuit against the tabloids and Ava St. John? The official charge against them would be malicious defamation," she added, cutting an eye in his direction.

Darwin stopped in his tracks, a Teflon-coated baking sheet in his hand tilting toward the floor. "Are you serious?"

"Very. I think you have grounds for a civil suit. I also feel you should sue for no other reason than sheer principle. Two of the tabloids actually reported that you and Ava engaged in illicit sexual conduct based solely on a photo I think we can prove was manipulated. They blatantly lied.

"Ava has substantiated that lie with more lies, innuendo and overt comments that have cast a negative light on your reputation. I think they should all be held accountable for their actions."

Darwin's head bobbed up and down . He laid the baking sheet against the counter, sliding four slices of Texas toast on top, and then slid the pan into a heated oven. "Do you think we can win?" he asked, turning back to face her.

"I think we'll eventually settle, but we want the attention, as well as a very public apology. And it's that public attention we want more than anything else. We want people to know that you aren't the man they're making you out to be. I also think it will help us find out what the link between Ava and Ella is."

"So you believe me about Ella?"

Bridget smiled, nodding her head. "I believed that you weren't capable of doing what you'd been accused of. You just never gave me the chance to say so."

He nodded his head ever so slightly. "Sorry about that."

Bridget shrugged. "Did you know both women came from the same small town? How coincidental is that?"

"How did you find…" Darwin started, pausing to peer into the refrigerator for a bowl of grated Parmesan cheese "…that out?" he finished, tossing her a quick look.

"I did a little homework. It's amazing what a girl can find out if she digs in just the right places."

Darwin came to a standstill, turning to face her. His gaze locked with hers as he studied her intently. "Why are you doing all of this?" he asked. "I mean, I know why I want you to help me, but why are you actually doing it?"

Bridget pondered his question for only a brief moment. "I understand that your integrity means everything to you. You haven't gotten this far in life being a man others couldn't look up to. And now that you are a public figure you have the opportunity to be an admirable role model for other young black boys. I don't want anyone or anything to taint that. You mean too much to me to ever let that happen," she said, her voice dropping softly.

Darwin beamed and as his face glowed, it looked as if a heavy weight had been lifted from his shoulders. He reached to give Bridget another kiss, allowing his cheek to linger just briefly against her cheek. "Boy, I'm glad you're my girl."

Not sure how to respond, Bridget found herself blushing, her face flushing with heat. Opting to say nothing at all, she turned back to the table she'd been setting and lit the tall candles that sat in an arrangement of freshly cut flowers.

The mood in the room shifted and their dinner conversation touched every subject except Ava and a pending lawsuit. Both were grateful for the reprieve, their minds overly saturated by thoughts of what had happened to Darwin and the potential fallout. Bridget marveled at how easy the exchange between them was. They laughed and joked about things that were silly, of no true value, and both felt as if their spending time together was the most natural thing for them to do. Both Darwin and Bridget liked the fit, the way they meshed so comfortably with one another.

The evening moved into Darwin's family room, the duo cuddled comfortably against each other on the sofa. The television was on, but the volume had been turned down low, barely audible over their chatter. Turning her attention to the screen, Bridget reached for the remote and turned up the sound. TV One was showing a classic Tyler Perry comedy and before they knew it both were in near hysterics, laughing loudly at the lunacy of Madea and her kin.

Bridget kicked off her sandals and twisted her body sideways. She pulled her legs up on the arm of the couch and leaned her torso back against Darwin's chest. The man wrapped his arms around her, pulling her comfortably into him as she leaned her head back and snuggled against his shoulder. Together they enjoyed the televised mirth, but it soon became obvious that they were enjoying being in such close proximity more. They grew comfortable in that position, neither giving any thought to moving during the commercial breaks.

The aroma of patchouli incense billowed from a small burner on the coffee table and in the dimly lit room, the faint glow of the television provided most of the light. Darwin traced his fingers up and down the length of her bare arm, marveling at the sheer beauty of her dark skin, its rich color melding nicely against his own. The scent of her perfume was intoxicating and he inhaled deeply, sucking in the scent of her as if his life depended on it. Thoughts of touching her, and tasting her, and feeling himself lost within her raged like wildfire across his mind.

He cupped his palm beneath her chin and lifted her mouth to his, tasting the soft silk of her lips. The touch was easy and sweet, just the barest caress of flesh against flesh. He deepened the embrace, his lips skating anxiously across hers. Darwin captured her mouth beneath his, his tongue seeking sanctuary with hers. He could feel his heart begin to race, perspiration beading against his brow.

Bridget shifted upward, both of her palms pressing hot against his chest. Darwin's own hand reached out to stroke the length of her back, his fingers snaking across the shelf of her buttocks. Bridget moved against him, pressing the fullness of her breasts against his chest, her abdomen kissing his. He boldly reached one hand up between them to cup her breast, his fingers dancing against the protrusion of nipple that swelled hard and full beneath his touch. The other hand trailed seductively along the edge of her skirt, tickling the line of her thigh as he tiptoed to the edge of her black silk panties. Heat radiated from her core and with his eyes closed, Darwin imagined he could hear her heart beating in sync with his, both panting heavily as they yearned for more.

He was suddenly aware of Bridget boldly stroking his upper thigh as she shifted her leg between his legs, her knee gently caressing the apex of his crotch. When she moved to undo his belt buckle, pulling at his pants zipper, his nerves suddenly kicked into overdrive. Sensation failed him and fear reared an ugly head to spoil the moment. His body tensed as he grasped her hands beneath his own.

"Bridget, stop, please," Darwin muttered, his voice cracking. There was a tear in the corner of his eye and Bridget watched as it dropped onto his cheek and rolled down over his chin. He eased his body away from hers, moving to the other end of the couch. The space between them was suddenly a wide gully of discomfort, confusion and quiet chaos.

"Is something wrong?" she asked, her expression concerned.

He shook his head. He stammered, searching for a response that would ease them out of the moment. "I…I…just…"

As his gaze moved away from hers, she sensed his discomfort, then suddenly remembered what the problem was. Bridget moved back next to him and pressed both of her palms to his face as she kissed his mouth. She wrapped her arms around his shoulders and neck and hugged him tightly. "I don't care," she whispered into his ear. "It will happen for us when it's supposed to."

"What if it doesn't?" Darwin whispered back. "What if I can't ever—"

"Shh." She brushed her mouth against his for a second time. "Hush. Figuring out other ways that we can bring each other pleasure will be half the fun. Right now, though, you have other things on your mind. I understand that. We're sitting up here playing house like we haven't got anything else to do. Once the pressure's off and you can relax I'm sure everything will be just fine."

Darwin hugged her back, holding her tightly. "I sure hope you're right, Bridget. I want to make love to you so badly that it hurts."

"See. Desire is half the battle. The rest will fall into place when it's time. Now just isn't the time."

Wanting to believe her, Darwin nodded his head. He reached for the lamp on the table at his side and switched on the light. Taking a quick glance at his wristwatch he brushed his palms against his pant leg and tossed Bridget a quick glance. Although he didn't want to say so out loud, he desperately needed to be alone.

She smiled sweetly as if reading his mind. "I should head on home. I have a ton of research to do to prepare my brief and get your case filed. I should probably get to bed early. Besides, a girl needs all the beauty rest she can get."

Darwin forced himself to smile back. "You won't need much sleep then." He brushed his index finger down the line of her profile.

"Flattery will get you everywhere, Mr. Tolliver."

"That and my banana cream mousse."

"Yeah, that mousse was good."

He gave her a quick wink as he followed her to the door.

Bridget turned, moving to stroke his arm. She caressed him warmly before she stepped outside. "Thank you for dinner, Darwin."

"I'm usually better company than this, Bridget. I hope you don't…"

She stalled his words with another gentle squeeze to his upper arm. "Just say good-night and if you get a chance, give me a call tomorrow," she said.

Darwin nodded his head, then grimaced, his face twisting as if he were in pain. "I completely forgot," he said, slapping his palm to his forehead. "I'm not here tomorrow. We're shooting off-site and I'll be away for a few days."

"That's okay," Bridget responded. "You have to handle your business."

"But I will call. Every chance I get. I promise."

Bridget led the way out his front door as Darwin walked her to her car, wrapping her in one last hug before making sure she was secure behind the wheel of her automobile. He stood with his arms crossed over his chest,

watching as she pulled out of the parking area and headed
down the road. When the last flicker of her taillights turned
the corner out of his sight, he headed back inside, closing
and locking the door behind him.

He stood with his back against the door frame, leaning
on it for support, his hands pushed deep into his pockets.
He was experiencing sensory overload, every nerve
ending in his body feeling as if it were ready to explode
from sheer stress. It felt as if the weight of the world had
fallen on his shoulders and he couldn't find the strength
or the energy to keep it from crushing him into the ground.
He heaved a deep sigh, blowing a gale of warm breath out
past his parted lips.

Moving into the family room, he fell across the chenille
sofa, stretching his body from one end of the unit to the
other. He thought about Bridget. He had loved the feel of
her in his arms, how nicely they fit against one another.
He would have given anything to have swept her up in his
arms to carry her into his bedroom to lie against the freshly
washed sheets he'd put on the bed. He'd wanted to press
himself into her, to revel in the feel of her body wrapped
around his own. His heart and his mind hadn't needed any
encouragement, but his manhood had made it clear that
he needed some serious assistance. He couldn't help wondering if anything fazed Bridget, her calm and collected
demeanor seeming to take it and everything else in stride.
As much as he'd wanted her gone just minutes before, he
now wished her back. He would have given almost anything to have her still there lying by his side.

Bridget couldn't believe herself. It had only been an incredible dinner, a bottle of expensive wine, dim lights and

incense, and she'd been ready to drop her panties right there on the man's sofa. She could still feel his hands on her body, her skin feeling as if he'd burned an imprint across her flesh. Just thinking about his touch was causing her to breathe heavily and she rolled down the window, allowing the night air to blow into her face.

She couldn't begin to imagine what Darwin was thinking about her and the way she'd behaved. She shook her head. *Lord, my mother didn't raise me to be so easy,* she thought. Although it broke her heart to see him so distressed by his predicament, Bridget was grateful for the diversion. Two dinners didn't make a relationship and she hadn't intended to act so brazenly. Bridget was sure Darwin had women throwing themselves at him all the time. Ava had been proof of that. She surely didn't want to give the man the impression that she was that way, and had he not stopped her, there was no telling what she would have done.

She had wanted him. Badly. Had his fingers crept just an inch closer to her secret treasure it would have been all over. All day she'd been fantasizing about the two of them, barely able to concentrate on anything else. She had envisioned the two of them making love over and over again, only managing to disentangle their bodies from each other for brief moments. She'd imagined the long, lingering kisses Darwin would plant against her body until they both got slick and sweaty. And then there would have been showers, warm, wet escapades beneath the spray of a double showerhead. Bridget had foreseen them kissing, caressing, climaxing and dozing off in each other's arms. Then one would gently awaken the other with more kisses and caresses, and it would start all over again. Her fantasies had been fueled knowing she would be spending the evening in his company.

The loud horn of a passing vehicle brought her back to reality and Bridget gasped loudly, her attention moving back to the road ahead of her. Darwin was surely messing with her concentration and all she really wanted was to turn her car around to head right back into his arms.

Chapter 11

Ella was glad for the day to be over and even happier that it was the end of her workweek. She was looking forward to the weekend and the two-day reprieve from her responsibilities at the station. The pressure had increased tenfold and it was starting to wear on her energy level. She was also weary of Darwin Tolliver and the permanent pout that seemed to fill his face every time he was in her presence. She'd figured he would be over himself by now but she'd been wrong.

Moving into her galley kitchen she pulled an open bottle of Chianti from the refrigerator and poured herself a large glassful. She didn't have an appetite for food but had spent most of the afternoon looking forward to coming home and kicking back with some Boney James on her CD player and a good bottle of wine.

Kicking off her shoes, she slipped out of her clothes and dropped down against her living room sofa. She drew her forearm over her forehead, closing her eyes as she settled down against the cushions.

Boney was blowing a soothing tune across her spirit, the easy syncopation of the saxophone like a freesia-scented balm filling the air around her. Ella didn't like it, but she had to admit things weren't going as well as she'd hoped. Reaching for the wineglass resting on the coffee table, she swigged a large mouthful and then a second.

Although her plan hadn't backfired altogether, it hadn't played out as nicely as she had plotted. She'd predicted the public interest, certain that her baby sister would generate plenty of attention to herself and Darwin. And where she'd anticipated Mr. Nice Guy Darwin Tolliver would have shrugged it off, perhaps even being amused by all the attention, the man was instead acting like someone had accused him of bloody murder.

As well, the station's owners had been overly concerned at first, their confidence in Darwin wavering substantially. A few of the sponsors had even threatened to pull their advertisements, citing Darwin's behavior as grounds to revoke all their contracts. Idle threats to get their rates reduced, Ella mused. It had almost been catastrophic before she had swooped in to save the day and make things better. The significant increase in the show's Nielsen numbers hadn't hurt, either, the *Cooking with Darwin Tolliver* show rising to number one in its time slot and holding strong.

Go figure, she thought, rolling her eyes and her moving head from side to side. Ava had tried to warn her about playing Darwin Tolliver, but the man had been convenient. Ella didn't have anything against Darwin. In fact, for the most part she had liked the man as much as she liked any man. Although he would not have been her first choice for hosting the new show, the powers that be had loved everything about him. He was too pretty for her tastes, though, and he reminded Ella of the many pretty men who'd used and abused her over the years. Men who'd made her feel insecure or unwanted, who'd misjudged her loving demeanor as weakness, thinking she was a doormat they could all walk over.

It had always been the pretty men with their chiseled good looks, bedroom eyes, athletic bodies and butter-toned voices that had fawned over Ava, giving her anything and everything her heart desired. They were the same men who had barely given Ella the time of day. Darwin could have been the poster child for all the pretty men in the world, Ella thought, and for that reason alone, it had been easy to play havoc with his life.

Ultimately, management was happy once again and they had more confidence in what Ella could and couldn't do. As long as she could keep the show at the top, a promotion was surely in line for her. Ella mused that she'd done a fair enough job of placating Darwin's bruised ego so that he shouldn't be any more of a problem. She also hoped by Monday morning he'd be back to his normal self, the incident barely occupying his thoughts.

She was starting to feel the effects of the wine on her empty stomach. Her nerves were still shaky, anxiety playing pattycake with her spirit. It was an ice cream moment, she thought, rising from her seat to go peer into the freezer. A pint container of Ben & Jerry's Chunky Monkey ice cream was waving for her attention. Grabbing the container and a spoon from the drawer, Ella moved back to the couch, sinking her utensil into the banana-flavored confection as she dug around for a few chocolate chunks and some walnuts. The ice cream melted against her tongue and half a pint later, the empty sensation in the pit of her stomach began to feel satiated.

She really should have avoided the ice cream, she thought as she savored the last few spoonfuls. Just that morning she'd been upset that she couldn't zip her size eighteen slacks and here she was gorging herself on sweets. Ella heaved a deep sigh. She'd recognized years ago that she ate for comfort and right then she needed a lot of comfort.

For just a brief second she thought about calling Ava. Then she thought better of it, imagining her sister's Friday night was being spent being wined and dined by her man of the moment. Even if she were home, Ava would only give her a lecture about taking better care of herself and Ella didn't need any lectures. In fact, she thought as she lifted herself from the sofa one more time, all she needed was that container of Cherry Garcia sitting next to a frozen TV dinner in her refrigerator. Just the sheer thought of another spoonful of ice cream seemed a better cure for everything that ailed her.

Ava hid behind a pair of designer sunshades and a large floppy hat. No one but the large black man behind the counter knew who she was and no one else in the video store bothered to lift an eyebrow to gaze in her direction. The store's owner had waved a hand in greeting when she'd entered, nodding a quick hello as he dealt with another customer. Ava was grateful for his silence, not wanting to be bothered with any attention.

Searching the shelves, Ava picked up five DVDs, taking stock of the store's weekend special: five movies for five days for five dollars. She was planning a quiet weekend, no company, no dates, her time all her own to do as she pleased. She had no intention of making up her face or even bothering to comb and brush her hair if she didn't feel like it. The refrigerator was already filled with her favorite junk foods and she had no plans to even think about exercise or dieting. She needed this time to regroup and recharge her energy levels. People had been pulling at her attention for weeks and she'd had more than enough.

The store was now empty and Wiley, the owner, leaned against the counter staring in her direction. He really was a nice-looking man, Ava thought, his round, umber-toned complexion projecting large black eyes, a broad nose and full lips. Wiley smiled and Ava couldn't help but smile back.

"So, how are you doing, Wiley?" Ava asked politely, moving to the counter with her selections.

"Just fine. How about yourself?" he responded as he entered her account number into his computer system.

Ava shrugged her narrow shoulders as she wrapped her arms around her torso, pulling her oversize sweater over her chest. "I can't complain."

"No one bothers to listen when you do," Wiley said, smiling broadly.

"Isn't that the truth," Ava answered.

Wiley looked from Ava to the computer screen and back to Ava. "Miss Ava, you have a late fee on your account from last month. Two movies came back three days late."

Ava nodded. "Sorry about that. I'll pay the fee now."

The man nodded as he tallied up her bill. "Your total is twelve dollars and thirty-six cents."

Ava passed him a credit card, her hand quivering ever so slightly as he brushed his thick fingers against hers. Wiley smiled again.

He pointed to the DVD on top of the pile. "This was an excellent movie. You're going to love it," he said, sliding the pile from the counter into a plastic bag. "It's some of Denzel's best work, I think." He passed the bag to Ava, then slid the credit card receipt forward for her signature. He watched as she scribbled her name across the tab and passed it back to him.

"Thanks, Wiley," Ava said, not bothering to move from where she stood. She slid the sunshades off her face, allowing her eyes to meet his. He met her gaze and held it. She motioned as if to speak, then thinking better of it, pulled the shades back on and said nothing.

"Is everything okay, Miss Ava?"

"Don't call me that. You and I have known each other too long for you to be calling me Miss. And it makes me feel old. I've told you before, please, just call me Ava."

The man chuckled softly as he nodded his head. "Ava. That's a very pretty name."

"Thank you."

"So, is everything okay, Ava?"

She shrugged again. "I was just thinking that you seem to spend all of your time here in the store."

"I'm a man trying to build an empire. I do what I have to do."

"What about your girlfriend? I imagine she would want you home over the weekends, right?"

Wiley leaned on his elbows, resting his chin against the

back of his hand. "We're not together anymore. It didn't work out. She said I work too much. Go figure," he said with a low chuckle. "Seems I'm all alone again." He gave her a broad grin as he continued staring into her eyes.

Ava was suddenly at a loss for words and she clutched her bag closer to her chest. "Well…I…" she stammered. "I guess…I should be going."

"Enjoy your movies."

She nodded. "Thanks. See you next week."

"I look forward to it," Wiley said, giving her a quick wink. "You have a good weekend, Ava."

Moving toward the door, Ava waved goodbye, then disappeared out into the cool evening air. As she eased her car out of the shopping center's parking lot, she couldn't believe her nerves had her shaking like a leaf on a tree. She hadn't ever met a man who could move her to stutter and giggle so foolishly, so she was unnerved by her reaction to that man.

Ava had been a patron of that video store for over ten years, since she first settled in Seattle, moving to be near Ella. The previous owners hadn't been overly friendly, and Ava hadn't been inclined to befriend them or any of the young high school students who had manned the cash register.

Five years ago, Ava had come in one day for her usual monthly selections and Wiley had been behind the counter. He was a gregarious man with a large frame but it was clear that he wasn't overly athletic. He only stood an inch or so taller than Ava's five feet four inches and in her four-inch stilettos she towered easily above him.

He'd blessed her with his trademark smile, introducing himself, and though he wasn't typical of the men Ava was usually attracted to, there had been something about him that had captured her attention. Ava had begun to look forward to seeing him although they both maintained a politely distant relationship. But it had been Wiley who'd changed the direction of Ava's life, a casual comment steering her on a path she'd not considered before.

It had been a rainy Saturday night and Ava had come in bedecked in a formal, candy-apple-red satin ball gown. Her date for the evening, a United States senator with some considerable prestige, had stood her up, not even bothering to call to cancel their dinner plans.

Ava had been livid, her anger furrowing her brow, but she'd made light of it, even spinning a joke or two over the situation. Wiley had laughed and then jokingly commented that Ava needed to write a book about the tribulations of her love life. Two years later, Ava St. John was reborn, a national bestselling author making the rounds on the talk show circuit. And through it all Wiley still smiled when she came in for her movies, treating her no differently from how he'd treated her that very first day.

It wasn't long before Ava was settled comfortably on the sectional sofa in her family room, in oversize flannel pajamas with a chenille blanket wrapped around her body. The first of her five movies had begun to play and a large bowl of freshly popped popcorn tossed with peanut M&M's, Goobers and Raisinets rested in her lap.

As she pulled a handful of the mixture into her mouth, she reflected on just how uneventful her Friday nights really were. Few would have imagined that the infamous Ava St. John rarely had a real date most weekends and wasn't even remotely involved with a man who was actually interested in her. Although the autobiography that she'd written read like good fiction, if Ava was totally forthcoming, she'd have to admit to embellishing a few of the events that had gotten her noticed.

Proclaiming herself the misunderstood mistress of some select politicians and an accused war criminal during a campaign year had hardly been anything to brag about. In fact, one reviewer had called her tome a "walking waste of breath" and since sex scandals had been around since the days of Sodom and Gomorrah, Ava knew that she truly hadn't accomplished anything by sharing the dust and dirt in her closet.

But she'd liked writing and the process of publication had been her true source of accomplishment, a nice reward for her fragile ego. Since then she'd penned some two hundred pages of fiction that she hoped to sell. The story was about two sisters who closely resembled her and Ella, except that her sisters actually loved each other.

Ava heaved a deep sigh, reaching for the remote to the DVD player to rewind what she'd just missed. Thinking about Ella and the mess they'd both made of their lives tended to be a huge distraction. This last fiasco, though, was weighing heavily on Ava's conscience. There had been something about Darwin that she had liked, something she could see in that brief moment that had made him stand out as a man above other men. His smile had been genuine, reminding her of her friend Wiley, and he hadn't been taken in by Ava's charms. In fact, nothing about him had been enamoured with Ava and she could appreciate that he hadn't fawned all over her hoping she would be a conquest he could brag about to his friends. The man was clearly made from moral fiber that would not be compromised and both she and Ella had made light of that. What they said about payback might prove to be prophetic, Ava mused, and that very thought was haunting. She heaved another sigh, shoved a second handful of popcorn into her mouth and lifted her eyes back to her movie.

Chapter 12

They'd talked on the telephone every day for over a week, their conversations lasting for hours on end. The business trip for Darwin to tape at an annual food festival in San Francisco had not just been an excuse to keep them apart, although, if the truth were told, both would have to admit they were still reeling from their last encounter alone. The moment had been more awkward than either had been willing to admit but by day number ten, Darwin knew he needed to face the problem with Bridget and not without her. Being without her was killing him, twisting his heart into a tight knot.

His flight had gotten in late and though he probably should have gone to his own home and waited for daylight before heading to Bridget's, he'd instructed the limousine driver to leave him and his luggage at her front door. He stood anxiously outside waiting for her to answer the doorbell. The elderly woman across the way watched him with a wary eye, never once moving from her stance in an opened window. Darwin's exuberance greeted Bridget as she pulled the door open.

Wrapping his thick arms around her waist, Darwin lifted Bridget off the floor as he swung her in a tight circle. He kissed her, hard, his tongue dancing inside the warm cavity of her mouth. Bridget clasped both of her hands around the back of his neck and kissed him back. He tasted sweet, like strawberry-flavored bubble gum, and she was overcome with glee, laughter filling her spirit.

Carrying her through the entrance, Darwin pushed the door shut with his foot. The knot in his chest began to unwind, the empty, sinking feeling from the days before dissipating into thin air.

"Boy, did I miss you," he murmured, his lips still lingering against hers.

Bridget nodded, wrapping the length of her legs around his waist. Darwin moved to the living room sofa, dropping down against the cushioned seat as he cradled her against his lap. They kissed again.

From the stereo, Keb' Mo' was singing a love song in a brilliant shade of sky-blue. The echo of his voice flooded the room. Keb' Mo' was singing about having lost his love but the sheer beauty of its emotion moved Darwin to think about what he shared, right then, in that moment, with Bridget. His thoughts were interrupted by the telephone ringing. Bridget kissed his cheek, then reached for the receiver.

"Hello?"

She paused, listening to the party on the other end.

"Thank you, Mrs. Gibson. Yes, ma'am. I will. You have a good night," Bridget concluded before hanging up the phone. She giggled, shaking her head in his direction, then lifted her body from his lap. Skipping to the front door, she came back seconds later pulling Darwin's bags behind her.

"You forgot your luggage," she said as he laughed with her.

"I did forget," he responded. "I hadn't given that stuff a single thought since the car service pulled out of the parking lot. All I could think about was holding you."

Bridget waved her head from side to side, her smile widening. Heat flushed her face, the hint of a blush caressing her cheeks. She moved to sit back down beside Darwin on the sofa, pulling her legs beneath her buttocks as she leaned her body against his. Darwin wrapped both arms around her torso, pulling her close to him. They sat quietly together, neither saying a word as they reveled in the familiarity they'd been missing.

The lights in the room were dimmed and Darwin sensed that Bridget had been elsewhere in her home before his unexpected arrival.

"Did I interrupt something?" he asked.

Bridget shook her head, cracking a slight smile. "Not really. I was just reading."

"Anything good?"

"Maureen Smith's last book."

"I don't know her work. If it's any good maybe you'll let me borrow it when you're done."

"Maybe," Bridget said coyly.

Darwin chuckled and they cuddled against each other, shifting positions against their seats. Darwin let his fingers glide along the length of her bare arms, the warmth of her skin teasing his fingertips. Someone's reggae was playing in the other room, the beat sultry and heated as it resonated through the house. For a quick minute Darwin imagined himself nuzzled between Bridget's legs, the two of them making love right there on the carpeted floor. The image was so vivid that he could feel himself break out into a cold sweat.

Bridget sensed the sudden rise in tension and gently stroked his forearm. "Are you hungry?" she asked, easing her body slightly away from his. "I can make you a sandwich."

Darwin shook his head. "No, I just…" He paused, sitting forward in his seat, his hands cupped together in front of him. He cut his eyes in her direction, meeting her stare, then allowed his gaze to drop to the floor. He cleared his throat before continuing. "Bridget, I know things with us seem to be happening kind of fast and I'm really hoping that I'm not feeling all these emotions by myself." Darwin took a deep breath. "Because I'm really feeling you." He looked back up at her.

Bridget's smile was intoxicating as she sat staring at him. Darwin was mesmerized and he leaned in to press his lips against hers. Sweet didn't begin to describe the moment. When he pulled away he was visibly shaking, every nerve ending in his body quivering with nervous energy.

Bridget reached out to hold his hand, clasping his fingers between hers. Heat flushed her cheeks for a second time and she suddenly felt anxious. She'd wished this moment more times than she cared to count and now that it was actually happening, the words were caught in the dry cavity of her throat. Her eyes misted, saline pressing at her lashes. She stammered, stopped to gather her thoughts before attempting to speak. "I really care about you, Darwin. You know that I've had a crush on you since forever, and now…" A tear dripped against her cheek and Darwin pressed his lips to capture the moisture. He gently brushed the back of his hands against her closed eyes.

He pulled her back against him, cradling her in his arms. "I know it's scary," he said, acknowledging the emotions that were consuming him. "But when I was away, all I could think about was getting back to you. Is that crazy?"

"This is new for both of us but it feels right. I really like how it feels."

Darwin grinned, nodding his head. "Me, too."

"So, where do we go from here?" Bridget asked, her voice dropping to a low whisper.

Darwin pondered the question just briefly. "The last time we were together I told you I was glad that you were my girl. I meant that. You should know that I'm very possessive. I don't want to see anyone but you and I don't want you seeing anyone else but me. You're not seeing anyone else, are you?"

Bridget giggled. "No."

He heaved a deep sigh. "Good, 'cause I want you all to myself."

They went quiet for just a brief moment, smiles blessing both their faces.

Darwin took a deep breath. "I may be asking too much, but would you go with me tomorrow to see my doctor?"

Bridget shifted her body to face his. "It's nothing serious, is it?"

He shrugged. "I never picked up that prescription and maybe I'm being presumptuous, but I figured since that problem of mine affects both of us that you might want to hear what the doctor has to say."

"Darwin, I hope you don't think we have to consummate this relationship for us to be together. Please tell me this is about more than our just having sex."

"Of course I don't," he said, shaking his head vehemently. "And how I feel about you doesn't have anything to do with our having sex, but I'm not going to lie to you. I used to enjoy sex. A lot. I was very good at it as a matter of fact. And I would like to enjoy it with you. I meant what I said about wanting to make love to you."

Bridget could feel the blush resurfacing to her face, the heat rising to tint her cheeks. She nodded. "If you want me to go with you then you know I will. I will support you however you need me to."

Darwin reached out to hug her again, his warm breath blowing against the line of her ear as he pressed his cheek to her cheek. He whispered softly, "Thank you. I really didn't want to do it alone."

"You don't have to, Darwin. I'll be right there with you."

Darwin heaved a sigh of relief. "I should probably call myself a taxi." He looked down to the watch on his wrist. "I didn't realize it was so late."

"You can stay here, if you want," Bridget said, her eyes shimmering. "I do have a spare bedroom," she added, a sly smile pulling at the edges of her mouth.

"Really? You wouldn't mind?"

"Of course not. Unless you just really want to leave?"

Darwin grinned. "You know I don't."

"Then it's settled. You're spending the night." Bridget rose to her feet. "I'll go put clean sheets on the bed."

Darwin stood up with her. "May I ask you a question?"

The woman turned about to face him. "Yes?"

"You do want to make love with me, don't you? I mean, if you aren't ready to take this to the next level, I'll understand. You would tell me if I were rushing this, wouldn't you?"

Bridget's smile widened, her expression radiating warmth and light. There was a gleam in her eyes as she stepped in toward him, pressing her body to his as she reached up to wrap her thin arms around his neck.

"Yes, I do. I want to make love to you very much, but I won't stop caring about you if it doesn't happen. But, don't you know you've already taken me to heaven with just your lips?" she asked, her tone tinged with seduction.

She reached up to kiss him, her mouth skating easily against his. Darwin parted his lips, searching out her tongue as the embrace deepened. The kiss didn't last long enough and when Bridget pulled away from him, Darwin found himself hungry for more. His eyes widened with excitement, a full grin painting his expression as Bridget moved out of the room.

At the bottom of the stairwell, she turned back to face him. "I need to ask you a question," she said, meeting his gaze. "What's happening with us?"

Darwin grinned and shrugged his shoulders. "I don't know if I have a word for it yet. But I hope it lasts always."

She eyed him curiously, confusion in her expression. "Always? What does that mean?"

Moving to her side, Darwin stared deeply into her eyes, falling headfirst into the intoxicating stare. "When it comes to me, you and the subject of love, always means forever," he whispered and then he kissed her one more time, emotion spinning a tight web around them.

The digital clock on the nightstand read ten minutes past three o'clock. Bridget was only slightly startled when she awoke to Darwin snoring lightly beside her. His body was spooned around hers, the heat from his flesh washing warmth over her flesh. She couldn't remember the last time she'd wakened to a man in her bed and a man who wasn't curled on the other side of the mattress with his back to her.

Moving to the edge of the bed, she gently lifted Darwin's arm from around her waist and slid the length of her legs from beneath his. He was naked from the waist up, his bare chest rising and falling easily with each breath. His legs were covered by a pair of well-worn cotton sleeping pants that fit him snugly through the hips and thighs. As she eased herself off the mattress to the floor, rising to her feet to stare down at him, Bridget couldn't help but grin as if she'd just won the big prize at the state fair.

He was beautiful, she thought, his mouth opened ever so slightly as he slept soundly, blowing breath past his lips. His dark complexion was a stark contrast against her bright white sheets, his smooth, deep, dark-chocolate tone seeming to her like liquid marble.

Thoughts of the spare bedroom had been lost the moment they'd made it to the top of the stairs. Darwin had refused to let her go, his mouth dancing from one end of her body to the other. Bridget pulled her fingertips to her lips, then dropped a hand on her thigh, suddenly reminded of Darwin's touch. Her mind dwelled on the memory of his kisses.

She'd led the way into the guest bedroom, showing him where he could find fresh towels and anything else he might have needed. She'd been nervous and had chattered nonstop, afraid that he might disappear if she allowed a moment of silence to pass between them. Darwin had changed into his nightclothes and then had stood in the doorway of her bedroom watching her as she'd brushed her hair before tying a silk scarf around her head. He'd stared at her with sad, puppy-dog eyes that didn't even begin to compare to Biscuit's and she'd fallen out laughing at his absurdity.

Before either of them knew it they were sprawled across her bed watching a late-night episode of *In Living Color* on BET. The mood shifted when the station aired a series of video classics on the show *Midnight Magic*. The tones were sultry and sensuous and they both had fallen right into the moment. Darwin had eased his body so close to hers that she couldn't begin to see where he stopped and she started. Just the nearness of him had caused her chest to tighten, her breath coming in short, harsh gasps. Bridget had felt her composure beginning to slip away from her.

"Heaven, huh?" Darwin had whispered as he drew his face to hers, inhaling the sweet scent of her skin, his warm breath blowing along her profile. Bridget had only been able to nod her head as his mouth touched hers, his lips brushing her lips, and the breath she'd been holding was drawn out of her as he kissed her harder. A low moan had formed in the back of her throat, moving him to keep kissing her, to not stop teasing her lips with his own.

His mouth never left hers as his hands had caressed her

skin, his fingertips searching out the lines of her hips, tracing an easy path over her abdomen and buttocks. At one point Darwin had cupped his palms around her face, his fingers gliding into her hair as he'd stared deeply into her eyes and she'd known, in that moment, that there was no other place she could imagine being.

Darwin shifted his body against the bed, mumbling softly in his sleep. The gesture made Bridget smile even more as she continued to watch him. Closing her eyes, she eased back into the memory, remembering the feel of his tongue as it had slid like velvet over her lips and into her mouth. She'd been so mesmerized that she barely realized it when Darwin had slid the straps of her nightgown off her shoulders, gliding the garment off her body. He'd rolled her from one side of the bed to the other and suddenly she'd been completely exposed, bare black skin shimmering beneath the faint lights that flickered from the television set.

His hands had explored every square inch of skin and where his fingertips had lingered, his mouth had followed. Darwin had kissed a slow trail down the length of her neck and across her shoulders. He'd brushed his lips around the curves of her breasts then had slowly suckled one breast and then the other, each of her nipples swelling full and hard in his mouth. When she felt her back arch off the bed, her body moving with a will of its own, she'd known there was no turning back.

He'd continued to lick a wet, glistening path down-ward, pausing to press a kiss to her belly button, and then he'd leaned on his elbows to stare up her. "Let me show you heaven," he'd whispered, his tone teasing. Bridget had suddenly felt light-headed, her body trembling with anti-cipation. Darwin had moved himself between her thighs, hooking his thumbs into the elastic of her lace panties as he slid them off her body.

When she'd felt his breath blowing against her secret treasure, his fingers dancing with precision in her moist chamber, she'd called his name out loud, chanting it over and over again. Then he'd eased the tip of his tongue expertly against her sex and she'd lost complete control, her body convulsing with sheer pleasure. The experience had been nothing like anything she'd ever experienced before and he'd brought her to a point of no return, gasping for air beneath him as he'd laid his head to rest on her stomach, his arms holding her close.

Just reflecting back on the moment caused a quiver of energy to shoot up Bridget's spine. Shaking the sensation from her head, she moved into the bathroom to still the call of nature that had awakened her in the first place. Climbing back onto the bed, she watched him for a while longer, drawing a light finger across his cheek.

She loved him. She loved everything about him. She'd loved him even before she'd been willing to admit it, actually missing him after those holiday get-togethers when he'd gone his way and she'd gone hers. There had been a reason for them to come together now, in this space, she mused, reflecting back on the events that had led them to this point. Fate had arranged this dance and was directing their moves and Bridget was glad for it. Fate had led her to the door of her dreams and a higher power had answered her prayers. Curling back against him, she smiled as he wrapped her back into his arms, pulling her close against him.

"Everything okay?" Darwin asked, slumber guiding his words, his eyes still shut tight.

"Everything is perfect," Bridget whispered. Then she closed her own eyes and fell back to sleep.

She never heard the alarm clock. It was the telephone ringing that finally pulled her from deep slumber and when she opened her eyes, her bed was empty, Darwin nowhere in the room. The ringing phone stopped quickly and Bridget assumed it had clicked over to the answering machine in her home office.

The aroma of freshly brewed coffee and something decadent that she couldn't identify wafted up from the kitchen below. Bridget stretched her body up and outward, yawning widely. Rising from the bed, she moved into the bathroom, performed the usual morning toilet, and then slipped her naked body into a pair of baby-blue sweatpants and T-shirt. When she reached the lower level, moving into the kitchen, Darwin was on her telephone, chatting easily. Bridget stood watching as he laughed and smiled into the receiver tucked between his ear and his shoulder as he held a steaming mug of hot brew between his two hands.

When he caught sight of her, he grinned widely, tossing her a quick wink of his eye. "Good morning, beautiful," he said, moving to kiss her cheek. He returned to his con-versation. "My baby girl just woke up…yeah…I'd love to…okay…I'll talk with you later," he said and then he held out the telephone toward her. "It's Jeneva," he said as he passed her the receiver.

Bridget continued to eye him as he moved first to the oven to peer inside and then back to the stove top to pour another cup of coffee into a second mug resting on the counter.

"Hello?"

Her best friend giggled into the receiver. "My, my, my. It must have been some night, *baby girl!*"

Bridget grinned. "Good morning, Jeneva. How are you?"

"No. The question is how was he?"

"You sound like Roshawn now."

"If I were Roshawn I would have asked Darwin."

Both women laughed heartily.

"I was shocked when he answered the telephone," Jeneva said. "I dropped my toast on the floor."

Bridget cut an eye toward Darwin, who stood watching her, a full grin gracing his expression. She grinned back.

"Jeneva, let me call you back. I haven't had a cup of coffee yet and Darwin is cooking something that smells absolutely incredible."

"It's his breakfast casserole. It's to die for! And scones. He told me."

"Well, I'm glad you know." Bridget chuckled.

"Don't worry about calling me. You two are coming to play bid whist tonight. We'll talk then. Love you!"

Bridget shook her head. "Love you, too. Bye!"

As she hung up the receiver, Darwin wrapped his arms around her, hugging her tightly. "Hope you don't mind me answering the phone. The name and number came up on the caller ID and I didn't think you'd have a problem with my picking it up."

She shook her head. "Not at all. How are you this morning?" she asked, nuzzling her cheek against his bare chest. "Did you sleep well?"

"Very well," he said as he kissed her forehead. "Are you hungry?"

She nodded. "I hear this meal is to die for. One of Jeneva's favorites, I gather?"

"One I make regularly. I was going to serve it to you in bed."

"You still can. I have no problems going back upstairs and crawling back under my covers."

Darwin slipped his hand beneath her T-shirt, allowing his palm to cradle her breast as his fingers caressed the rise of nipple that suddenly pressed candy-hard against the cotton fabric. His other hand skated around her back and down her spine into the back of her sweatpants. He cupped her right butt cheek in his palm, gently caressing the globe of tight flesh. He pressed his mouth to her ear and whispered. "I enjoyed last night. I hope you did, too?" he asked.

She giggled, heat rushing to her face. "Yes, very much," she responded as she pressed herself against him, planting a light kiss against his lips. "Very much."

Darwin smiled. "Good. Then I'll make sure breakfast is just as tantalizing," he said, giving her a quick squeeze before letting her go.

Bridget took a deep inhale of air. "You just take care of the food," she said, still smiling. "Then I get to do dessert."

Darwin chuckled. "That sounds interesting," he said as he watched her grab her cup of coffee and head back in the direction of her bedroom.

She tossed him a quick glance over her shoulder. "I promise you, it will be," she said, before disappearing back up the stairs.

Darwin stood staring after her, the prospect of what might happen between them moving his temperature to rise. A quiver of electricity shot through the pit of his stomach and sensation strained against his nerve endings.

Rushing to the oven, he pulled the hot pan from inside, then prepped the breakfast plates. He also filled a bowl with sugared strawberries and placed champagne glasses onto a wicker tray. When everything was ready, the presentation capped with a single rosebud in the center of the display, he raced up the stairs, anxious to get to the meal and even more excited about what might possibly follow.

Chapter 13

The smirk across Bridget's face was all-telling and she imagined that everyone who saw her could tell what she and Darwin had been up to that morning. Breakfast had been better than imagined, the brie and sausage casserole and pineapple mimosas beyond decadent. She'd ended the meal by giving Darwin a full-body massage, kneading every muscle in his body with a concoction of coconut and mango seed oils that she'd purchased from the Body Shop. Between her own hands, the thumb thongs and the footsie roller, she'd managed to caress and relax every ounce of tension out of his body.

They'd spent a fair amount of time just lying side by side trading light, easy caresses as they talked about their plans for the day and every random thought that had crossed his or her mind. After an extended shower together, both savoring the flow of hot water in her large shower and the heated steam that had permeated the room, Darwin had dressed and headed for his own home, having to stop to pick up Biscuit from the overpriced pet-hotel he'd kenneled her in.

Bridget had headed in the opposite direction toward the county courthouse where she now stood at the counter waiting for the clerk to date stamp and file the stack of legal documents in front of her.

The county administrator greeted her warmly. "Hi there, Counselor," she said with a large smile adorning her round face. "Where have you been hiding? It's been a while."

"Not too long, I hope," Bridget responded.

The woman shook her head. "So, what do you have for me today?"

Bridget pushed a large stack of documents forward. "I need to file these, please. It's civil litigation."

Bridget pulled into the parking lot of the Seattle Medical Center just seconds after Darwin had parked and shut down the engine of his own vehicle. For a brief moment the two sat side by side staring at each other.

Bridget knew how difficult this was for Darwin. They'd talked about his feelings that morning, how inadequate he was feeling by his predicament. Darwin was a true alpha male, his dominant spirit unable to comprehend the why and wherefore of what was happening to him. He was a man who exuded confidence in everything he did and that confidence was powerful and sexy, that certain *je ne sais quoi* that made people want to be near him, or be like him. He was also a consummate leader and a rule breaker, setting his own standards, exceeding the expectations of

KIMANI PRESS™

An Important Message from the Publisher

Dear Reader,

Because you've chosen to read one of our fine novels, I'd like to say "thank you"! And, as a special way to say thank you, I'm offering to send you two Kimani Romance™ novels and two surprise gifts – absolutely FREE! These books will keep it real with true-to-life African-American characters that turn up the heat and sizzle with passion.

Please enjoy the free books and gifts with our compliments...

Linda Gill

Publisher, Kimani Press

Peel off Seal and Place Inside...

FREE GIFTS SEAL
PUBLISHERS
THANK YOU

We'd like to send you two free books to introduce you to our new line – Kimani Romance™! These novels feature strong, sexy women and African-American heroes that are charming, loving and true. Our authors fill each page with exceptional dialogue, exciting plot twists, and enough sizzling romance to keep you riveted until the very end!

KIMANI ROMANCE ... LOVE'S ULTIMATE DESTINATION

Two NEW Kimani Romance™ Novels
Two exciting surprise gifts

YES! I have placed my
Editor's "Thank You" Free Gifts
seal in the space provided at
right. Please send me 2 FREE
books, and my 2 FREE Mystery
Gifts. I understand that I am
under no obligation to purchase
anything further, as explained on
the back of this card.

PLACE
FREE GIFTS
SEAL
HERE

168 XDL ELWZ   368 XDL ELXZ

FIRST NAME   LAST NAME

ADDRESS

APT.#   CITY

STATE/PROV.   ZIP/POSTAL CODE

Thank You!

Offer limited to one per household and not valid to current subscribers of Kimani Romance.
Your Privacy – Kimani Press is committed to protecting your privacy. Our Privacy
Policy is available online at www.eHarlequin.com or upon request from the Reader
Service. From time to time we make our lists of customers available to reputable
firms who may have a product or service of interest to you. If you would prefer for
us not to share your name and address, please check here. ☐

The Reader Service — Here's How It Works:

others. Darwin made the game up as he went along, writing his own rules, and impotence had placed him on a playing field he couldn't begin to maneuver. But he was learning to improvise, and though Bridget couldn't begin to imagine where he might be able to take her if he were at full capacity, he was being exceptionally innovative as they explored the intimate side of their new relationship. She only wished that she could return the pleasure as wholeheartedly so that he was feeling as intensely satisfied as he had made her feel.

She smiled as she moved to exit the car, greeting him as he exited his own. "Hey, you!"

"Hey, yourself. Get all your errands run?"

"I did. How about you? How's Biscuit?"

"Glad to be home. She's mad with me though. Wouldn't even let me cuddle her. Just hopped onto her favorite chair and ignored me."

"Poor daddy. That's what you get for not taking her with you."

"Next time I'm leaving her with you," he said as he wrapped his arm around her shoulder, leaning to give her a quick kiss on the mouth. He took a deep inhale of breath, blowing it out in a large gust.

Bridget squeezed his hand and they headed for the entrance, taking the elevator to the second floor and the office of Dr. Owen Page, one of the area's most renowned urologists. It was only a matter of minutes before the two of them were escorted from the office waiting area to one of the rear examination rooms. Bridget's nerves were instantly assuaged the minute she stepped into the room. Spinning in a slow circle to take in the view, she grinned, her gaze moving from the walls to Darwin and back again.

"Wow!" she exclaimed. "This is too cool!"

Darwin nodded his head as he took a seat on the examination table. "I thought the exact same thing the first time I saw it," Darwin said. "Doc has an interesting sense of style."

The nurse at his side was wrapping a black blood pressure cuff around his bicep. The woman smiled. "It's definitely something to talk about," she said, her blond head bobbing eagerly. "It's quite an impressive collection."

Bridget turned her attention back to the walls. The decor was like nothing she'd ever seen before in a physician's office. The doctor was clearly an avid fan of western memorabilia. Every square inch of wall space was adorned with mementos from the wild, wild west.

There was an old rifle mounted above the door frame and two ten-gallon hats resting on wall hooks. There was a saddle, a jar filled with etched belt buckles, framed images of horses and cowboys, a vintage gun holster, a bull skull, an Indian headdress, a cabinet filled with old medicine bottles and vintage doctor supplies and a profusion of knickknacks too numerous to inventory without a few hours of time. Bridget and Darwin were so busy scrutinizing each item that both jumped when the doctor came into the room.

"Darwin, my man, how's it hanging?" Dr. Page said, extending his hand in Darwin's direction.

"Owen, your choice of words leaves a lot to be desired. How's everything going with you?"

"I can't complain, my friend. Can't complain at all. How about yourself?"

Darwin shrugged. "Things have been better. That's why I'm here, remember?"

The doctor smiled. "Well, let's see if we can't do something about that." The man turned his attention to Bridget. "Hello, I'm Owen Page."

Bridget shook the outstretched hand. "It's a pleasure, Dr. Page. I'm Bridget Hinton."

"Bridget is that special lady I was telling you about," Darwin said, an unexpected blush flooding warmth over his cheeks.

Dr. Page nodded his head. "I'm glad you're here for Darwin, Bridget," the man said as he looked down to the file folder in his hand. He scanned it briefly before speaking again. "Darwin, your blood pressure is slightly elevated."

"Probably just my nerves," Darwin responded.

The other man smiled again, cutting a quick gaze in Darwin's direction. "Probably, but I want to check it again myself just to be sure," he said, reaching for the cuff that hung from the wall. The man continued speaking as he worked. "Well, the good news is that the last wave of tests we took all came back negative. So, as I told you before, it doesn't appear that your condition is being caused by something medical. Did you call that psychologist I recommended?"

"Not yet," Darwin said, his gaze skirting toward Bridget and down to the floor.

"Do you plan to call him?" Dr. Page asked.

Darwin shrugged but didn't bother to respond.

"Well, it's an option I think you should seriously consider," the doctor said. He jotted a quick note into Darwin's folder. "Your blood pressure is one-twenty-five over eighty-five. It's coming down and that's good. Now, any questions before we go on?" He looked from Darwin to Bridget and back to Darwin.

Darwin cleared his throat. "Would you please explain to Bridget what's going on? I tried, but you know how I am," he said, a shy grin filling his face.

The doctor turned to face her. "Why certainly! As you know, when things are working properly, sexual performance is a three-step process. The man becomes sexually aroused, the penis responds by becoming erect and then stimulation of the penis causes ejaculation. In Darwin's case, step two isn't happening, and of course, that makes step three difficult or impossible to complete. Although he may be stimulated, the penis does not become erect."

"And you don't know why?" Bridget asked.

"Think of the penis like a balloon. If a balloon has no air in it, it's limp. As you inflate a limp balloon with just a little air, it becomes elongated and rigid. The penis uses a similar mechanism, but instead of using pressurized air to become rigid, the penis uses pressurized blood. That's one reason why we monitor Darwin's blood pressure so closely. If he suffered from high blood pressure or what we call hypertension, that and the medications to treat it could cause his problem."

"Really?"

The doctor nodded. "And worse. High blood pressure could actually cause a heart attack as well as other problems. Did you know African-Americans have the highest rate of high blood pressure in the world, affecting one out of every three persons? We also know that hypertension affects 36.4 percent of black men aged twenty and older compared to 25.6 percent of white men, plus they develop it at an earlier age than their white counterparts. But his blood pressure isn't Darwin's problem."

"And medication can fix him?" Bridget queried, tossing Darwin a quick smile.

"We hope medication will alleviate the symptoms but we still need to narrow down the cause."

"So, how does Viagra work?" Darwin interjected.

The doctor shifted in his seat. "Darwin, when you get aroused, the arteries leading into the penis open up so that pressurized blood can enter quickly. You get an erection. With you, your arteries aren't opening up properly and we need to open them."

Bridget winced. "That actually sounds like it would hurt."

Both men laughed.

Dr. Page shook his head. "It won't. The pills will help the process but you have to understand that it's not like you take the pill and suddenly you have an erection that lasts nineteen hours. You still have to be actively involved."

"I don't understand," Darwin said.

"You need to take your dose about thirty minutes before you want to engage in sexual activity. Then you need to do the kissing and cuddling to stimulate an erection. Lots of foreplay. Once you get excited, the rest should come back to you."

Darwin rolled his eyes. "Gotcha!"

"And, don't forget you'll still need protection. Have sex, but make sure you have safe sex, please."

Bridget blushed, feeling the rise of heat burning her cheeks.

"Unless you two are thinking about having children," the doctor concluded, "and then I would recommend you both have an AIDS test first. Are you thinking about children?"

Bridget shook her head vigorously, a thoughtful reflection crossing her face. She stammered, her eyes widening as she looked at Darwin. Both of them laughed nervously.

Dr. Page looked from one to the other. "Too soon for that, huh? Oh, well. Any questions?"

Darwin shook his head and looked at Bridget, noting a frown that crossed her face.

Bridget's smile quickly returned as she crossed her arms over her chest. "Now, you're sure about that nineteen-hour erection, right?"

The doctor chuckled. "Sorry. Won't happen, and if it does, we'll have a whole other problem to contend with."

Darwin shook his head from side to side. "So what now?"

The doctor jotted more notes onto his pad. "My nurse will come back with a sample for you. It's only seven pills. And there'll be some papers for you to sign saying we gave you a sample at no cost. Unfortunately, your insurance company probably won't cover the cost of the pills if you decide to continue with them and they're expensive. Very expensive."

"Hopefully, I won't be on them for too long, will I?"

"Hopefully not, but I can't say for certain. We still need to identify the cause and I still think you should go see Dr. Sinclair. So, call and make an appointment to talk with him."

Darwin rolled his eyes for a second time. The doctor shook his head and turned to Bridget. He gave her a quick wink.

"It was nice to meet you, Bridget. Feel free to call me if you have any other questions and try to talk some sense into his hard head."

Bridget smiled. "I will, Dr. Page, and thank you."

"Please, call me Owen. Darwin and I have been friends since high school. We go back a long way." He gripped her hand between his own. "The fact that he brought you here tells me you have a very special place in his life. So, I look forward to getting to know you."

"Thank you, Owen," Bridget responded.

She watched as the two men exchanged a quick palm slap and one-armed hug. Then the doctor exited the room as quickly as he'd come in. Darwin turned to stare at her and she reached out to wrap her arms around his neck as she kissed his cheek.

"Are you okay?" she asked softly.

Darwin nodded. "Yeah. I feel a little silly, but it'll pass. It's not often that I have to have a conversation about Darwin Jr. with my doctor and my woman in the same room."

Bridget laughed. "Darwin Jr.?"

"I used to call him Chuck but the name just doesn't fit right now."

"Thank goodness. I don't like Chuck."

Mischief gleamed in Darwin's eyes. "Oh, you would have liked Chuck. You would have liked Chuck a lot."

"I think I'm going to like Darwin Jr. just fine," she said with a giggle as Darwin pressed his lips to hers to give her a quick kiss.

He laughed with her. "Let's just hope we can get the old boy to work. If that happens, I'll let you name him," he said with a wry smile.

"Oooh," Bridget cooed. "Now, a girl could have some fun with that!"

The day had been long for both Darwin and Bridget, so as they leaned over the edge of the Anacortes Ferry, holding each other up, both were grateful for the lull of the water below and the few minutes of quiet they could share. The sun was still posturing in a blue sky although an influx of darkening clouds seemed to want to prove the weather predictions right with the threat of pending rain.

Bridget leaned back against the man's chest as he wrapped his arms around her torso. She felt good in his arms, Darwin thought, and he wasn't overly anxious to let her go. He took a deep breath, inhaling the delicate scent of her perfume as it danced in the air with the salted spray of the ocean.

She had asked him if what they were feeling was love. Darwin couldn't help but ponder the question more closely. He hadn't yet said those three words to Bridget but he knew something real was happening between them. If he were honest with himself he would have to admit that he'd been fighting his feelings for Bridget since forever. There had been no denying the attraction he'd felt but he had surely done battle with the sentiment that had consumed him as they'd gotten to know each other. The casual flirting had only served to mask what he'd really been feeling and even when he had walked away from the not-so-subtle maneuverings of their friends and family, his heart had been held hostage by the swell of emotions he had for her.

He pressed a kiss to the top of her head as he nuzzled his face into her hair. The silken strands were scented with a coconut moisturizer, the fresh aroma billowing up into his nostrils. Tightening his grip, he pulled her closer to his heart, wondering why it had taken him this long to figure out where he belonged.

Bridget suddenly turned around to face him, spinning

in his arms as she wrapped her own around his waist. Staring down into her face, Darwin sensed something weighing on her spirit, her expression too serious for so calming a moment.

"What's wrong?" Darwin asked as he leaned to whisper in her ear.

Bridget met his gaze and held it. She took a deep breath before speaking. "I think there's something important we need to talk about before we go any further with this relationship," she said, her tone beyond serious.

Darwin nodded his head. "We can talk about anything. You know that."

She waved her own head. "It's about something your doctor said today, and, well…" Bridget paused as Darwin looked at her curiously. "I think you should know that I don't want children. I love kids, but I've known for a long time that I don't want to be pregnant and I don't want to adopt. I don't want to be a mother."

Darwin's expression changed from curious to shocked, the magnitude of her statement spinning through his mind. "Okay," he said finally as he released his grip and moved toward an empty bench. Bridget followed behind him, taking a seat at his side.

"You need to know that, Darwin," Bridget said softly. "Have you thought about having children of your own?" she asked.

Darwin nodded. "When Mac and Jeneva had Alexa I thought about it a lot. I think every man wonders at some point what kind of father he might be."

Bridget gave him a quick smile. "I'm sure you will make an amazing father," she said, her voice dropping to a loud whisper.

Darwin's mouth bent upward just a fraction as he forced himself to smile back.

Bridget continued speaking. "I might be making some assumptions about us and where we're going with each other but you needed to know how I feel and you need to know before this gets any more serious."

"You might change your mind, Bridget. Things could change," Darwin said, a thread of hope in his voice.

Bridget shook her head. Conviction painted her expression. "No. I won't. My heart's not in it, Darwin. I would never want to bring a child into this world knowing my heart wasn't into it."

Darwin blew a loud sigh. "For some strange reason I always figured every woman wanted to be a mom."

"Only some of us, Darwin. Not all of us."

Darwin blew another gust of air. Bridget dropped a light palm to his leg, kneading the flesh gently. Darwin forced another smile.

"Well, aren't we a pair," he said with an anxious chuckle. "But hey, if we can't solve my problem, then it really won't matter much, will it?"

Bridget wiped a tear from her eye. "Don't make light of this, Darwin. You will solve your problem and when that happens you need to be in a relationship with a woman who wants the same things you do. And, even if you don't, there are still options available to you. You can still be a parent."

"But I want that with you, Bridget."

"But, Darwin, I don't want that at all, not with anyone."

Darwin rose from his seat, moving back to the vessel's rail. He stared out toward the distance, his gaze resting on the rush of clouds gaining control of the sky. There was no denying the disappointment across his face. He had never imagined that so large an issue would ever be a problem between them but he had to acknowledge this threatened the future he'd been dreaming for himself.

Although parenthood had never been in the forefront of his mind, he always figured he would one day have a child or two of his own. He'd been by his brother's side when the world had welcomed little Alexa into the fold. He had felt his brother's joy as if it were his own, witnessing the brilliance of a miracle as Mecan first held his baby girl in his arms and realized just how magnanimous his capacity for love could actually be. Every time he saw them together, Darwin envied what Mac had, wishing for such in the back of his mind.

But there had been no missing Bridget's staunch convictions. She wholeheartedly meant what she said. There would be no compromise. His children would never be her children and parenthood would not be something they'd ever navigate together. If nothing else, Darwin understood that bringing a child into the world that she didn't want with everything in her would be a point of contention that could tear them apart anyway.

Bridget's hand pressed against his lower spine and Darwin closed his eyes at the sensation of her touch.

"I understand," Bridget said cheerfully. "It really is okay. We've had a great time together and no one can take that from us. We will always be friends, Darwin, even if we can't be anything more to each other," she said, trying to ease his visible discomfort.

Darwin searched her face, trying to read the lines of her expression. "Do you really believe that? Is that honestly how you feel?"

Bridget sucked in air, fighting not to cry. "I don't... I just want..." she stammered, suddenly at a loss for words. "I don't want to make this difficult for you," she said softly. "I just want things to be all right."

Darwin shook his head. "Well, things aren't all right." He turned back to face her, cupping her chin in the palm of his hand as he lifted her gaze to his. "I love you. I love you, Bridget, and I'm not ready to just let you go."

He stared into the dark depths of her gaze, her eyes misting with tears. Darwin choked back his own tears. "I love you, but suddenly I don't know where we go from here."

Chapter 14

Bridget and Darwin paused outside the front door of the Tolliver family's San Juan Island home. Darwin wrapped his arms around her, pulling Bridget into a tight hug. He brushed his lips over her forehead, the damp kiss burning hot against her skin. Taking a step back, he sucked in two deep breaths of oxygen then pushed the doorbell. When little Alexa pulled the door open both of them forced a wide smile across their faces, beaming down at the little girl.

"Hi, Uncle Darwin!" Alexa chimed, throwing her miniature body into his outstretched arms.

"Hey, pumpkin pie! How's my girl?"

"I was watching *Scooby-Doo* on the television," Alexa responded, kicking her legs to get back to the floor. She wrapped herself around Bridget's legs. "Hi, Auntie Bridget."

Bridget leaned down to kiss the top of the child's head, her thick, dark brown hair plaited in three neat braids atop her skull. She lifted her right foot up, her chubby leg extended straight out in front of her.

"See my new sneakers?" she said, twisting her foot from side to side. "These are for playing in, and I got a pair to wear with my nice pants, and I got Mary Janes to go with my dresses. They're red like Dorothy's in the wizard movie," she said quickly, finally pausing to take a breath.

"Wow!" Bridget exclaimed. "Red Mary Janes! I don't have red Mary Janes!"

Alexa giggled. "They don't have none in your size," she gushed, rolling her wide eyes skyward.

"Oh, is that the reason," Bridget responded as the child slipped her small hand into Bridget's, pulling her toward the back of the house.

Darwin watched as the two of them went past him, his smile still pulling his facial muscles upward. Mecan called out his name from the top of the stairwell.

"What's up, little brother?" he quipped, taking the steps two at a time to join him.

The two men slapped palms then gave each other a quick hug.

"It's all good, big brother. All good," the man said, his voice a low drone.

Mecan nodded, studying his brother closely. "Why am I not convinced?" Mecan said, crossing his arms over his chest.

Darwin shrugged, turning his eyes to avoid his brother's gaze. "Where's my sister-in-law?" Darwin asked, starting down the hallway Bridget and Alexa had just disappeared down. Mecan followed close on his heels and Darwin could feel his brother's stare burning straight into his back.

Easing into the kitchen, they found the women peering into the oven. Alexa was dancing excitedly between them.

"What's going on in here?" Darwin bellowed. "All the pretty girls left me!"

Alexa laughed heartily. "Mommy made chocolate cake!"

Darwin moved to Jeneva's side to kiss her cheek. "Mmm, chocolate cake!"

Jeneva laughed. "Hi, Darwin," she said as she returned the kiss.

"Is that the infamous Death By Chocolate chocolate cake?" the man questioned.

"It sure is."

Darwin shook his head.

Behind them Mecan joined in the laughter. "See what they keep doing to me," he said, patting the very small beginnings of a round belly. "That woman just wants to keep me in the gym. The things a man has to put up with in this house."

Alexa tossed him an annoyed look, moving to lean against her mother's leg. "Are you being mean, Daddy? That didn't sound too nice. Did it, Mommy?"

"No, girlie, it wasn't nice at all."

Mecan tossed both his hands into the air. "These two are always ganging up on me!" he said, pretending to pout, his bottom lip pushed outward toward his chin.

The little girl giggled again. "You're so silly!"

The adults all laughed with her.

Mecan gestured in his brother's direction. "Darwin, let

me pull you away for a minute," he said, his eyes locking with his twin's. "If you ladies would excuse us, please. We'll be right back."

"Can I still watch *Scooby-Doo*, Daddy?"

Mecan nodded. "Come on. Daddy will turn it back on for you," he said as he extended his hand toward his daughter.

As she took it, she reached out with her other hand toward Darwin. "Come on, Uncle Darwin," she chimed. "Daddy wants you to boy talk with him."

Darwin cut an eye toward his brother as he followed reluctantly. Bridget watched as they disappeared out of the room. A pang of hurt pierced her heart as she watched Alexa twisting both men around her pinkie finger. The look of distress that crossed her face did not go unnoticed.

"Bridget, is everything okay?" Jeneva asked, concern in her expression. "You look like you're about to be sick."

As Bridget turned toward her friend, tears welled up in her eyes. Jeneva held up her index finger, stalling the woman's response as she moved to the door to check that the others were out of earshot. Moving back to her friend's side, she gestured toward the kitchen table and both women sat down. Bridget swiped at her eyes with the back of her hand, brushing a trail of moisture over her cheeks. "What's wrong?" Jeneva asked again, her hand dropping against the woman's knee.

Bridget shook her head, her voice caught deep in her chest.

"Something is wrong," Jeneva persisted. "Let me help."

"Darwin wants children," Bridget finally whispered.

Jeneva leaned back in her seat and heaved a deep sigh. "And you told him you didn't?"

Bridget nodded. "I had to, Jay. There's no way I could have kept something like that from him."

"What did he say?"

"He told me he loved me but he wasn't sure where we can go from here."

Jeneva smiled. "But he said he loves you! So all's not lost."

Bridget swiped at her eyes again. "I can't believe this. I finally connect with the man of my dreams and it's over before we can get the relationship started."

"But it's not over."

"It can't work, Jay. He wants children as much as I don't want children. One way or the other one of us will end up being resentful. Better we cut and run before either of us gets hurt."

"But you're already hurting."

Bridget's eyes filled with tears again. "I wanted this so badly, Jay! I love Darwin. I love him very much."

"Enough to reconsider having children?"

The two women sat staring at each other as Bridget pondered the question. Her head waved from side to side as she answered.

"I don't want kids, Jay, and I have to be honest about that."

Jeneva had known the answer before Bridget had spoken. They'd had this conversation before and with both her pregnancies and Roshawn's three, Bridget had been adamant about not wanting to be a mother. Jeneva had been honest when she'd told Bridget that she couldn't understand the sentiment, motherhood being as natural to her as breathing, but she had respected her friend's decision. It was not for her to judge whether or not Bridget was right or wrong, but to just support her when she needed her most.

Jeneva wrapped her arms around Bridget's shoulders and hugged her. She desperately wanted to assure the woman that it would all work out and she and Darwin would have the fairy-tale ending of happily ever after, but Jeneva herself wasn't sure she believed it.

Behind the privacy of Mecan's office door the two brothers were navigating a conversation similar to the one being held in the kitchen. Darwin was settled against a leather recliner, his shoulders rounded with weight as he leaned his head in his hands, his elbows pressed into his thighs. Mecan sat in the seat opposite him.

"So, you two were just having a casual conversation about kids and she told you this?"

Darwin shook his head. "Bridget had gone with me to Owen's office to pick up my Viagra sample and Owen made a comment about protected sex and having kids. I guess Bridget figured we needed to discuss it since it's an issue for her."

"So she doesn't want children at all."

"No."

"And you do?"

"I just always assumed I'd have a family and children of my own. And I figured if I ever got married the woman in my life would want that with me."

"This thing with you and Bridget is still pretty new. Maybe…"

Darwin tossed him a cold stare. "There is no maybe. I love her. I know that. I can't imagine my life without her." His gaze dropped back to the floor.

"And you *can* imagine your life without a son or a daughter of your own?"

The silence in the room was palpable, heavy and pervasive as the two men sat staring at each other. Darwin didn't have an answer to his brother's question and Mecan didn't know what else there was for him to say.

There was no denying the albatross hanging like dead weight between them. The cold, intermittent rain that fell from the sky compounded the dark silence on their return trip. The rest of their evening had been uncomfortable at best, everyone trying to pretend that all was well when nothing at all felt right for Darwin and Bridget.

Their family had turned the tide of all the discussions. They'd talked about the progress Jeneva and Mecan's son was making, Mecan's job, Darwin's new show and his issues with Ava, Ella and the pending lawsuit. They'd talked about the weather, vacation plans, summer trends and other assorted trivia that had nothing to do with anything. Darwin had been grateful for his brother's quick humor, the teasing and jocularity that had kept them all laughing until it had been time to catch the last ferry. And now it seemed to him that all his issues with Ava were suddenly insignificant.

As they sat staring out toward the dark night, Darwin reached for Bridget's hand and held it, entwining his fingers with hers. Once or twice he pulled her hand to his lips and kissed her palm, his full lips just barely grazing the soft flesh. Both purposely avoided continuing the discussion that had moved them to this mood and there was no mention of any future dreams that might have involved them both.

Bridget wanted to ask Darwin what he was thinking and

how he was feeling but she was afraid to hear his answers and so she waited, hoping he might volunteer the information. So, when he had nothing at all to say, she found his silence as cutting as if a knife had been plunged deep into her heart.

Darwin's emotions were a whirlwind of highs and lows. He'd finally stopped reeling from the fact that his body was failing him in the bedroom and now here he was reeling from the fact that he could see his heart about to be bruised and he didn't know if he could stop it. He found it difficult to believe that just hours earlier he was imagining the night ending much differently. He'd also imagined a much different future but that suddenly seemed out of sync, as well.

He watched Bridget from the corner of his eye. He loved to watch her, awed by every delicate feature. Her beauty was timeless. The arch of her eyebrows, the glow in her large eyes, the fullness of her mouth and her round, dimpled cheeks were classically gorgeous.

He so wanted to tell her that everything would be fine, that nothing would ever come between them, but he was scared, actually frightened that this one issue would be bigger than they would ever be able to handle. He knew that when he did say something he would have to be as honest as he could ever be. She deserved no less from him. This could never be about *hoping* they could make it, but *knowing* beyond a single doubt that it would work.

He kissed her palm again then leaned into her side as she rested her head on his shoulder. They both heaved a sigh at the same time, anxiety blowing out into the damp night air. Darwin tightened his grip on her hand. When the time came for deep conversation he wanted his heart to promise Bridget forever.

* * *

Bridget closed her front door, tossing Darwin one last wave before he got back into his car and pulled out of the parking lot. As she stood staring out into the dark she fought back the rush of tears that threatened to fall like rain from her eyes. After locking the entrance and securing her house for the night, she headed straight up the stairs and into her bedroom, throwing her fully clothed body across the padded mattress.

Her timing could have been better, she mused, reflecting back on all that had happened that day. But telling Darwin how she felt about children would have been no easier if she'd waited a day, a month or a year. His response would have been the same, maybe even worse if time had found them even more committed to each other.

Darwin's reaction had been typical of the many responses she'd experienced over the years. The looks of astonishment and disbelief as if there was something not quite right about any female who didn't want the responsibilities of motherhood and all that entailed. Bridget had felt the brunt of many an opinion on what was right and wrong for her womb. Although most had been voiced in genuine concern, there had been a few that had just been out-and-out nasty for no apparent reason other than to soothe an evil spirit.

Even those closest to her had questioned her sanity, pondering whether or not her decisions were founded in selfishness or something else they just couldn't comprehend. But Bridget had always known that were she to ever walk that path it would be the worst thing she could ever do to herself and any child made to suffer that burden because of her.

Bridget had much love for her own mother, but had known for most of her existence that the woman who'd given birth to her had no more wanted to be a mother than the man on the moon. Although Bridget knew her mother had loved her, had sacrificed to raise her well, she also knew the woman had done so reluctantly, dismayed by her own resentments.

Bridget had felt it in the hugs that were few and far between and the looks that were never quite as warm and caring as she would have liked. She'd also seen the difference when Jeneva's and Roshawn's mothers had both interacted with their daughters as the girls had grown up, their relationships profoundly different from the one she'd shared with her own mother.

Although she and her mother had never discussed it outright, Bridget had known instinctively that Bernadette Hinton hadn't wanted to be anyone's mother. And the only time the elusive Mrs. Hinton had even ventured an opinion about Bridget's decision, she'd said to Bridget what she'd wished someone had been able to say to her so many years earlier.

"Don't do it if you can't give it all your heart and soul, girl. It's not fair to you and it won't be fair to your baby. And it doesn't make you a bad person, either. If it's right, you'll know it. If it's not, you'll know that, too. But trust your heart. Don't let anyone steer you from what you know deep down to be true."

Her mother had kissed her then, pressing her lips to Bridget's forehead, and Bridget sensed it was the one and only time her mother had honestly believed she was doing right by her daughter.

Over the years Bridget had come to understand that the

life her mother had dreamed for herself was a far cry from the one a night of unprotected sex with Dwight Hinton, the high-school Lothario, had handed her. The time being what it was, Bernadette had lost sight of her options and she'd become the dutiful wife and mother everyone else had expected her to be. Bridget had been adamant that she would never feel betrayed by what others expected of her, oblivious to what she wanted and needed for herself. She would never be as unhappy as her mother because of a decision she could control.

Bridget sighed, no more tears left for her to cry. She rolled onto her stomach and pressed her face into a pillow. It smelled of morning-fresh scented fabric softener. She wished it smelled of Darwin and the rich scent of the cologne he wore. She peeked at the digital clock on the nightstand. It was almost four o'clock in the early morning. She and Darwin had talked for hours before he brought her home, both wanting the other to understand why they felt the way they did. When he'd finally accepted there would be no changing her mind, Darwin had asked for space, desperate for time and distance to help him resolve the wealth of emotions he was suddenly feeling.

Bridget had understood, needing her own time to work through the hurt and the inevitable loss she was anticipating. Needing her own space to make sense of it all.

Chapter 15

Ava saw the man coming and instinctively knew it wasn't a coincidence that he was there. Although people from all walks of life showed up at her book signings, police officers in their distinctive blue-and-black uniforms rarely made a point of pushing ahead of the line, cutting boldly in front of those waiting eagerly for her attention. But this officer did, and as Ava met his deep blue gaze, his eyes the color of ocean water, she knew that her luck had finally run its course.

"Ava St. John?"

"Officer, to what do I owe the pleasure?"

Ava gave him a demure look, her eyes widening just slightly as she smiled, her mouth parting just enough for her to push her tongue over her lip just a hint. The man was not moved.

He lifted the folded paper in his hand out toward her. "You've been served, Ms. St. John," he said as she took the document from him.

She watched as he spun back around on the heels of his highly polished government-issue shoes and exited the building. The crowd gathered watched her intently as she opened the legal record and scanned its contents.

There was no masking the rush of annoyance that suddenly consumed her, irritation shifting her mood from hot to cold in a heartbeat. She couldn't believe it and everyone holding a copy of her book in the bookstore that afternoon witnessed her astonishment.

Ava turned to the store manager standing by her side. The petite Asian woman seemed flustered by Ava's sudden mood shift.

"I'm sorry, but I have to go."

"Excuse me?"

"Go. I have to go, so I'm done here. It's an emergency."

"But you're supposed to sign for another hour. We have a line," the other woman uttered, her expression shocked.

Ava's gaze shifted from the woman's face to the line of patrons waiting for her attention. She shook her head. "This can't be helped. I'm very sorry."

"Ms. St. John, this is highly unusual. We can't just leave these people hanging."

Ava was headed in the direction of the door, the store manager right behind her.

"Ms. St. John!"

Ava stopped short and spun around quickly, the other woman just inches from running into her.

"Look," Ava said between clenched teeth. "I said it was an emergency. Now, I have to go. If you have a problem with it, then sue me. It would seem everyone else is!" Then Ava stormed out of the store and into the Bellevue Square mall, the bookstore's crowd staring curiously after her.

Ava could barely see straight as she headed toward the parking deck. When she reached the upper level she handed the valet the requisite ticket to collect her vehicle. As she waited for the young man to return she pulled her cell phone into her hand and dialed. The instrument rang in her ear as she waited for it to be answered on the other end.

"Bayer, Younger, Gleason and Associates. How may I direct your call?"

"Joshua Bayer, please."

"Please hold the line while I transfer you."

Ava rolled her eyes, taking a quick glance over her shoulder to see if anyone was watching her.

"Mr. Bayer's office. May I help you?"

"This is Ava St. John. I need to speak with him now."

"Mr. Bayer is—"

"I said now," Ava snapped. She could feel the woman on the other end bristle.

"I'm sorry, Ms. St. John, but Mr. Bayer is in a meeting and—"

Ava interrupted the woman for a second time. "I'm sorry," she said, taking a deep inhale of breath. Ava suddenly realized she was being overly rude and rude wasn't going to get her what she needed. "Please, forgive me. I'm just very upset and I have no reason to take it out on you, but I really do need to speak with Joshua. Please, it's extremely important."

His assistant nodded into the receiver. "I understand.

If you'll hold the line, Ms. St. John, I'll see if he can take your call."

"Thank you. Thank you so much."

"Just hold one minute, ma'am."

One minute quickly turned into two and then three as Ava stood tapping her foot anxiously. The valet finally returned with her car and Ava didn't bother to acknowledge him with a small tip as she jumped into the driver's seat and spun the tires out of the garage. The telephone was still pressed to her ear as she continued to hold on for Joshua Bayer. By the time he answered she'd already run two yellow lights and a red one as she sped in the direction of the man's office.

"Ava, what's wrong?" Joshua queried as he answered the call. "My assistant said you sounded upset."

"I'm being sued, Joshua," Ava shouted just a little too loudly. "A man named Darwin Tolliver is suing me. Can you believe it?"

"Doesn't he have that new television cooking show?"

"That's him."

"And did you do whatever it is he's *alleging* you did?"

"What does it matter, Joshua? I just need you to get me out of this mess."

Her attorney chuckled. "Okay, I'm going to put Melanie back on the phone so she can schedule an appointment for you."

Ava pulled her car into an empty parking spot and shut down the engine. "Tell her now is as good a time as any, Joshua. I'm downstairs."

Ava could almost see his head waving from side to side as he spoke. "I declare, woman!"

"Joshua, please," Ava said, her voice dropping to a seductive whisper. "I need you and you promised you'd always be here for me."

"Yes, I did, didn't I?"

"You did and you have never broken a promise to me."

"Ava, you drive me absolutely mad sometimes."

"But you still love me, right?"

Joshua paused, then sighed. "Either that, or I'm as crazy as you are. Come on up. I don't have much time."

The man stood waiting to greet her as she stepped off the elevator onto the twelfth floor. Heads turned as Ava swept ahead of him toward his office, a plush executive suite that only select clientele ever saw the interior of.

As Ava dropped onto the sofa, she pulled the official complaint from her handbag and dropped it onto the low coffee table.

"I can't believe this is happening, Joshua," she said, angst tinting her words. "This is all Ella's fault," she concluded with an obvious pout.

Closing the office door, Joshua dropped down beside her, leaning to kiss her cheek. He reached for the papers and began to read. The first time he looked up at her, Ava only rolled her eyes. The second time she sucked her teeth and glared. But the third time she fumed.

"It was not my fault! Why are you looking at me like that?"

Joshua chuckled. "This isn't going to be pretty, Ava. Did you really…"

"Just make it go away!" Ava whined. "It really doesn't matter if I did it or not!"

"Actually, it does matter. In this situation, the truth is the only absolute defense you're going to have. So, I need to know the truth."

"The truth is none of this would have happened if Ella wasn't such a—"

Joshua interrupted her, his index finger waving in front of her face. "From this moment on, you have no comment and you definitely are not to do any more press for a while. Luckily, I think they want the tabloids more than they want you. We might be able to negotiate our way out but it'll probably cost you something."

"How much something?"

He shrugged. "I don't know. I'll have to meet with his attorney to see if they're interested in dealing. Of course, you won't assume any liability for what happened. We don't want any fault assessed against you, even if you are guilty as sin."

"And you think they'll settle?" Ava rolled her eyes.

"What I think is that they're banking on us settling just to make it go away. As far-fetched as their claims may seem, Ava, they might be able to get a judge and a jury on their side. If I remember correctly, you're not the most popular person with a few of our more illustrious statesmen. Many a government official has a judge or two that he plays golf with on a regular basis and for more reasons than they just like the game. A favor here or a favor there in retaliation for some of the secrets you spilled in your book might make this a very expensive case for you to fight and win."

The man paused, rereading the page he'd just reviewed. He read it out loud, disbelief punctuating each word. "Slander. Interference of contractual relations related to loss of business and clients. Damage to his professional reputation." The man looked back at Ava. "Was it really necessary for you to go on television and boast about your little tryst with the man? You certainly can't deny what they have on tape or that you said what you said."

Ava rolled her eyes, her growing ire steeped in much attitude.

Joshua was not amused as he continued. "We could certainly fight it, but in the end you have to decide which is the cheaper route to go."

He looked back down to the papers in his lap, flipping them quickly. Then he smiled, a wide grin crossing his face.

"What?" Ava asked, looking at him curiously.

"Mr. Tolliver is being represented by the law office of Bridget Hinton."

"Do you know her?"

He nodded. "I do. Very well." He draped his arm around Ava's shoulder and gave her a tight squeeze. "Don't you worry about a thing, Ava, my darling. You don't have anything at all to be concerned with. I promise to make this go away faster than you can blink. You have my word."

Ava smiled. "I do love it when you talk dirty to me!"

The black man staring back at Darwin was small in stature, barely standing an even five feet tall. His outward appearance with his bow tie, black suspenders and wire-rimmed reading glasses belied his intimidating stare, deep baritone voice and his straight-to-the-point demeanor.

Dr. Franco Sinclair was asking him hard questions and Darwin suddenly realized he didn't have any answers. It was becoming more apparent with each passing moment that he really didn't know what he wanted for his life as well as he'd initially thought. Issues the good doctor was raising had never crossed Darwin's mind before and things didn't seem so cut-and-dried anymore.

Unlike his twin brother, Darwin had been a rebellious child, always doing what he wanted no matter the consequences. There had never been any concrete plans where he was concerned, each new day seen as an adventure he only needed to conquer. Occasionally he was simply oppositional for the sheer pleasure of being contrary. And, with each accomplishment, every goal met, Darwin had become complacent, expecting that no matter what the obstacle, the outcome would always weigh in his favor.

Mecan had been as blessed but Darwin always envied that his brother had managed to settle down and find comfort and satisfaction so easily, building an ideal family unit. He'd wanted the same for himself and had just assumed it would come when he wanted it, but he was recognizing that he only wanted it because his brother had it and his mother wished it for him.

Dr. Sinclair's booming voice interrupted his thoughts. "Darwin?"

Darwin shook his head, looking back up to meet the man's intense stare. "Sorry. I don't know. I've never thought about it before."

"Maybe you should. You say you want to have children because that new life will embody the love you two feel for each other, but really, how much of that is just your ego talking?"

"But isn't it a natural progression for couples to want children?"

"Not necessarily. It's unquestioned cultural conditioning that says they should want children."

"But it will also help us to cement our relationship."

"If that's the case then your relationship is already destined to fail. Any relationship too weak to survive the lack of kids probably won't last long or prosper after they arrive."

Darwin didn't bother to respond, still staring at the man, his hands twisting idly in his lap.

The doctor cleared his throat as he rose from his seat. "One of your first steps is to rethink your mind-set. From an early age, we are all told that we'll have children of our own someday. We accept it and just ask how many and when. But if the answer is never, then alternatives begin to have more meaning for us. Life is about choices and when we walk down one path we sometimes rule out another."

"Do you have children, Dr. Sinclair?" Darwin asked.

The man nodded yes. "Two boys, both in college now."

"Would you have regretted it if you hadn't had them?"

"I would have regretted if I'd had them when I really didn't want them."

The two men stood staring at each other as the doctor continued speaking.

"Really evaluate why you feel the way you do, Darwin. Understand your rationale, then you'll be able to make better decisions one way or the other."

"Any other advice, Doc?"

The man smiled. "A wise man once said that having children will make you no more of a parent than having a piano makes you a pianist. Know without any doubts that you really want to be a good parent before you opt to have children." The man looked down to the watch on his wrist. "Let's talk again next week. Same time work for you?"

* * *

Darwin had gone into the studio early, a half mile of paperwork on top of his desk awaiting his attention. For the umpteenth time he'd picked up the telephone to call Bridget and for the umpteenth time he stopped himself, not having a clue what he needed or wanted to say. She hadn't called him, either, so he imagined she was feeling as out of sorts as he was.

Boy, Darwin thought, love wasn't supposed to be so difficult. So why was it he couldn't get the darn thing right? He sighed.

The expression on Bridget's face the last time he saw her was haunting him. Not even a blind man could miss the hurt in her eyes, the pain she'd tried to hide behind her beautiful smile. Not only had Darwin seen it, but he'd felt it also, the emotion drilling a hollow void straight through him. By the time he'd made his way to his own home, the emptiness had filled with a wealth of sadness and loss.

He twiddled an appointment card in his hand between his fingers. His meeting with the doctor had gone as well as could be expected. Their first meeting had been brief, just long enough for Darwin to realize that not only wasn't it going to be easy for him, but that it was something he needed to do for himself.

His brother had been right about him needing to take inventory of his life, to finally settle down and actually take time with the many blessings that had been bestowed upon him. Darwin hadn't realized just how hard he'd been running or what he'd been running from until Bridget had stopped him still in his tracks.

He was suddenly startled from his thoughts when Ella burst into his office, raging like a madwoman on a rampage. Darwin jumped in his seat, his reflections suddenly assaulted by a barrage of anger and hostility. Ella slammed the morning newspaper onto his desktop. An exceptional photo of himself stared back at him. The headline was bold and brief: Chef Cooks Tabloids In Court.

Darwin smiled warmly as he greeted her. "Good morning, Ella. How are you this morning?"

"What in hell do you think you're doing? How can you sue over something so trivial?"

"It's easy. The information they printed was totally false. They were given ample opportunity to retract it and they didn't. Since it's my name they disparaged, I have every right to seek legal recourse. I'm surprised you don't support me."

Ella glared. "Don't you think you should have talked with me first? How do you think the studio is going to feel about this?"

"My attorney has had a number of conversations with the station's legal department before we proceeded. They have no problems with the lawsuit."

Ella's face raged with ire, the wealth of it creasing lines across her forehead and tightening the muscles along her jawline until she looked as if her head might explode. "You went over my head. I can't believe you'd do something so…so…" She stammered, too angry to find the words.

"So, what?" Darwin queried, his own tone even and controlled. "So unlike what you expected? Because you expected that I would just sit back and pretend absolutely nothing happened and what did happen wasn't a big deal? And we both know what did happen was a very big deal totally manipulated by your good friend Ava St. John."

Darwin came to his feet, moving to the other side of the desk to stand in front of her. "Ava St. John will pay for her lies and anyone who helped her will pay, as well. And I don't particularly care, Ella, whether you have a problem with it or not, because we're talking about my reputation here, not yours and not the studio's."

Ella bristled, her mouth opening then closing as she struggled to speak. Darwin's eyes were locked tightly with hers, his gaze just as angry and bitter. Turning from him, Ella stormed toward the door.

Darwin called out to her. "Ella, I don't think our working relationship is working for us anymore. My agent has asked the executives to assign me another producer and they've agreed. I felt it only right that I be the one to tell you first. I'm sure you'll agree that this is best for both of us."

Biting her tongue, Ella slammed the door behind her and stomped back down the hallway. The rest of Ella's day was tense. Darwin had the full support of the station and nothing she could think to say or do could change their opinions. She'd left a dozen messages on Ava's answering machine, but her sister was refusing to answer any of her calls. As Darwin finished taping the last of his shows for the week, every ounce of his magnanimous personality captivating his audience, she could only shake her head, glaring in his direction. None of it was supposed to have ended this way.

Two weeks, five counseling sessions and hours of introspection later and Darwin felt like a weight had been lifted off his shoulders. He took a quick taste of the cream sauce he was making, jotting down a note on the yellow-lined pad atop the counter. Sprinkling just a touch of salt into the mixture, he stirred it, then pushed it off to the side.

A whole chicken rested in a shallow pan in the refrigerator and Darwin moved it from the cooler to the counter where he was working. He stood staring at the raw meat briefly, mulling over his options. From the other end of the room, a low cough pulled at his attention, and he turned to face the young woman clearing her throat.

"Hi, Rhonda. What's wrong?"

"Nothing, Mr. Tolliver. I just came to see if I could be of any help."

Darwin nodded. "Actually, I could use a hand. I'm trying something new and if you'd like to write down the ingredients and steps for me as I go along I'd appreciate it."

The young woman hurried over excitedly. "Not a problem, sir."

Darwin chuckled. "Do you like to cook, Rhonda?"

"I'm not very good but it's fun to try."

"Well, then, we need to get you in the kitchen more. I find it's the most relaxing thing in the world to do."

"Is that why you've been here more than in your office lately?"

Darwin cut an eye in her direction. "Has it been that obvious?"

"I just know you've been under some stress for a while now and lately, when you get here, the first place you come to is the kitchen."

Darwin filled the empty cavity of the chicken with whole garlic cloves, sprigs of fresh parsley and an apple sliced in four quarters. Rhonda reached for the pen and pad and jotted it down, noting how he rubbed the meat with a tablespoon of olive oil before resting it back into the baking dish.

Darwin said, "Cooking helps me deal with the stress."

The woman smiled. "So, what are we making?"

"It's a simple roast chicken with a white sauce but I'm trying to infuse more flavor into the bird."

"Are you planning to do this one for the show?"

"Actually, I'm thinking about writing a cookbook. What do you think?" he asked, looking up to meet her gaze.

'Wow. I think that would be cool."

"So do I. I think a Darwin Tolliver cookbook would probably do very well."

There was a brief moment of silence as Darwin put the finishing touches on the dish and placed the pan into the oven. Rhonda followed his movements, noting all the details she thought would be important. As Darwin wiped his hands on a cotton dishcloth, she cleared her throat for a second time.

"Mr. Tolliver, this might not be any of my business, but…" she started, then paused, suddenly appearing nervous.

Darwin turned to stare at her. "Yes?"

"Well, lately, Ms. Scott has been acting very strange."

Darwin rolled his eyes. "You mean stranger than normal?"

"I mean scary strange. I've seen her watching you a few times when she thought no one was looking and she looked really weird. And yesterday, I caught her stabbing a pile of your promotional photos with a pair of scissors. That was way scary."

"I wouldn't worry about it," Darwin said dismissively. "She's just angry that I won't work with her anymore. It'll pass."

Rhonda's head bobbed slowly against her thin neck. "I hope so. She makes me nervous. I don't like her very much."

Darwin grinned. "Rhonda, I don't think she likes herself. But let's not talk about Ella. Ever make risotto before?"

Bridget listened to the message Darwin left on her answering machine and smiled. She was amused that Ella was clearly chagrined by his actions and she found Darwin's comments almost comical. The man was highly pleased that Ella and Ava would be getting their comeuppance.

Darwin had been giddy with excitement and absolutely oblivious to the fact that he hadn't bothered to call her for almost three weeks. Or so she thought until she heard his second message and the grin across her face glowed like a full moon. He apologized for the distance, for taking so long to realize they could work things out if they truly loved each other. He told her he missed her, was thinking about her and had much he was anxious to share with her.

Maybe Jeneva had been right and all really wasn't lost, Bridget thought. She was hopeful and she fully intended to hang on to every ounce of it.

The next message captured her full attention. She wasn't surprised to hear from Joshua but she was shocked to learn he was representing Ava St. John. He was anxious to speak with her, advising they should be able to settle the complaint easily. He left his cell phone number and asked her to please call.

What Bridget found particularly annoying with his call was the total disregard he had for her. She had heard it in the inflection of his words. Joshua Bayer had always considered himself the better attorney but Bridget was about to prove him wrong.

She laughed out loud, moving from her office to the kitchen. Her man was going to be on television in ten minutes. He was making a meal of wild mushroom ravioli with eggplant and goat cheese, and red snapper à la Tolliver in thirty minutes. She'd downloaded the recipes from the station's Web site and everything, except the onions she needed to chop, was ready for her to cook right along with him.

Joshua Bayer slammed the telephone down against the desk. Annoyance sat like bad foundation on his pale face. He pushed the button to the intercom and summoned his secretary.

"Yes, Mr. Bayer?" the young woman answered.

"Would you please bring me Ava St. John's file, then get her on the line for me. I need to speak with her today."

"Yes, sir."

Joshua heaved a deep sigh. Ava's problem wasn't going to go away as quietly as he'd predicted. He and Bridget had only spoken briefly but she'd made it quite clear that her client wasn't even remotely willing to let this go away quietly. Not only was he seeking damages, but he was also demanding a very public retraction of every statement and innuendo that had been made about him, as well as an apology from Ava, to run in every national publication and media outlet. That and a cash settlement of one million dollars would settle his claim and keep them out of court.

Joshua had thought he could convince Bridget to leave Ava out of it. She had the tabloids on the line and would probably settle her case for a sizeable sum. Both knew the tabloids carried significant media liability insurance for situations just like this one.

Bridget had been blunt about being able to prove her case. The info had been published and Ava had been directly identified as the source of that information. The remarks and comments could easily be construed as malicious in their intent and the media attention had exposed the man to public ridicule and contempt. The man's integrity, virtue and reputation had been impeached and the truth was clearly on his side.

As well, the photographer had signed a statement that he'd been paid by Ava to be there at that precise moment and had been given direct instructions about what was going to happen and what he was expected to capture on film. Even the limo driver had admitted his culpability in the incident. Bridget had just enough evidence to prove her client had been set up and everything pointed to Ava having instigated the situation for her own personal gain, a media ploy to promote her book and further her career. Bridget fully intended to use what she had against Ava unless they could give her something else to work with.

Bridget hadn't bothered to even blink at Joshua's veiled attempts at intimidation and coercion, and his other persuasive efforts had been laughed at. She'd given him an ultimatum and a deadline within which to comply.

The buzzer hummed on the intercom. "Mr. Bayer? Ms. St. John is on line three."

"Thank you."

Joshua's gaze moved to the view outside. The sky was dark, the residue from a morning rain hovering overhead.

He pulled the telephone receiver back into his hand. "Ava, it's me. I can't fix this without giving them something to work with. We need to tell them about that crazy sister of yours."

Chapter 16

Their second breakfast was decidedly better than their first. As Darwin approached the corner booth where she sat waiting for him, Bridget couldn't help jumping to her feet and throwing herself into his arms. It was so out of character for her that even she was surprised by her own exuberance. Darwin laughed heartily as he swung her in a tight circle, pure joy washing over them both.

"Never again," Darwin whispered into her ear as he gave her earlobe a gentle nibble.

She met his gaze as he eased her back to the floor, a questioning look on her face.

"Never again will anything come between us. Never again will I let my fear put any distance between us." He clasped both his hands around her cheeks and lifted her lips to his, kissing her mouth as if he were kissing her for the very first time. He stared back into her eyes. "I love you, Bridget. I love you very much."

Bridget kissed him again, savoring the soft curve of his mouth as it meshed so sweetly with her own. She hugged him tightly. "I love you, too," she said, the beauty of it ringing around the restaurant's dining room.

The small crowd gathered suddenly burst into cheers and applause and both looked around, embarrassed that they had been so oblivious to everyone else in the room. Darwin waved with one hand as he clutched her elbow with his other, guiding her back to their seats.

Their waitress, a buxom woman with an old-fashioned beehive hairdo, stood grinning at them, her order pad and ballpoint pen clutched between her thick fingers. "Congratulations," she said cheerily, her booming voice boasting a Southern drawl. "Are you going to set a date?" she asked curiously.

"A date?" Bridget responded, her gaze moving from the woman to Darwin and back.

"For the wedding. You did say yes, didn't you?"

Darwin laughed, nodding his head. "Oh, she definitely said yes," he answered, his own grin as wide as an ocean.

Bridget could feel herself blushing, color rising from her chin to her brow. She nodded. "The man promised me forever. How could I say no?"

"Well, how about two glasses of our freshly squeezed orange juice to kick off your celebration?"

"And a cup of coffee, too, please," Bridget said.

"Make that two cups," Darwin added.

The older woman jotted quickly onto her notepad. "Coming right up," she said as she headed for the kitchen.

Darwin reached out to clasp Bridget's hands between

his own. He leaned over the table and kissed the tips of her fingers. Bridget smiled at him, a twinge of nervous energy piercing her tummy.

"So, how are you?" she asked.

"Much better now," Darwin said.

"That's good, because we've got a long day ahead of us."

The man nodded. "I'm ready for it, Bridget. More than you know. And you and I have a lot to talk about. I have so much I need to say to you."

"We can get to that later."

He shook his head vehemently. "No. You gave me the space I asked for and I appreciated that. I needed some time to think because there was so much happening between us so fast. I know you had to be feeling the same pressure."

"I think my concerns were a little different from yours, but yes, I was feeling it, too."

"So now I owe you an explanation and some answers. I owe you that and you deserve to know just what I'm thinking and feeling."

"Darwin, it's not like—" Bridget started before they were interrupted, the waitress returning to the table with their beverages.

"Have you decided what you want to eat?" she asked as she set the cups onto the table.

Darwin answered first. "I'm not sure yet. How about you, baby?"

Bridget's nodded. "I have. I would really like two eggs over easy with an English muffin and an order of crisp bacon."

"And you, sir?"

"That actually sounds pretty good. I'll have the same thing and add a side order of your oatmeal pancakes to my order, please."

The woman reached for the two menus that sat unopened on the table. "I'll bring your meals right out."

"Thank you," the two said simultaneously.

Bridget watched as the woman strode off in the other direction. Darwin watched Bridget, waiting to hear what she'd started to say before they'd been interrupted.

Bridget smiled, took a deep breath, then continued speaking. "I understand that what I told you knocked you offside. I expected that. I was hurt that you pulled away from me, but I understand that, as well. But I don't feel like you owe me any explanations. You have every right to feel the way you do. You want children. I don't. And I have the right to make that choice for my life."

"Yes, you do. But it's a choice that we both will be making for *our* life together. I wasn't kidding when I said that I couldn't see myself without you. What I've discovered is that I *can* see myself without children. I don't have to donate my sperm to feel like my life is complete. But I can't even begin to think what my life would be like if you weren't in it. Without you, I can't see myself whole."

"And you honestly believe you and I, just the two of us, can build a future together?"

Darwin nodded and then said, "No."

A look of confusion crossed Bridget's face. "No?"

"No. I believe you and I and Biscuit can build a future together."

She giggled. "How could I forget Biscuit!"

"That's just so like you, woman!" Darwin rolled his eyes at her.

Once again, they were interrupted by the waitress. It took less than a minute for her to deposit their breakfast order onto the table and disappear again.

"Seriously though," Darwin continued. "It has taken a whole lot of self-reflection and some hard questions from my shrink for me to really understand what I want and why."

"So you finally called the doctor?"

"Yeah, and don't you ever tell my Uncle Jake. You know he doesn't believe in telling your business to strangers. He'd have a heart attack!"

"That old adage that we're supposed to resolve our problems around the Sunday dinner table, huh?"

"Exactly!"

Bridget sighed a soft sigh. "So what now, Darwin? Where do you and I go from here?"

"Now, we enjoy our breakfast, get through all this media stuff you've got me scheduled for today, and then tonight—" Darwin paused, leaning forward in his seat. "Tonight, I just hold you in my arms and show you how much I love you."

Bridget was taken aback by the all-embracing gaze that seemed to caress her entire being. The sentiment behind Darwin's stare was so overwhelming that she couldn't help but be moved to tears. Her eyes misted and she gasped, an influx of air filling her lungs. With both hands she fanned her face, fighting not to let the rise of water clouding her eyes fall.

Darwin moved from his seat to her side, sweeping her into his arms. He pulled her to his broad chest and held her close. "Just hold on," he whispered into her ear. "When you need to let go of everything else, you just hold on to me and I'll be right here to hold you up."

"Forever?"

"Always."

Once they got past the apologies, the pronouncements and all the other waves of emotion, Bridget felt as if she'd been reenergized. She barely tasted the eggs and bacon on her plate, all her senses focused on the man at her side. By the time they arrived at *The Morning Show*'s affiliate station for Darwin's first public interview since news of his lawsuit hit the airwaves, Bridget felt as if she were walking on air, everything about her light and buoyant.

Darwin's interview was to be a face-to-face session with the entertainment correspondent, a man of some sizeable girth with two double chins. His cold demeanor when he greeted them belied the jolly manner he portrayed on camera. Bridget sensed he planned to go on the attack and when she had an opportunity she pulled Darwin aside and said so.

"Be careful with him. Don't let him goad you into saying anything negative. We don't want to attack or criticize Ava. We want to build upon your credibility. Make you shine."

Darwin gave her a quick wink. "Yes, ma'am. I'll do well. I promise."

"You'd better," Bridget teased. "Otherwise you're going to owe me a bigger retainer."

"What? You mean you're not going to give me my other check back?"

"Oh, heck, no!" Bridget answered.

"But I'm your man, aren't I?"

"And this is business. I don't play like that."

"Boy, you're hard, woman!" he said with a deep chuckle.

Bridget laughed with him. Minutes later she stood in the station's green room, watching the monitor. The weather, a series of news recaps, two commercials, and then Darwin's face filled the screen. He was breathtaking and Bridget could feel the energy he exuded spilling out over the airwaves.

"We're here this morning with one of Seattle's favorite sons, Mr. Darwin Tolliver, chef extraordinaire! Darwin is the newest food network host who's making quite a name for himself in kitchens across the western seaboard. Welcome, Darwin!"

"Good morning, and thank you for having me."

"You've become quite a staple in some homes. To what do you owe your success?"

"Hard work and an overall love for what I do. I love good food and I love to share good food with other people."

"Well, I sure do like to eat, myself and I had the pleasure of tasting one of your meals." The man grinned into the camera. "That dessert just blew my diet to pieces!" he said with a loud laugh.

"And it was actually low calorie," Darwin said, laughing with him. "I guarantee it didn't bother your diet in the least."

"So why did you take up cooking for a living? Some folks might think it's an unusual job choice for a young man such as yourself."

"Actually, there was a time when it wasn't unusual at all for black men to be cooking for a living. It was quite common to hear a black chef being described as an epicure. These men had skills that surpassed most French chefs. Men, and women, who had the Midas touch with whatever food they prepared."

"Really? Why was that?"

"Because they could create culinary masterpieces that easily surpassed boiled collard greens and barbecued pork. There is a tradition in the black home of preparing exquisite meals served with meticulous care. In fact, the Southern kitchen was one of the few places during slavery where the creative talents of blacks could run free, and in that hotbed of experimentation they excelled."

"I have to ask this question, Darwin, because I know a lot of our viewers want to hear it directly from you. You've had a lot of media attention on you lately. First there was the press about your rendezvous with the author and film personality Ava St. John. And now there's the pending lawsuit you've filed against her and three very prominent tabloids. So, tell us the truth. Was there any truth to the rumors about you *socializing* with Ava St. John?"

"Chefs don't have time to socialize. We're too busy making sure everyone else has a good time to have any time for ourselves."

The man chuckled. "Be honest, now. A good-looking man such as yourself surely has time for a personal life."

"Well, if I do, it would be just that—personal. Nothing I would need or want to share with the public. A man has to have some privacy and I would hope the public would respect that. I'm sure you wouldn't want your private life splashed all over the national media, would you?"

"Unfortunately, I don't have beautiful women like Ava St. John chasing after me," the man answered with another deep laugh. "But back to you. You fully maintain that there was nothing personal going on with you and Ava?"

"Not a thing."

The show's host stared back into the camera. "You heard it here, folks. *Cooking with Darwin Tolliver* airs on your local station Monday, Wednesday and Friday at seven o'clock Pacific time. Let Darwin Tolliver show you how it's done!"

The camera panned back to Darwin as the other man continued to speak. "Darwin, thank you and I look forward to sharing a meal with you again. In fact, I'm hoping you'll give me the recipe to that dessert."

Darwin beamed. "Thank you! It's been a pleasure to be here."

In the green room, Bridget was thoroughly pleased. The interview had gone better than expected. The publicity would serve his case well. It was only a matter of time before Darwin's talents would clearly outshine the public's need for scandal.

By the end of the day both Darwin and Bridget were past ready for some time alone. Both welcomed a few minutes of silence as they returned to Darwin's home. Darwin had moved right into the kitchen to the stainless steel kettle to make them both a cup of hot tea. In the other room the lights were dimmed, a fire flickered hot in the fireplace and soft music played in the background.

The temperature outside had dropped significantly and there had been a chill in the air by the time they'd left his last interview. The session had gone even better than the five before it, but Darwin had grown weary of answering the same questions over and over again, and his face actually hurt from having to smile so much. Darwin knew his signature chocolate tea would be a welcome treat to warm their bodies and their spirits and ease them into a quiet evening.

Bridget dropped down onto the sofa, Biscuit cradled in her lap as the dog snuggled against her. Darwin stopped what he was doing to watch the woman as she cooed at the animal. Eyeing the two of them together brought a wide smile to his face and he couldn't resist laughing out loud.

"You're going to spoil my dog," he said, shaking an index finger in her direction.

Bridget laughed with him, mirth rising from somewhere deep in her chest. "Yes, I am," she said as she scratched his pet behind the ears and rubbed her belly. "Act right and I might spoil you, too," she added, cutting her eyes in his direction.

"You'd better," he answered, moving back to the Belgian chocolate and Earl Grey tea leaves that were steeping in two cups of hot water.

A few minutes later he moved to her side, a tray of assorted cheeses, water crackers and sliced prosciutto in his hand. He sat the tray on the table in front of her, then dropped down beside her, his body resting heavily against hers.

"I thought you might like a snack," he said softly, his energy level suddenly deflating. "When you're ready, I'll whip up something for dinner."

Bridget cradled her body against his, pulling his arms around her waist. Biscuit moved to the end of the sofa and settled down in the corner of the cushion, eyeing both of them curiously before closing her puppy-dog eyes. Darwin pulled Bridget against him, welcoming every inch of her softness to his body.

An easy silence descended over them. Bridget closed

her eyes, content. She felt safe and secure in Darwin's arms, the sensation a new experience for her. As they lay together across the cushions, Darwin's hands dancing a slow drag up and down the length of her arms, she sensed that he was as satisfied as she was, both of them having found that one place that would always be home for them. As if reading her thoughts, Darwin pressed his lips to her cheek and kissed her, allowing his mouth to linger gently against her flesh.

Bridget suddenly yawned, every muscle in her body moving to expel the exhaustion sweeping through her. Darwin found himself yawning, as well.

"Why'd you do that?" he teased. "Don't you know it's contagious?"

"Sorry. I didn't realize just how tired I was," she said, yawning for a second time. "I should probably just head on home."

"Stay with me tonight," Darwin said, his tone just shy of a command. "I mean, you know that you can, don't you?"

"I don't know if that's a good idea," Bridget responded, hesitancy wavering in her voice. "We still have so many things to work through, Darwin."

"We do, but that doesn't mean we shouldn't spend our time just enjoying each other's company. I told you this morning that all I want to do tonight is hold you. Besides, I can't do much of anything else, remember?"

"I remember that the doctor gave you some pills for that problem."

"That he did, but…" Darwin paused.

"What?"

He shifted upward in the seat, turning so that they were facing each other. "But I'm not ready to take them. I need to work through some issues first and then see if things work out without medication."

"Anything you want to talk about?"

"Eventually, but not tonight. We're both tired and I need to understand them myself before I can explain it to you."

Bridget nodded her head but said nothing. Darwin waited and when her silence felt as if it were deafening, he asked with concern in his voice, "You're not offended, are you?"

"No, of course not. I just hope you don't think you have to always pull away from me to work through things that are bothering you. I think we'll have a serious problem if you do."

"No," Darwin said, shaking his head emphatically. "I don't feel that at all. Never again, remember? I'm not ever pulling away from you as long as you'll have me. And I hope you'll keep me around for a very long time."

Bridget shrugged, a demure look painting her expression. "I guess we'll just have to see, won't we?" she said, her voice dropping an octave.

Darwin reached with both hands to tickle her abdomen. "You think you're funny. Don't be playing with my emotions, woman. It could get very ugly around here!"

Bridget roared with laughter, fighting to move herself out of his grasp. The duo fell to the floor giggling, the dog rising to stare at them both. Rolling against the floor, Darwin drew the length of his body down against hers as he pinned her to the floor. He held her wrists captive above her head, his pelvis pressed into hers as he clutched both of her legs between his knees.

Both were breathing heavily and as he stared down at

her, his whole body wallowing in the thick depths of her gaze, Darwin was suddenly consumed with yearning. He dropped his face toward hers, his mouth meeting her mouth as he kissed her, his hunger radiating with intensity. The kiss deepened as he sought out her tongue, sucking the appendage gently into his mouth to savor the taste of her. The kiss lasted forever as he gently nibbled at her top lip and then her bottom one, his lips gliding with ease across hers.

When he finally broke the connection the heat in the room had risen tenfold and perspiration beaded his brow. Darwin eased down beside her, spooning his body against the length of hers. He wrapped his arm around her waist and pulled her taut against him. They stared into the ripple of fire, marveling at the brilliance of the colors that appeared to be dancing in sync with the rising heat.

Miles Davis was floating through the room, the mood of the music a beguiling transition into a memorable evening. When the sun rose the next morning, pushing its way through a cushion of lush clouds, the couple was still sleeping soundly in front of the fireplace, the gas log burning as brilliantly as when they'd drifted off to sleep.

Chapter 17

Ella rocked her body back and forth, her knees pulled up to her chest, her arms wrapped tightly around her. She stared at the formal letter resting on her coffee table, the television station's logo printed in dark letters across the top of the crisp, white letterhead. The president of the company had handed it to her personally, just minutes after he announced her termination; her services were no longer required. The man had cited her problems with their new star as being an issue, the working relationship between her and her peers having eroded beyond repair.

This was all Darwin's fault. She'd been watching him as he'd paraded around the station, soliciting support from everyone who bothered to hear his concerns and offer an opinion about that lawsuit. He'd been confident and cocky, his innocuous disposition turning the tide in his favor.

People had started to question her attitude and behavior, actually falling for his complaints that she should have done more, been more supportive, believing that she herself had caused all the commotion that had cast a shadow of doubt on his integrity.

The man was whining, Ella thought, pouting like a big baby. She reached for the drink that rested on the floor beside her, moving the empty ice cream container out of her way to reach it. She took a big sip, swirling the bitter fluid around in her mouth before swallowing it. Maybe Ava had been right, she reflected, thinking about the initial conversations between them. Maybe she had underestimated the man. His carefree, happy-go-lucky behavior had overshadowed the man's serious nature. His response had been totally unexpected and she hadn't been able to work him around to her way of thinking the way her sister probably could have.

A wave of anxiety cramped her stomach and she suddenly felt nauseous. Rolling onto her side, she curled up into a fetal position against the carpeted floor. It seemed like ages since she'd felt this awful, the trepidation consuming her reminiscent of that one time, long ago, when things had gotten so bad that her parents had sent her away for treatment. They had called it a mental care facility for young adults with emotional problems but Ella knew that it had been a hospital for crazy people. Her mother had thought her crazy because of all the time she spent trying to hurt her sister, Ava, the little girl with big, innocent eyes who was always in her way. The child had been a nuisance and all Ella had wanted was for her to be gone for good.

Ella thought about Ava. The woman still had not responded to her messages. Her little sister had cut her off completely and Ella didn't have a clue what she was planning to do and how she intended to handle this problem. She would have to talk to Ava before it was too late. Ava couldn't say anything to anyone about her participation. "Ava will take care of me," Ella said out loud, taking another mouthful of her drink. "She'd better," the woman continued, saying, "I'm the big sister. She'd better do what I tell her, or else."

Ava moved from her sofa to the television set to exchange the DVD in the player for another. She'd been watching movies back to back, the blinds drawn shut to darken the room as though she were in the theater. She hadn't bothered to shower since picking up the lot of films the night before and still wore the pajamas she'd woken in. The telephone ringing barely distracted her as she waited for the answering machine to answer the call.

Moving back to the sofa, she listened as Ella left another message, screaming at her to pick up the telephone. The screaming turned to begging followed by a minute of silence before the woman started yelling all over again. The night before, after having sneaked past the guard, Ella had stood outside knocking on her door for hours but Ava had refused to answer the door, pretending she wasn't even at home. She knew from the sound of her sister's voice that when they finally did speak it would not be a pleasant conversation. Rarely was anything between her and her sister pleasant.

She'd become too accustomed to Ella's mistreatment, wishing with every prayer she could muster that the two of them could be friends. But instead of getting better, it only got worse with each passing year and Ava was suddenly tired of trying so hard.

Ava reached into her bowl of popcorn, popping a handful of kernels into her mouth. She didn't want to admit it, but Ella's problems were bigger than she could fix by her lonesome. No matter how much she wanted it, nothing she could do would ever make things right for Ella. Her mother had tried to explain that to her the first time Ella had been sent away, but even then there had been no understanding of it.

Ava had vague memories of that time, remembering how distraught her parents had been by what Ella had done. Ava remembered that it had only been a game, one of the few times her big sister had offered to play with her. Ava's father had taken them to one of his job sites and the lure of the big sand pile had been too much to resist. "Play nice, girls," the man had admonished from his desk as they'd gone racing out the door.

Ava didn't remember much after that. Her parents had told the story frequently over the years, how fourteen-year-old Ella had buried her beneath the sand, cutting off her air. It had only been by the grace of God that her father had come to see what they'd been up to, finding his lifeless eight-year-old just in the nick of time. Ella had been indifferent, unable to understand what the fuss was all about, and Ava remembered the animosity harbored in her sister's eyes.

And now, here she was enduring another of her sister's messes. Well, no more, Ava thought to herself. Enough was finally enough and she'd had her fill. First thing Monday morning she would set the story straight. She would tell them everything and hope that an earnest apology would make Darwin Tolliver go away.

She was forever hitting the rewind button on her remote, she thought as she maneuvered her movie back to the last scene she'd actually watched. "Enough is finally enough," she said as she settled back against the cushioned pillows, staring at the television screen that hung against her wall.

Ella was furious when the guard at the entrance refused to allow her to pass. "Ms. St. John is away," he said smugly. "She's left explicit instructions that no one be allowed access to her home."

Ella shook with rage. "I'm her sister. I need to check that everything is okay," she hissed between clenched teeth.

The man shrugged broad shoulders. "I can't help you. I'm sure her neighbors are keeping an eye on things."

Shifting her car into Reverse, Ella hit the gas, backing out into the street like a wild woman. The guard continued to watch her as she shifted into Drive and sped back in the direction she'd come from, tossing him an icy glare before she pulled out of sight.

Ella drove for some time, having no idea where she was going. Her head hurt, a severe migraine coursing through her skull. She had to figure out a way to fix this. She didn't understand why Ava was avoiding her and it made her even angrier to imagine that her baby sister might actually turn against her. Ava worshipped her and she couldn't let anything change that. Ava would surely do what she needed if only the woman would talk to her.

Raging, Ella screamed at the top of her lungs into the cool night air. The man in the car beside her sat staring, a baffled expression crossing his face. Ella stared back, the man reminding her of Darwin and his pretty face. Then she screamed a second time, baring her teeth like a caged animal. She reached for the small-caliber, semiautomatic handgun that rested on the passenger seat beside her. Clasping the pistol in the palm of her hand, she turned to look at the stranger a second time as she pulled the weapon into her lap. The man tossed her a nervous smile, then pulled into the intersection. Ella looked up to see that the light had turned green. The driver behind her honked his horn and she loosened her grip on the gun, letting it drop to the floor beneath her feet. Tossing the driver a quick wave of apology, Ella took two deep breaths, gripped the steering wheel with both hands and made the right turn toward downtown and the television station.

As Rhonda exited the building she couldn't help but notice Ella Scott sitting alone in her car, staring at the entrance door. Ella looked crazed, her hair jutting in every direction atop her head. Her eyes were glazed as her stare skated back and forth. The woman appeared distraught, not her usual calm and collected self, and Rhonda thought for just a brief moment about going to see if she could be of some assistance. The moment passed, though, when Ella's gaze locked with hers and the woman snarled in her direction.

Rhonda was startled by the gesture and found herself clutching her handbag closer to her side as she rushed in the direction of the car. She heard the woman calling her name but she ignored her, pretending not to hear a thing as she got into her car, started the ignition and pulled out of the parking lot.

Rhonda couldn't begin to imagine what Ella was

thinking. Everyone had been whispering about her being terminated from the company and though Ella wasn't one of her favorite people, she was saddened by the turn of events that had gotten Ella to that place. She sensed that Ella was a bit more than disgruntled and Rhonda didn't mind admitting that the woman scared her to death. She'd had more than her fair share of Ella's Dr. Jekyll and Ms. Hyde moments, having borne the brunt of a few too many tantrums when Ella hadn't been happy about something. Rhonda had chalked each experience up to her being the intern, the employee most expendable and usually relegated to all the dirty jobs no one else was interested in doing.

As she made her way onto the highway entrance ramp, she pondered whether or not she should call someone and report her last encounter with Ella. Making her way through the evening traffic, she thought better of it, figuring it was probably wiser to just mind her own business and leave the poor woman alone.

Joshua Bayer stood in front of Bridget's front door. The designer suit he wore fit his lean frame nicely, but by the way he was pulling at his sleeves one would have thought the garment was too small and very uncomfortable.

Bridget watched him for a brief moment, peeking through the curtained sidelights. The man was hardly his usual self, his calm demeanor seeming just a touch anxious as he waited for her to answer the door. She paused, her hand resting on the doorknob as he rang the bell for a second time. She pulled the wooden structure open just as he was having second thoughts about being there in the first place.

Joshua pulled at his sleeves and then his lapels, adjusting the silk jacket around his torso. "You need a proper office if you're going to be meeting with clients," he said in greeting.

Bridget chuckled, waving her head from side to side. "I have an office, but thank you for being concerned. Since I don't plan to make a habit of meeting with clients on the weekends, I'm considering you an exception."

She held the door open wider to allow him entry. As he stepped over the threshold, Joshua leaned to kiss her cheek.

"Good morning, Bridget. I appreciate you seeing me on such short notice."

"Well, you said it was important that we talk. It's the least I could do for an old friend."

Joshua looked around her space, taking in his surroundings. "Very nice," he said casually, pushing his hands deep into the pockets of his trousers.

"Thank you. So what's this about, Mr. Bayer?" Bridget asked, crossing her arms over her chest. She didn't bother to offer the man a seat, so the duo still stood in her foyer.

Josh cleared his throat as he twisted his hands together in front of him. "Ava St. John would like to meet with your client to see if the two of them might be able to resolve this problem amiably. Obviously, I advised her against it, but she's insisting so I'm obliged to ask. I thought you and I might be able to facilitate something for tomorrow. That is if your client would be interested."

Bridget stared at him, her eyes locked on his face, his eyes dancing everywhere else. "We already discussed the terms of any settlement. My client isn't going to change his mind."

"I understand that but as I said, my client is insistent." A flush of vibrant red colored his ivory cheeks.

"Oh, my," Bridget cooed, amusement tinting her words. "Have you been smitten by Ms. St. John's charms, Joshua? This is so unlike you."

Joshua blushed again. "She's a good friend, Bridget. You know how much I value my friends."

"I do, which is the only reason I'm going to do this. But tomorrow's not good. Does nine-thirty Tuesday morning work for you?"

The man gestured with his head. "My office or yours?" he answered, glancing around the room a second time.

Bridget smiled. "Mine," she said, jotting down the address of the new office space she'd rented onto a scrap of notepaper. She passed it to him and he stood staring at it briefly before putting it into the breast pocket of his blazer. He smiled almost shyly as he moved back to her front door.

"I think once you hear what Ava has to say we'll be able to bring this case to a close or at least to a quicker settlement," he said.

Bridget shrugged as if disinterested. "Maybe. Maybe not. In any case, we'll see you on Tuesday," she answered.

Joshua paused in the doorway, turning back to face her. "Thank you, Counselor. I appreciate your time."

"Enjoy the rest of your weekend, Josh."

The man winked, gave her a quick salute, then rushed out the door. Bridget shook her head as she watched him race toward his car. There had only been one other case where Joshua Bayer had known he was defeated. She remembered the moment well when he'd had to present a sizeable settlement check to the opposing attorney, a look of concession painting his face.

She'd proven herself a formidable opponent without stepping into a courtroom and Joshua's demeanor showed her he was feeling it. Bridget grinned broadly as she closed her front door. She was going to enjoy seeing that look on Joshua's face one more time.

Bridget and Jeneva were laughing so hard neither could catch her breath. Roshawn giggled with them, the trio only midway through what could easily be an hour-long telephone call.

"You have to stop, Roshawn," Bridget finally managed to utter. "That's just too funny!"

"I swear you don't have an ounce of good sense," Jeneva added.

Roshawn chuckled. "Well, I don't care what either of you say. I will not cut my son's hair until it's time for him to go to high school and I might not do it then. His braids are just too cute!"

"No wonder your husband is having a fit. It must be driving him crazy that people think Dario is a little girl."

"Angel will get over it," Roshawn mused. "Besides, my child is all male and just like that daddy of his. Give me some time, though. I'll fix those bad habits."

"So," Jeneva said, changing the subject. "Did *baby girl* tell you about her tryst with my brother-in-law, Roshawn?"

"Don't start, Jay."

"Who's starting? I just asked a question."

"I can't believe you didn't tell me," Roshawn exclaimed. "So, you done finally got you some and from a real man, not the battery-powered kind?"

"Darwin and I are enjoying a mutually satisfying relationship that I don't need to discuss with you two," Bridget responded.

"Oooh, that's what I'm talking about!" Roshawn exclaimed. "Give us the details."

"I'm not giving you two a thing."

"Well, at least he's cured," Jeneva interjected.

"Cured? Of what?" Roshawn asked.

"Well…" Jeneva started "it was…well…"

"I cannot believe you!" Bridget groaned. "How did you find out?"

"Find out what?" Roshawn asked.

"Mecan told me."

"Darwin is going to kill him!"

"Mecan tells me everything. Darwin knows that. But why didn't you tell us? You know we would have been there for you."

"Tell us what?" Roshawn interrupted. "Someone tell me something."

Bridget sighed. "Darwin has a personal male problem we're dealing with."

"Personal male problem?"

Jeneva giggled. "It's an equipment issue. His equipment won't work."

"Oh," Roshawn said, understanding seeping over the telephone line. "You're kidding, right?"

Bridget shook her head, switching her telephone receiver from one ear to the other. "Neither one of you is funny. This is serious."

"I guess it is," Roshawn said with a deep chuckle. "I swear, Bridget, if it's not one thing with you two it's another."

"I don't know what you're talking about. Darwin and I are just fine, thank you very much."

"Uh-huh," Roshawn said, rolling her eyes as if the other two women could see her.

"We are. Intercourse does not make a relationship, Roshawn."

"If you say so."

"Well, I do. In fact, I can personally attest to the fact that where my boo may be lacking in one department, he more than makes up for it with other expertise."

"Meaning?" Jeneva queried.

"Meaning Darwin may be penile challenged, but he is definitely not orally challenged."

"Now that's what I'm talking about!" Roshawn chimed.

"Too much information," Jeneva quipped. "I'll never be able to look at Darwin the same ever again."

Roshawn laughed. "I'm looking at him with renewed respect. You go, girl!"

"If either of you says anything to Darwin I will personally kill you both."

The other two women laughed.

"My lips are sealed," Jeneva responded.

Roshawn was still giggling. "Would I do something like that?"

"I mean it, Roshawn," Bridget admonished.

"Oh, lighten up. I am not that bad."

"Yes, you are," Jeneva said with a light giggle.

Roshawn sucked her teeth. "I don't know why I'm friends with you two cows!"

"You did not just call me a cow!" Jeneva exclaimed.

"Yes, she did," Bridget teased. "That heifer has some nerve."

The trio laughed again.

"Well, answer me this," Roshawn finally asked. "Are you happy, Bridget?"

Bridget smiled into the receiver. "Happier than I ever imagined myself being."

"He loves you very much," Jeneva said. "He told me and Mac that."

"I love him, too," Bridget responded, a wide grin blessing her face.

"Well, then all my hard work has finally paid off," Roshawn concluded. "Gosh, I'm good."

"Oh, please!" Jeneva snorted.

"Please nothing. First you and Mac, and now Bridget and Darwin. I'm good, girl!"

"You're a fool!" Bridget and Jeneva both chanted simultaneously.

Roshawn laughed. "I love you heifers, too!"

Chapter 18

Darwin and Mecan sat in a middle pew at Mt. Zion Baptist Church. Alexa slept soundly between the two men, her head resting in her father's lap, her black patent leather shoes and white ankle socks propped against her uncle's leg. Reverend Dr. Samuel Berry McKinney stood majestically in the pulpit preaching the morning sermon. Bridget and Jeneva sat with the women's choir, both draped in flowing white gowns that reflected the prism of light filtering through the stained glass windows and filling the sanctuary.

The family had enjoyed a quick breakfast together before rushing to Sunday school and the morning worship service. As Darwin stared at the colorful appliquéd tapestry that hung over the baptistery, one ear listening to the minister's words, he was grateful for the refuge, the entire morning a welcome balm for his spirit. He also cherished the moment of thanksgiving knowing he had much to be thankful for.

The previous day had flown by, time seemingly lost as he and Bridget had spent the afternoon and evening together. They'd talked, laughed, shared and had just experienced the simple comfort of being by each other's side doing absolutely nothing and expecting even less. Darwin hadn't known how pleasurable it could be to have a woman cater to him as Bridget had, the woman refusing to let him lift a finger in the kitchen as she prepared their dinner and dessert. He'd watched her from the sofa as she'd maneuvered her way around the kitchen, actually surprising him with her expertise.

By the end of the evening they'd shared their dreams, exchanged wishes, and had realized that they could do and be more together than either could have ever begun to imagine. Suddenly his impotence and her convictions about children seemed irrelevant in the larger scheme of what they wanted from and with each other. Darwin had known beyond any doubts that they had surpassed what he had wished for and he had admitted that his big brother had been right all along.

He reached an arm around Mac's shoulder and gave him a hug. Mecan tossed him a quick smile, then turned his attention back to the pastor. Darwin looked down to the little girl sleeping so soundly between them, her father's large palm gently caressing the waves of curls atop her tiny head. He was suddenly overcome with emotion, knowing that he'd been blessed with an incredible family and with Bridget beside him, things would only get better with each passing day.

He shifted his gaze to Bridget's face and met her stare. Her expression was caressing as she smiled at him, joy shimmering in her dark eyes. Darwin's stomach tumbled with anxious energy and he was suddenly impatient for the service to be over so he could make his way to her side and simply hold her hand. As if reading his mind Dr. McKinney concluded his speech, gesturing for the choir to grace them with one last song as he led the congregation in benediction.

Outside, the two men stood patiently, waiting for their women to catch up. Alexa lay against her father's shoulder, oblivious to everything around her.

Darwin grinned. "They must have worn her out in Sunday school this morning," he said, laughing lightly.

His brother laughed with him, waving his head. "I don't know what I'm going to do with this girl."

"What can you do except love her to death."

"So, you and Bridget seem to have worked things out."

"Yeah. I think so. In fact, I want to ask you a favor."

"What's that?"

"Will you be my best man?"

Mecan grinned, a wide smile filling his dark face. "You know I will. When? Have you asked her yet?"

Darwin shook his head no. "I think I'm going to do it tonight. And if she'll have me, I'm hoping she'll want to do it soon. Like next week soon."

"That's really soon."

"I'd marry her today if I could."

"Well, that's not going to happen," Mecan said, rolling his eyes.

"Why would you say that?"

"Bridget won't even think about getting married if

Roshawn isn't here. And Jeneva wouldn't allow it. Those three sisters would have a fit if you even thought about it."

Darwin chuckled. "I know that's right."

Mecan nodded as he shifted his daughter against his chest. "Just like I couldn't marry Jeneva until you were there. It just wouldn't have felt right."

The two men exchanged a look and smiled. Both turned as Jeneva called out Mecan's name, she and Bridget moving to their sides.

"Hey, you," Bridget whispered as she lifted her mouth to his and kissed him.

Darwin wrapped his arms around her and hugged her tightly. The other couple stood staring at them as Jeneva pressed a hand against her baby girl's back.

"That was a sweet solo you sang this morning, Miss Jeneva. Very sweet," Darwin said, leaning to kiss his sister-in-law's cheek.

"Why, thank you," she gushed, clutching her husband's elbow.

Mecan agreed. "You were beautiful, darling. I'm very proud of you."

"Well, I was scared to death."

"But you did it," Bridget interjected. "Who knew you could sing like that. Had the whole church tearing up."

"You sure they weren't tearing up in pain?" Jeneva said with a laugh.

The others shook their heads.

"You know better than that," Mac said. "You were great."

Jeneva smiled as she hugged him warmly. "So, where would you good folks like to go eat lunch?" she said, turning back to Darwin and Bridget. "I'm hungry."

At that moment Alexa lifted her head, looking around as she wiped at her eyes with her tiny fists. "I want macaroni," she said with a wide yawn.

Everyone laughed, shaking their heads.

"Uncle Darwin knows just the place for macaroni, girlie," he said.

Mecan was still chuckling. "Lead the way, little brother. We're right behind you."

Ella didn't bother to slow her vehicle or stop for the security guard at the gates. Racing over the speed bumps, she took the quick left and right turns toward the eastern cul-de-sac, screeching her tires as she pulled her vehicle to a stop in Ava's driveway.

Ava was standing in her front yard, mulling over the new foliage planted by her landscaper when her sister just missed slamming into her garage door. She braced herself for the tirade she knew would be coming and just as she expected, Ella jumped out of the car ranting like a wild woman.

"Why haven't you called me? I know you've been here. How can you treat me like this? What kind of sister are you?"

Ava slowly eased her gardening gloves off her hands. She met her sister's intense stare with her own look of annoyance. "What do you want, Ella?"

"What do I want? What do I want? What do you mean what do I want?"

Ava sighed, rolling her eyes skyward. "Exactly what I asked, Ella. What do you want from me?"

Ella swore, a string of colorful expletives filling the warm afternoon air. Ava looked toward her neighbors' yards, relieved no one was outside to witness Ella's meltdown. She turned her back on the woman, heading toward the rear yard of her home. Ella moved behind her, close on her heels, still spewing venom about absolutely nothing.

Ava was used to her sister's tantrums, the childish tirades when things weren't going her way. Their family had endured them more times than anyone had cared to count.

As they entered the home through the back door, Ava could only shake her head, already weary of what would prove to be a very long afternoon. She pulled a pitcher of cranberry juice from her refrigerator, poured two glasses full, then took a seat at the granite counter. Turning to stare at her sister, she waited for Ella to pause knowing that at some point the woman would tire, take a deep breath and shut down long enough for her to get a word in.

She slowly sipped her drink and waited. Ten minutes later her glass was empty and Ella was quiet, staring back at her sister as she waited for Ava to speak.

"Ella, I love you. You're my sister and I will always love you. But I can't do this anymore. Our relationship is too toxic. It's killing me and I can't…no, I won't…I will not do this anymore," she said firmly.

Ella twisted her face, her upper lip curling in a snarl as she crossed her arms over her chest. "Oh, don't be so melodramatic!"

Ava's eyes widened at the absurdity. "I'm sorry. You've just spent the last half hour screaming at me and I'm the one being melodramatic?" She rolled her eyes.

Ella sucked her teeth. "I just need to know what we're going to do about Darwin Tolliver."

"*We* aren't going to do anything. He's suing me. Not you. *I* plan to tell the man the truth, offer an apology and hope I can settle this for less than six figures. I'm meeting with him and his attorney on Tuesday. Then I plan to take a long vacation away from everybody and try to build a normal life for myself. Maybe even meet a man who's interested in marrying me and having a family. I don't have a clue what you plan to do, Ella. And, since we're being honest with each other, I don't much care." Ava took a long, deep breath.

Ella cussed again, cutting her eyes in the opposite direction. "You're a fool, Ava."

Ava shrugged her thin shoulders. "I have been foolish about a lot of things, Ella. But no more. That's why I'm not doing this with you ever again."

Ella tossed her hands up in frustration. "You can't tell them I planned this. No one can ever know I was ever involved, Ava!"

"Yes, I can, and I will. I'm not going to lie anymore. That's not the type of person I want to be."

The two women sat staring at each other. Before Ava knew what was happening Ella had picked up the second glass of juice and flung it across the room, throwing it against the cherry cabinets with all her might. Ava didn't flinch, having expected some sort of violent outburst from her sister. She didn't move, grounded in her seat as her gaze remained frozen on Ella's face.

Ella came to her feet, moving toward the door. She hissed between clenched teeth. "You'd better not tell, Ava. If you know what's good for you, you will not say one word."

Ava moved to her sister's side. She leaned to give the

woman a quick hug, a teardrop rolling past her lashes onto her cheek. Ella refused to hug her back, standing with her arms locked at her sides, her body stiff and cold. Reaching for the door, Ava pulled it open and held it as Ella moved back outside.

"Don't come back here, Ella. You're not welcome anymore. And please, don't call me. I'm not going to take your calls." She pulled the door open wider. "Be happy, Ella."

Ella stared at her sister, her eyes narrowed to thin slits. As she stormed back to her car, Ava dropped to the kitchen floor, drained of emotion. It had taken every ounce of her energy to get through those few minutes with her sister. Ella always managed to drain her energy and leave her spirit feeling battered and bruised.

She closed her eyes, pulling her knees up to her chest as she wrapped her arms around her legs. She leaned her cheek against her kneecaps, her torso pressed into her thighs. She didn't have any friends to call. She'd invested so much of herself in trying to be friends with Ella that she'd never bothered to build any lasting relationships with other women. She would have given anything to have a girlfriend she could call, whose shoulder she could cry on and who would tell her everything would be well.

There were a few men she was close to who might be consoling, but she understood that it wasn't the same. She didn't think her male friends would really understand the hurt she was feeling over Ella. She didn't understand the pain herself and had no words to even begin to explain it to anyone else. But she did hurt. She hurt for all the things she'd hoped to share with her sister. She hurt for the relationship that had never been anywhere close to what she'd imagined it could be. And mostly she hurt for Ella, knowing that in the end she would be fine and well, able to move on with her life, but that her sibling would probably not be so lucky.

Ava sighed, a low burst of breath blowing over her lips. She stretched her body up and outward, then came to her feet. Crossing over to the other side of the room, she reached for the telephone and dialed.

"Joshua, hello. It's me, Ava. What do I need to do to get a restraining order against my sister?"

This wasn't the first time Ava had told her to go away. Ella had heard it many times before. There was something different about it this time though, she mused. Something she couldn't see in Ava's eyes. Poor, sweet Ava may have actually grown a backbone, Ella thought to herself, remembering the chill she'd felt from her sister's icy stare.

Time would tell, though. On average it would only take a month or two for her to get back into Ava's good graces. Maybe this go-round it would take just a bit longer.

She pulled her car to a complete stop, looking left and then right in the intersection as she waited for the red light to change to a shade of green that she liked. She could still turn this around, she theorized. As long as she could keep Ava from exposing her, she could turn this around. As she thought more about it, she figured some clever manipulation might even help her to get her job back at the television station. Ella's eyes darted from point to point as she talked herself through a number of possible scenarios that would have them all apologizing for their mistreatment of her, begging her back into all of their lives.

Tears streamed down Ella's face, confusion sweeping over her spirit. Even if Ava did squeal, she could fix this. Convincing Darwin that she'd only done it to help him and his career would be easy. She could find the words to convince him just what she'd been able to do all for him. She could show him if she worked it just right.

Ella tightened her grip on the steering wheel, maneuvering her way through the Sunday traffic. A wide smile filled her face. It would take some work, but she could do this. By Tuesday, she'd be on top of her game again and no one would be able to say a thing. Ava wasn't the only daughter who could shine.

Chapter 19

Laughter resonated through the entire house as Darwin and Bridget relaxed on his enclosed patio with their feet up, reclining on his wicker settee. They sat basking in the simple beauty of the evening's sunset. The day's blue sky had disappeared behind striations of gold, saffron-yellow and mulberry, colors that were so vibrant, so luxurious that both knew it was a work of art no earthly body could even imagine creating.

As they lay side by side, Darwin's arms wrapped around her torso, the sun finally disappeared over the horizon, a palette of dark blue and black covering the night sky. The brilliance of sunshine was replaced by a full moon that loomed large and majestic above them. As they inhaled the ambience of the warm evening air, Darwin knew he couldn't have picked a more perfect moment to ask Bridget to marry him if he'd meticulously planned every single detail.

"Would you do me a favor, please?" he asked casually, shifting upward in his seat as he pressed a kiss to her forehead.

"Of course. What?" Bridget responded.

"There's a package lying on my bed. Would you bring it here while I pour us another glass of wine?"

"What is it?"

"Just something I want you to see," Darwin said with a wry smile.

Bridget came to her feet, eyeing him curiously. "Something good?"

He shrugged, his eyes smiling. "Just something I thought you'd be interested in."

Bridget smiled back. "Go pour that wine. I'll be right back," she said, heading inside toward the rear hallway. Bridget was thoughtful as she eased past the foyer to the other side of the man's home. The energy between them had suddenly shifted, renewed electricity coursing through the evening air. She sensed Darwin was up to something but she had no clue what that might be.

As she moved into the master bedroom she could hear the man humming in the other room. An oversize item wrapped securely in brown paper lay in the center of the king-size bed. From its outward appearance Bridget was certain that the twenty-six-by-thirty-inch package couldn't be anything but a new painting for Darwin's collection. Clutching it securely, she moved back into the family room where Darwin stood waiting for her, an anxious expression gracing his face. Bridget rested the package against the sofa.

"Open it," Darwin said, gesturing in her direction. "I'd like to know what you think."

"Did you buy another Holston painting?" Bridget asked as she began tearing at the wrapping.

"No. This one's by John Holyfield."

As the last of the brown wrapper fell to the floor, Bridget took a step back to admire the original work of art. Darwin moved to her side and passed her a newly filled glass of red wine.

"It's called *Soul Mates*," Darwin said softly.

Bridget nodded her head, a wealth of emotion suddenly sweeping over her. The image was extraordinary, a beautiful black couple standing one behind the other in a garden of flora and butterflies beside a body of calm water. It was a wonderful depiction of love and the sheer joy of two people lost in the bliss of each other.

"It's absolutely beautiful," she said, her voice almost a whisper.

Darwin watched as she continued to stare at it. A sly smile crossed his face as she lifted her glass to her lips to take a sip of her drink.

"I was thinking that this would be a wonderful piece for our new home," Darwin said nonchalantly, his gaze focused forward.

Bridget cut an eye in his direction. "Our new home?"

He nodded. "I was thinking we could put it in the bedroom. And, I would like to see the Holston you have and my two on their own wall in the living room. What do you think?" he asked, turning to look at her.

Bridget giggled. "How much wine have you had to drink?" she said, taking another sip from her own glass.

It was then that she noticed the shimmer of white gold floating in the sea of red spirits.

"What…what's this?" she said, stammering.

Darwin gave her a dull look, feigning ignorance. "Something wrong?"

Bridget grinned, reaching two fingers into her crystal goblet. "There's something in my drink."

Darwin shrugged as she pulled a two-carat, blue-diamond engagement ring into her hand. "How'd that get there?" he said smugly.

"Darwin!"

The man grinned, pulling her drink and the ring from her hands. Setting the goblet onto the coffee table, he dropped down onto one knee in front of her, pulling her left hand into his. Bridget pressed the fingers of her other hand to her lips, fighting back a rush of tears threatening to spill from her eyes.

"Bridget, I love you. You complete me and my soul would still be lost if it weren't for your love. You are my soul mate and I want to spend the rest of my life loving you, and protecting you, and bringing you as much happiness as humanly possible. Would you do me the honor of being my wife?" he asked as he slipped the ring onto her finger.

Bridget's head waved up and down as the first tear trickled past her lashes. "Yes," she whispered, dropping down to wrap her arms around his neck. "Yes, yes, yes," she chanted over and over again.

The couple was laughing and crying as Darwin hugged her tightly. He couldn't begin to expound the emotion spinning through him. It was as if every ounce of doubt, every moment of discontent that had consumed him weeks before was slowly dissipating into oblivion. He stared down at her, inhaling every inch of her as if she were the source of all his oxygen, the lifeline that would keep him standing.

Bridget met his gaze, losing herself beneath his intense stare. Bridget could feel her heartbeat quickening, the organ beating fiercely in her chest. The sensation was overwhelming, drawing the breath from her body, and she gasped, every nerve ending from the top of her head to her toes trembling with joy. In all her lifetime she could never have dreamed a moment as perfect as that one. "I love you with all my heart, Darwin," she said, her eyes brimming with joy, her whole face radiant.

"You are so beautiful," Darwin whispered, leaning as he tenderly kissed her on the lips. His touch was a soft, feathery brushing of his flesh against hers, his lips moving gently.

For the first time Bridget noticed the soft jazz playing over the sound system, a seductive saxophone blowing into the room. The tones were sultry and inviting and she found herself being mesmerized by Darwin's touch and the promises that danced against her skin. As if fueled by her own desire, a surge of yearning suddenly swept through Darwin's being as he crushed her mouth with his own, intensifying the kiss. Easing his tongue past her lips and the line of her teeth, he danced in the moist cavity, caressing her tongue with his own.

Time seemed to stop. Without realizing it the two of them moved down against the carpeted floor as Darwin eased his body above hers. Bridget was totally overwhelmed by the blissful pressure of the man's mouth, his touch pure, sensual ecstasy. Moaning quietly, Bridget pushed herself even more firmly against him, blending her body into his as she returned the embrace.

The sensations sweeping through them both were over-whelming. Bridget's nipples had suddenly hardened and she knew that they were clearly outlined against the fabric of her cotton top. They strained unbearably against the material of her bra, aching to be released. Warmth was spreading like ivy through her groin, the familiar tingling sensation spreading through her torso and into her limbs.

Darwin stroked her hair and her shoulders, one hand moving down the curve of Bridget's back to the line of her waist as he pulled her even closer. They both groaned, and again, tilting her head back so she could see him, Bridget stared into his eyes. Darwin moved his mouth back to her lips, tasting how exquisite she was as he sucked the breath from her.

Bridget gasped, breathless, as she moaned his name over and over again against his mouth. As she pressed her nose into his neck and inhaled the delicious scent of his cologne mingling with his desire, she heard herself whim-pering ecstatically. Her mouth drew a slow trail across his throat to his earlobe, lingering as her tongue caressed the curve of his ear and the single diamond stud that pierced his lobe.

Darwin could feel Bridget moving against him as she slowly rotated her hips, grinding her pelvis up and into his body. The heat in the room was suddenly consuming, the wealth of it burning from somewhere deep in both their midsections and radiating flames through every nerve ending. Bridget moaned his name again, warm breath blowing against his mouth as she opened herself to him.

He pulled at her clothes, suddenly desperate to feel her naked flesh warm against his own. The buttons on her white cotton blouse popped as he pulled anxiously at the material to expose a lace bra that contrasted nicely against her dark complexion. His hands danced against the fabric, his fingers gently caressing the protrusion of nipple that seemed to be begging for his attention. He caressed her slowly, his palms gliding like silk over the smooth slopes and hollows of her back, his fingers skimming and fondling her lightly as he explored.

Darwin stared down at her, his gaze dancing with hers. There was an urgency that neither could deny as he pulled at the zipper to her slacks and pushed the fabric down over her hips. Bridget lifted her buttocks from the floor and Darwin boldly caressed and held the smooth swell of her buttocks in his palms, moving his hands over the rounded flesh as he kneaded her with his fingers. A white thong snaked against the deep crevice between her butt cheeks and Darwin pulled hurriedly at the thin string, ripping the garment away from her. Bridget groaned and without a thought, opened her thighs to him, a shiver of sensual excitement shooting through her as he suddenly encountered silken, moist heat.

Rising only slightly, Darwin pulled at his own clothing, tossing his dress shirt into the corner before releasing himself from his pants. Bridget's small hands moved over his chest, gliding down to his belly button, and on to the waistband of his pants. She pulled at his belt, fumbling with his zipper, and her insistence moved him to grin widely. Darwin pushed his denim jeans and his briefs down to his ankles, then shifted slightly so he could kick them off one foot and then the other. His heart raced as he moved back against her, her breasts pressed tight against his chest.

Bridget wrapped the length of her legs around his

buttocks, her heels pressed into the back of his thighs. Darwin immediately felt a deliciously soft warmth and smoothness against his pelvis, the lips of her sex pressing against his maleness. The intimate heat and wetness made his head spin and he groaned loudly, unable to contain himself. "Oh, how I want you," he cried, his words dancing with the music that billowed through the room.

Bridget stared up in complete awe, tears burning against the back of her eyelids. Their eyes met and held, Darwin's gaze a sweet caress that was too comforting for her to express. The woman reached forward and gently cupped her hands around his face, her fingers burning against the curve of his cheeks. She brushed her thumbs over the hard line of his jaw, tracing the tips of her index fingers over his eyelids and the profile of his face.

When he dropped his mouth back to hers, Bridget lost complete control. For some time she writhed and rubbed herself boldly against his body as he devoured her breasts, suckling the nipples and surrounding swell hungrily.

Bridget groaned, her breathing coming in short, harsh gasps.

Darwin moved with her, relishing the urgency, the intoxicating need that was consuming them both. He rolled his hips, sliding and pressing himself against her. He nibbled like a starving man at her neck and shoulders, growling as he marveled as the sweet taste of her skin. In unison, they pressed and rubbed each other with a slow, sensual, undulating rhythm.

"Oh!" Bridget gasped, throwing her head back. "I'm on fire," she moaned into his chest.

She clutched his back, her nails raking the length of his broad shoulders and up and down his torso. Control was lost completely as she strained for release. Darwin's hands burned with each touch, the imprint of his fingers skating over every inch of her flesh. His lips were still locked with hers and she could feel her mouth swelling full from the attention.

Darwin's breath blew hot against her ear as she pressed her face into his neck, sucking against his Adam's apple. "That's it, baby," he urged, continuing to move with her. He stared down at her, moved by the expression of lust that painted her face. "Don't stop. Oh, yes!" he encouraged as he rocked harder and faster against her, matching her rhythm. Both glistened with perspiration, sweat pouring in streams between them.

Bridget could feel her orgasm coming. She closed her eyes tightly, curving herself even closer against him as she writhed beneath him. With a small, gasping cry she froze. Her body suddenly tensed, her hips jerking uncontrollably as short, tense shivers ravaged her body. Darwin continued to move against her, moving her to climax as he held her tightly. She quivered in his arms and with a final shudder seemed to collapse beneath him.

Still lying against her, Darwin lay still, limply stretched out on top of her, then he slid his body over to his side and lay down beside her. Tears spilled over his cheeks, his own swell of emotion peaking. Every muscle and nerve ending in his body had wanted to perform, but performance had once again failed him. He cried, shaking with frustration, and Bridget pulled him closer, wrapping all of herself around him. She pressed her lips against his cheek, murmuring softly. She whispered into his ear, her tone caressing.

"Hold me," she said softly. "And just let me hold you."

Darwin nodded his head. "I'm sorry," he whispered back, tightening the grip he had around her.

"Shh. Don't you dare. You have nothing to be sorry for," Bridget said. "If I can spend the rest of my life just falling asleep and waking up in your arms, then I will know what it means to have found heaven on earth. I couldn't ask for anything more because you are absolutely amazing. I love you so much. The rest doesn't matter. We'll work through it."

Darwin nodded. "I know. And I know things won't always be this way. I'll get my mojo back."

She smiled. "And I know that. And then I can make you feel as wonderful as you make me feel."

"Just being with you makes me feel incredible." Darwin laid his head against hers, pressing his cheek next to her cheek. He marveled at what an exquisite creature she was. Bridget admired the ring on her hand, the symbol of the future she would share with a man who brought her more joy than she could have ever imagined. She smiled as he spooned his body against hers.

Reaching for the throw that rested on the arm of the sofa, Darwin wrapped the cover around their naked bodies. Together they lay content, staring toward the image of *Soul Mates* propped against the sofa's cushions, and outside, the full moon shimmered down over them.

Chapter 20

When Bridget opened her eyes it took a moment for her to adjust to her surroundings, realizing that she was in Darwin's bed, the morning sun streaming in through his large windows. She swiped at the sleep that was threatening to hold her hostage, shifting her body against the warmth of the mattress. As she took a deep inhale, the sweet aroma of baking apples, cinnamon, nutmeg and rich butter teased her nostrils. She was reminded of the apple pies her mother used to bake for her father and a wide grin pulled at the muscles in her face. She lifted her hand to stare at the exquisite diamond that adorned her finger, remembering in vivid detail the previous evening's pleasure and the man's proposal.

She jumped, startled for just a brief second when Biscuit moved against the pillow beside her, leaning to lick

Bridget's face. She giggled, pulling the pup to her chest as she rubbed the dog's belly.

"Good morning, Biscuit," Bridget cooed. "What's that daddy of yours up to?"

Biscuit's tail wagged eagerly, excited by the attention.

Pulling herself up and out of the bed, Bridget moved into the man's bathroom to brush her teeth and wash her face. After freshening up, she searched his bureau drawer for a T-shirt, slipping the white cotton garment over her naked body, then with Biscuit at her heels, headed down the hall to search out Darwin.

The man was standing in front of an opened refrigerator door when she and Biscuit stepped into the room. His expression lightened as he grinned widely. "It's about time, sleepyhead! I was beginning to think you were going to sleep the day away," Darwin said jokingly. He pulled a stick of butter and a container of heavy cream into his hands. He was closing the appliance door as Bridget moved to his side.

"It's all your fault," Bridget responded, leaning to kiss his cheek. "Good morning."

"Good morning. How's it my fault?"

"You know what you did to me last night," she said, color flushing her face. "And you did it over and over and over again. I don't know what got into you."

Darwin's grin widened. "I did, didn't I?" he said, blowing breath against his fingernails and then brushing his fingers back and forth across the breast pocket of his shirt. "A brother got skills," he said with a deep chuckle.

Bridget rolled her eyes skyward. "I don't know if brother was all that now," she said coyly.

Darwin wrapped his arms around her. "Ouch! You hear

that, Biscuit?" he asked, leaning to stare down toward the animal sitting at his feet.

Biscuit yipped, her tail wagging back and forth.

Darwin turned back to Bridget. "Just cut a brother down, why don't you!"

Bridget giggled. "Can't let that big head of yours swell too much now."

She pressed her lips to his, her mouth gliding against his mouth. He tasted like coffee with sugar and cream, a sprinkle of sweet painting his mouth. Bridget was suddenly hungry.

"What smells so good?" she asked, leaning to peer into the closed oven.

"Apple strudel. Something new I wanted to try. As soon as I whip up a batch of butter cream frosting and fry a few slices of bacon we can eat. And your coffee is on the counter. It should still be hot."

Bridget smiled. "What time do you have to be at the station?" she queried as she reached for her mug.

"I don't. I took the day off. We have a lot to do today."

Bridget eyed him curiously as she savored her first sip of morning brew.

"Planning a wedding in one week won't be easy," Darwin mused, catching her gaze.

"One week? You're kidding, right?"

Darwin shook his head. "Nope. Sunday is my birthday and I thought that would be a perfect day to get married."

"But that's so soon," Bridget exclaimed, her eyes widening in surprise. "Are you sure you want us to get married so soon?"

Darwin took a seat on the bar stool beside her, spinning so that they were face to face. He pulled her hands into his.

"Bridget, I have never been so sure about anything as I am this." His expression was suddenly serious. "Woman, you have a hold on my heart that I can't begin to explain. If I don't know anything else, I know that you, Bridget Hinton, will wear my name well. I can't imagine any other woman who could be Mrs. Darwin Tolliver. The sooner I make that happen, the sooner I'm going to feel like my life is complete."

A tear trickled down Bridget's cheek. "I love you," she whispered, pressing her forehead to his.

"I love you, too," Darwin said as he hugged her tightly.

He held her, neither saying a word, and then he jumped suddenly as if he'd been stung by something.

"My strudel!" he cried out, rushing to the oven as he slipped a padded oven mitt onto his hand. "I'm about to burn our breakfast!"

The rest of the morning rushed by. Both were anxious for a brief moment of downtime when Darwin suggested they take a bag lunch to Kubota Garden. Maneuvering through midday traffic, he stopped to pick up roast beef, cheese and a thick loaf of French bread, a pasta salad and two tumblers of lemonade from a small sandwich shop in a corner of Seattle Bridget had never experienced before. From there, the man drove north on Martin Luther King, Jr. Way to Ryan Avenue. One left and two right turns put him on 55th Avenue and into the Kubota Gardens parking lot.

As they stepped out of the car both knew they couldn't have picked a more perfect day. The sky was a brilliant shade of blue, the air was warm and the sun looked as if it had been positioned expressly to shine down over them.

Kubota Gardens was an astonishing twenty acres of

hills and valleys owned by the city of Seattle and maintained by the department of parks and recreation. The gardens featured a bevy of streams, waterfalls, ponds, rock outcroppings and an exceptionally rich and mature collection of plant life. The place was a magnificent sanctuary with significant cultural and historical ties to the community.

Hand in hand the two walked past the bronze sliding entry gate, pausing briefly at the overlook to take in the expanse of the impressive plantings. Flora bloomed abundantly, spatterings of bold, bright color punctuating a deep-green canvas. The setting was serene and tranquil and both could feel a calm washing over their spirits.

"I'd forgotten just how beautiful it is here," Bridget said, her eyes skating over the landscape.

"It's one of my favorite spots to run to and hide when I need a break," Darwin said softly.

"Darwin, I hope you don't ever feel you have to hide from me," Bridget said as she squeezed his hand.

"I might be hiding *with* you, baby. But I will never, ever hide *from* you."

She nodded. "You promise?"

"I promise."

Continuing along the paths, they made their way to the Japanese garden, the most traditional part of the garden with its spring-fed pond and stones that dated back some twelve thousand years left from the last glacier. Bridget paused for just a quick minute but Darwin continued to pull her along beside him. He didn't stop until they reached an area called Fera Fera Forest. He guided her to a stone bench that sat beneath a large cedar tree surrounded by a wealth of blue hydrangea in full bloom.

"Oh, my," Bridget gasped as she took in the view. Her gaze met his and the two stood staring at each other until Darwin leaned in to kiss her mouth. Making themselves comfortable, the two ate in silence, neither needing to speak. The food disappeared quickly and then both settled back against the bench, Bridget resting her head against Darwin's chest.

They cuddled against each other, lost in the ambience of the outdoors. Around them birds chirped joyously in the tall trees and the scent of fresh, clean air danced with the perfumed aromas of the flowers in full bloom and the warm rays of the summer sun.

The quiet was suddenly breached by a child's high-pitched laugh, the toddler running past them as he chased after a butterfly. The little boy's parents were right behind him, both smiling at his antics as they walked side by side. The couple smiled and tossed Darwin and Bridget a quick wave as they continued on their stroll.

For reasons she couldn't begin to explain Bridget felt herself tense, her body stiffening anxiously against Darwin's. The motion didn't go unnoticed.

"What's wrong?" Darwin asked, his voice seeming to echo in the warm breeze.

Bridget shrugged her shoulders, her gaze still following behind the little boy and his family.

Darwin persisted. "Something's wrong, Bridget. Tell me."

"Do you think you might miss out on moments like that if you marry me?" She tossed him a quick glance before turning to stare out into the distance.

He looked confused, his expression asking what she was talking about.

"Moments like that," she said, pointing after the family. She watched as the child's father swept him up into his arms and onto his shoulders, the short length of the boy's legs wrapped around his father's neck.

Darwin stared where she pointed. Then he shrugged. "No. I know you and I will make our own moments."

"But—"

"But nothing," Darwin interrupted. "I'm sure there are going to be times when you and I both are going to have what-if moments or moments of regret. And I'm sure neither one of us will be able to stop ourselves from wondering how things might be if we'd done something differently. But I know that as long as I have you by my side, loving me back, then there will be little in this world that I will ever miss out on."

Bridget smiled, then changed the subject. "Did you know hydrangea are my favorite flowers?" she asked, admiring the cobalt blossoms surrounding them.

"Mine, too, but just the blue ones. That's why this is one of my favorite spots."

"One day I want to have a yard full of them."

"And a rose garden. I love roses, too."

"Really?"

He nodded. "Did you know you can eat the petals?"

"Rose petals? For real?"

"Yep. They can be a nice addition to the right salad or an omelet, and they're great to garnish with. You would be surprised by the number of flowers and plants that are actually edible: dandelions, nasturtiums, pansies, even violets. Can't use too many at one time though. They'll give you gas."

Bridget laughed. "I guess they'd stop being pretty

then." She curled up closer to the man, pulling her knees into her chest as she leaned against him.

"Did you know you snore?"

Darwin chuckled. "That wasn't me. That was you."

Bridget giggled with him. "I don't snore!" she retorted cheerily.

"Woman, you sound like the rush hour trains rolling into New York's Grand Central Station!"

Bridget gave him a playful punch in the arm. "I do not!"

"Choo, choo!" Darwin teased, making strange train noises.

The duo giggled a while longer, then fell back into the tranquility of the peace and quiet. They sat for some time, watching an elderly couple who were themselves watching birds, a middle-aged man practicing Tai-Chi techniques and three teenage girls who were giggling nonstop as they talked fashion and boys.

Bridget broke the quiet. "No one will ever love you as much as I love you, Darwin. Don't you ever forget it," she said softly.

Darwin pressed a kiss to the top of her head and hugged her tightly. Bridget closed her eyes, giving in to the sensations sweeping through her, and she imagined the two of them spending the rest of their lives right there in that space, together and happy.

Chapter 21

The local weatherman had predicted cloudy skies with intermittent rain showers for the entire day. Intermittent didn't begin to describe the swell of water that had been pouring out of the sky since she first awoke. As Bridget stood in her kitchen watching the morning news and weather report, she could only shake her head at the ensuing flood warnings.

Her enthusiasm over the day's meeting with Ava St. John and her attorney had diminished with the previous day's sun-filled sky and moderate temperatures. There was something foreboding about the climate shift with its dreary atmosphere, Bridget thought. When she awoke that morning she'd been tempted to cancel but Darwin's early-morning telephone call and anxious anticipation had dissuaded her. The man was eager to be done with this mess with Ava. Bridget knew that once they settled with her, the tabloids wouldn't be too far behind, particularly if Ava admitted to lying about having had an affair with Darwin.

The previous day had been a whirlwind of things the duo'd had to accomplish and neither could have picked a prettier day to do them in. Bridget was still in awe that by that very time the following week she would be Mrs. Darwin Tolliver, every dream fathomable having come true.

With a good deal of cajoling, Dr. McKinney had agreed to marry them immediately following the Sunday service. Her parents were actually planning to be in town and not away on one of their vacation jaunts, Roshawn would be landing at the Seattle airport early Friday morning, and the Tolliver clan—Mama Frances, Uncle Jake and sister Paris—were flying in on Saturday. The only major details still to be handled were what Bridget would wear and if she needed to buy new shoes.

Bridget wrapped her arms tightly around her torso and hugged herself. Taking a quick glance toward the digital clock on her microwave oven, she dropped her coffee mug into the sink and hurried back up to her bedroom to dress. She had just enough time to shower, change and get to her office to unlock the door. And if she got tangled in a minute of traffic she would surely be late. That definitely wasn't the impression she intended to start the meeting with.

An hour later Darwin was waiting in the building's lobby when she stepped inside. Behind her, the sky had opened just as she'd stepped out of her automobile, soaking her raincoat and leather shoes. She shook the moisture to the polished floors as Darwin shook his head at her.

"Where's your umbrella, woman?" he asked smugly, wrapping her in a deep bear hug.

Bridget rolled her eyes. "I swear that cloud parked itself directly over my parking space and waited for me to get out of the car. I can't believe how it's pouring out there."

Darwin chuckled. "Let it rain all it wants to now as long as the sunshine comes back on Sunday."

Bridget grinned. "I know that's right! It's supposed to be sunny and warm all day Sunday."

"What's happening Sunday?" Joshua interrupted, making his way inside the building.

Bridget cut an eye toward Darwin, then extended her hand to the opposing attorney. "Good morning, Mr. Bayer."

"Good morning. I hope I wasn't interrupting?"

The couple shook their heads.

"Not at all," Darwin answered, slipping a possessive arm around Bridget's waist. "We were just discussing our wedding plans."

Joshua could not hide the stunned expression on his face as he glanced from one to the other. "Well. Oh, my. Congratulations," he muttered, his gaze meeting Bridget's. "What a pleasant surprise."

"Don't look so sick, Joshua," Bridget said as the elevator finally landed, its heavy doors opening widely. She moved inside the conveyor, both men at her heels, and pushed the button for the fifth floor.

"I said I was surprised. Shouldn't I be?" the man wondered. "The last time we talked you had just started seeing someone and now you're engaged."

Darwin chuckled. "What can she say. I was just that persuasive."

Josh laughed with him. "I'd say so." He extended his

hand. "Congratulations. I'm very jealous. She's an amazing woman."

"Yes. She is," Darwin said, shaking the man's hand.

As the elevator deposited them on the upper level, Bridget led both men down the short expanse of corridor to the office entrance. Inside, she turned on the lights and pointed in the direction of the conference room.

"Make yourself comfortable, Josh. Would you like a cup of coffee?"

The man waved his head yes. "Since it's too early for a real drink that'll be fine."

"Just give me a quick second," Bridget responded. "The machine is new."

"Need a hand?" Darwin asked.

Bridget smiled. "Sure," she answered, giving him a wink as he followed her out of the room.

Josh watched them leave, noting the playful gestures the two exchanged. He had never known Bridget to be so at ease, her carefree attitude a nice complement to the air of confidence surrounding her. As he sat waiting he had to rethink his reasons for having fired her in the first place. It wasn't hard to see that he'd made a huge error. He wondered if she might reconsider and come back to work with him, then chuckled under his breath, knowing that he wouldn't even think about coming back to work for himself.

The man glanced down to his watch, wondering where his client was. Reaching for the cell phone in his pocket, he dialed Ava's number and waited for her to answer the call.

The two sisters were standing toe-to-toe in the building's lobby when Ava's cell phone rang. She ignored the chime as she stood glaring at Ella.

"Why are you here? Did you follow me?"

"Someone has to stop you from messing things up completely."

"Did you hear a thing I said to you the other day?" Ella snarled. "Look, Ava—"

"No, you look. I told you before. I've had enough. I have to do what's right for me now. Not what's right for you. You are on your own. Now, I have an appointment to keep. Go home, Ella. Go home and leave me alone."

Stepping past her sister, Ava pushed the button for the elevator, staring up as she watched it descend from the top floor. She refused to glance back over her shoulder, turning only when the elevator doors opened in front of her and she stepped inside. As she hit the button to go up, her gaze met Ella's. For a brief moment the intense hatred and anger gleaming in her sister's eyes threw her offside. The emotion was so intense it knocked her breath away, air catching somewhere deep in her chest. She gasped out loud, even more unnerved as Ella smiled, her mouth bending into a twisted snarl that was anything but comforting. Neither woman said another word as the elevator doors closed between them.

Ella watched until the conveyor reached its destination. She pushed a hand into the pocket of her coat, wrapping her fingers around the barrel of the gun hidden in the lining. Ava had left her with no other choice. She would have to do whatever she needed to do.

Darwin didn't recognize the woman who swept into the conference room, greeting them all nervously as she moved to her attorney's side. Ava St. John, who'd reminded him of an overinflated balloon when they'd first met, appeared to have been deflated, hot air no longer filling her spirit. She was as attractive as he remembered, but there was a different energy sweeping over her presence. Her makeup was as meticulously applied, her hair swept into a conservative bun, and she wore a form-fitting, camel-colored linen pantsuit. But there was no hint of her earlier bravado and arrogance. There was no lingering boldness, no air of irrefutable confidence. The woman seemed almost fragile, on the verge of breaking into many small pieces. She smiled anxiously, appearing almost shy as she acknowledged him.

"Mr. Tolliver, good morning. I'm sorry that we have to meet each other again under such unpleasant circumstances." Her voice was barely audible, just a hair shy of being a whisper.

His head waved slowly up and down. "Ms. St. John."

She turned to Bridget and nodded her greeting. "Good morning."

"Good morning," Bridget said, a formal demeanor washing over her presence. "May I get you a cup of coffee, Ms. St. John? Or a glass of water, perhaps?"

The woman shook her head no. "I'm fine, but thank you."

Bridget gestured toward one of the leather chairs. "Then why don't we get this started."

Joshua and Ava took a seat on one side of the elongated conference table, and Bridget and Darwin took a seat on the other. Bridget directed her attention to Joshua.

"Since you asked for this meeting, Attorney Bayer, I'll let you start."

"Thank you. My client and I are hopeful that we can settle this business amiably. Ms. St. John is prepared to take full responsibility for her actions, as well as make a public apology to you, Mr. Tolliver, for the distress you were caused. She would also like to take this opportunity to apologize personally and perhaps explain how all of this came about in the first place." Joshua's gaze moved to Ava's face. "Ava, why don't you begin?"

"Thank you," she said softly, anxiously chewing on her bottom lip. "Against my attorney's advice I'm ready to settle this any way you decide, Mr. Tolliver. I have no excuses for my actions. What I did was wrong. I know it and I will do whatever I have to do to make amends for it." She paused, taking a deep breath, then continued speaking. "I don't know if I can make you understand why I did what I did, but I'd like to try and explain."

Darwin leaned forward in his seat, resting his elbows against the table and his chin against his folded hands. He motioned for her to continue.

"Everything that happened the night you and I met was planned. I was invited to that event to specifically meet you and try to seduce you."

Bridget jotted notes onto a lined white notepad. "Were you paid for your participation, Ms. St. John?"

"No. No. Nothing like that," Ava said, shaking her head vehemently. " I did what I did as a favor for someone."

"Some favor," Darwin muttered under his breath. He shifted back in his seat, crossing his arms over his chest.

"I'm not proud of what I did, Darwin. I'll be the first to admit that I haven't always made good choices. But I can tell you that I honestly don't think anyone was trying to hurt you on purpose. It just got out of hand and regrettably my participation further aggravated the whole mess."

"Ms. St. John, although we can appreciate your efforts to be forthcoming, you really are not telling us anything," Bridget said. "Who were you doing all of this for? I think Mr. Tolliver has a right to know."

Ava hesitated, her gaze shifting from Bridget's face to Darwin's, then to Joshua's and back to Darwin. She opened her mouth to speak but sputtered, suddenly unable to find the words. The last image of her sister flashed across her mind and she could feel a rise of perspiration dampening her silk blouse. She suddenly felt Joshua's hand pressing against her forearm.

"Ava?" Concern tinted the man's tone.

She shook the vision from her head. "I'm sorry." Her eyes locked with Bridget's. "I don't know if I can tell you who. I thought that I could but…" She hesitated for a second time.

Bridget cut an eye toward Darwin, then turned her gaze back to Ava. "Was Ella Scott involved with this at all?" Bridget asked.

"Ella?"

"Yes. Did Ms. Scott know what you were up to or was she responsible, in any way, for what happened?"

No one could miss the wave of anxiety that suddenly swept up and over Ava. The woman was visibly shaking, her hands twisting anxiously in her lap.

"Ella…she…" Ava stammered, tears burning hot against the back of her eyelids. She closed her eyes, taking a deep inhale of air that she held deep in her lungs.

Bridget moved as if to ask the question a second time when there was a harsh pounding against the closed door. Bridget cast a quick glance toward the two men, then rose from her seat to answer the knock.

"I need to hire some help soon," she said casually, trying to make light of the moment. "Excuse me, please."

Before she'd taken her second step, the large wooden structure was thrown open, slamming harshly against the wall. They all jumped, startled by the abrupt intrusion as all eyes swept to the entrance and the woman standing in the entranceway.

Voices all chimed simultaneously.

"Ella!"

"What the…?"

"Ella?"

"May I help…?"

Just as quickly the room fell silent as Bridget took a step backward. Her earlier sense of dread suddenly resurfaced with a vengeance. That apprehension was manifested in the sight of the gun waving from side to side in the other woman's hand. Everything seemed to spin in slow motion as Ella pointed the pistol directly at Ava's head. The next thing Bridget was aware of was Darwin pushing his way in front of her, using his own body as a protective shield.

"You don't have to be a hero, Darwin," Ella said with an evil laugh. "I'm not interested in you or your attorney."

"What are you doing, Ella?" Joshua asked softly.

"Since certain people won't listen to me," she said as she stroked the barrel of the gun against Ava's hair, "I have to take matters into my own hands. I need to clear things up. Ava here has just made a big mess out of it all."

Ava swallowed hard, her body shaking as cold metal tapped against the side of her skull. "Ella, please, don't do this," she whimpered, her tears beginning to stream down her face.

Ella shouted loudly. "Don't do what, sister dear? Don't fix your mess? Don't protect myself from all your lies? What should I do then?"

"Sister? You two are sisters?"

Ella looked toward Darwin, a look of surprise crossing her face. "You mean she didn't tell you?"

The man shook his head. "No. In fact, she was just telling us that she couldn't expose the person who was responsible. She was taking full blame for what you did."

Ella suddenly raged. "What I did? I didn't do anything, you smug little rodent! I was trying to help you, to help us. If you hadn't been such a crybaby we wouldn't be here right now."

Darwin nodded his head slowly. Out of the corner of his eye he saw Joshua take a small step toward the woman, the movement so slow and deliberate that no one else noticed. "You're right, Ella. I don't know what I was thinking," he said, taking a step to his right side. He pulled Bridget along behind him.

"Don't move," Ella shouted. She waved the gun at him, then Joshua and back again. "Both of you need to sit down. Now!"

The two men exchanged a quick look. Darwin lifted his hands, palms up as if he were surrendering. "Just stay calm. No one's doing anything. I just want to apologize for hurting you. I couldn't see the big picture back then, but I do now."

Ella chuckled. "I'm not stupid, Darwin. You can't fool me. I know exactly what you're thinking. You're just like the rest of them. You think I'm crazy, too."

"No. I don't. In fact, I think you're very smart. It took a lot to plan all of this out. Not just anyone could do something like that. I imagine it takes a brilliant mind to accomplish what you tried to do."

"That's right," she said emphatically. "I had it all figured out and everyone else messed things up."

"You can't blame Ava for anything, though. Ava didn't give you up. Ava was trying to protect you."

Ella rolled her eyes. "She would have told. I know it. She would have blamed all of this on me."

"I don't think so," Darwin said softly. "I can see that your sister loves you very much. She didn't want to see anything happen to you. She was willing to just settle, take the full blame and walk away. That's real love. I have a twin brother and I don't know if he would have done that for me."

Darwin felt Bridget move closer against his body, her forehead pressing against the line of his spine. She was clutching the back of his shirt with both hands, her body quivering against him. He wanted to wrap himself around her, to assure her that everything was going to be fine, but he knew he couldn't move. He couldn't do anything that might spook Ella and put any of them in any further danger. A slap of thunder shook the room as flashes of lightning seeped through the window blinds.

Ella slapped the palm of her free hand against her forehead. "I can fix this," she said, her gaze locking with Darwin's. "I can. I can fix this, and we can go back to working together," she rambled.

The man nodded, smiling ever so slightly. Joshua had eased even closer, his presence being ignored as Ella struggled with what she needed to do. The two men were having a silent conversation, eyes gesturing back and forth. Darwin sensed that it wouldn't be much longer before Joshua could make a move. He knew he had to keep Ella talking, focused solely on him until the man was in a better position to grab for the gun.

"Why don't you and I sit down and talk, Ella. Just the two of us. We can make plans and figure out how to get the ratings up."

"I know they're low since I left. They were only high because I was running things."

"Of course. I know that," Darwin agreed, nodding. "The show couldn't have happened without you, Ella."

"You better believe it. I tried to tell Ava, but she didn't care. She wasn't interested in what I could accomplish. Everything always has to be about her."

"That's not true, Ella," Ava whispered. "I do care about you."

"Shut up!" Ella pushed the gun into Ava's cheek for emphasis. "Shut your mouth before I shut it for you."

"Ella," Darwin interrupted, waving his hands slowly. "Don't pay her any attention. This is between you and me. We don't need Ava. Do we? Ava's clearly not as intelligent as you are."

Ella nodded. "That right. Her daddy always thought she was so special, but she wasn't. Always the center of attention, making people like her. Well, they'll see. They'll see that she's not special at all."

"That's right," Darwin continued. "We can make them all see that you're the one who's special. Very special."

Ella smiled, the harsh lines punctuating her expression suddenly softening. "I knew I could do this. I knew it."

Darwin smiled back. "Now would be as good a time as any," he said, staring Joshua straight in the eye.

Ella suddenly looked confused. "What?"

In that moment, Joshua grabbed for the gun, both hands clasped around Ella's clenched fist. Darwin rushed forward, using his own momentum to help knock the woman to the ground.

Ava jumped out of the way, rushing to the corner of the room. Bridget lunged for the telephone on the tabletop as the two men struggled with Ella on the floor. Just as she reached the receiver, a round of gunshots rang out through the room, the harsh noise followed by the muffled sound of metal striking flesh and bone, and a man's pitying scream.

Like snapshots rolling across a screen, Bridget looked to see the gun lying on the floor, Ella's limp body subdued beneath Joshua, and Darwin, sitting back on his haunches as he stared down toward his chest, blood splaying across his shirt. A crimson-red circle of dampness was spreading outward, forming an intricate pattern against the cotton fabric. Darwin's expression was a montage of disbelief and hurt, and then he looked up to meet her gaze, his mouth bending into an easy smile before he lost consciousness.

Chapter 22

There was an eerie silence sweeping through the sanctuary of Mt. Zion Baptist Church. Jeneva and Roshawn stood at Bridget's side, moisture flowing down all of their faces. Above them sunlight was streaming in bold striations through the stained glass windows, the weather a striking contrast to the days before. From one of the rear pews someone could be heard sniffling, the moment having moved the entire congregation to tears.

Mrs. Frances Tolliver sat in the first pew with her daughter, Paris, on one side and her late husband's brother, Jake Tolliver, on her other side. Behind them a host of family and friends filled the church. Everyone was overwhelmed. Mama Frances knew each of her children well, having had many conversations over the years about their dreams and expectations. She'd imagined many a moment for her offspring, but this event had not been one she would have expected for her youngest male child. She knew it was a time her child had even doubted having for himself. She looked toward her eldest son and smiled, Mecan meeting his mother's gaze with one of his own. He could almost see what the matriarch was thinking and he grinned broadly, his head bobbing ever so slowly. He turned his attention back to the minister.

Darwin sat in a wheelchair at Bridget's side, his head bowed in prayer, and his brother standing on his other side. When the pastor concluded the benediction, a loud amen ringing through the church, Darwin lifted his gaze back to Bridget's. The minister had touched them with his dedication, reminding them just how blessed they each were. Darwin, in particular, knew he had much to be thankful for. He looked down at the cast and sling on his left arm, feeling the tension of bandages that bound his torso. The bullets had torn through muscle and cracked bone, narrowly missing his heart and his lungs. Over eight hours of surgery and two weeks in intensive care had shed new light on the life and love he wanted for himself. His family had spent hours at his bedside, never once doubting that he would pull through, even when he himself wasn't quite so sure.

But here he was, just hours out of the hospital, alive and well, and with his friends, his family and an almighty God to declare his undying love for the woman beside him. In anticipation of the pastor's permission, he pulled Bridget down to him, reaching to kiss her mouth.

Dr. McKinney scolded him teasingly. "Did I say you could kiss the bride, young man?"

The whole room chuckled as Darwin smiled sheepishly.

"Okay. Now you may kiss your bride," the man said, tossing him a quick wink of his eye.

A round of applause and cheers erupted through the church as she leaned toward him, wrapping her arms around his neck and shoulders. Bridget hugged him tightly and both could hear her friends cheering them in the background.

A short while later, both Bridget and his mother were fussing over him as he sat against his living room sofa. It was a very nontraditional reception, an intimate gathering of his family and closest friends that filled their home to celebrate his recovery and their marriage.

"You need to be in bed," Mama Frances scolded softly. "You need your rest, Darwin."

Bridget nodded in agreement. "You should listen to your mother, honey."

Darwin rolled his eyes. "You women won't let me have any champagne…"

"No alcohol with that medication you're on. The doctor was very insistent," Bridget interrupted.

"…and now you want to send me to bed. Alone. What kind of wedding celebration is this?"

Bridget blushed. "I can't believe you!"

Mecan chuckled. "Believe it. He's always been a difficult patient."

Mama Frances nodded. "Both of you were. Couldn't get one of 'em to do what they were supposed to do. Lost count of the times their daddy and Jake had to use a switch."

"I'm too big for switches now," Darwin chimed.

"Won't take no bets on that if I was you," Uncle Jake interjected. "Yo' mama will wear your tail out if she has to. Don't think she won't. You might be grown but you still her child and Frances don't play like that."

Mecan and Paris laughed.

"We wouldn't test that if we were you." Paris giggled.

Mama Frances fanned her hand at the trio. She turned her attention to Bridget. "Don't you pay them kids of mine no attention. And if you need to take a switch to this one, I've got one with his name on it that you can use."

Everyone in the room broke out laughing.

Darwin leaned his head on his mother's shoulder. He made a coughing sound in his throat, patted his chest and then said in a child's singsong voice, "Mama?"

"What, baby?" Mama Frances asked, concern rising in her voice.

"Can I at least have me some wedding cake first?" he asked, batting his eyelashes at the woman. "Please?"

"Of course, suga'!" she chimed, jumping to her feet. "You have to eat some food first though. Let mama go fix you a plate."

As Mama Frances rushed into the kitchen, Darwin winked at his brother.

Paris shook her head. "I swear. Only you and Mac could get away with that."

Bridget laughed. "Just as long as you know you can pull that with your mother, but don't try it with me."

Darwin chuckled as the woman reached to kiss his mouth, drawing her fingers in a light caress across his cheek.

Conversation danced hand in hand with laughter throughout the home. Bridget moved from room to room, checking on each guest and periodically moving back to Darwin's side to insure all was well with him. Her parents sat out on the patio in deep conversation with her new mother-in-law, the two families bonding nicely. Outside in the yard, Mecan, Uncle Jake and Roshawn's husband, Angel, tossed a football around with the children, the men playing as if they were children themselves. Paris stood in deep conversation with Rhonda and Darwin's new producer, a tall man with a head of fire-engine-red hair and a smile as deep as the Grand Canyon. In the kitchen, Jeneva and Roshawn huddled around the kitchen table, whispering and giggling as though they didn't speak on the telephone every other day for hours on end.

Bridget joined them, dropping down onto one of the padded kitchen chairs. She grinned as both women reached out to hold her hands, the gesture a bond of their lifelong friendship.

"So, how are you doing, kiddo?" Roshawn asked.

Bridget nodded. "I couldn't be happier," she said, breathing a low sigh of relief.

"You had us worried there for a while," Jeneva said.

"I had myself worried," the woman admitted. "If anything had happened to Darwin…"

Roshawn squeezed her hand. "Don't think about it. Brother is doing just fine now. We just thank God that both of you are okay."

"Amen," Jeneva added.

"So, is that woman behind bars for good now?" Roshawn asked.

Bridget nodded. "She's been transferred to a high-risk mental care facility. She's clearly not competent to stand trial and might not be for a very long while."

"Did you see the full-page ad her sister placed in the newspaper?" Jeneva asked, her eyes resting on Roshawn.

"Not yet."

"It was a public letter of apology. Definitely not something you would see every day."

Bridget smiled. "The woman is actually quite impressive. A very classy lady. I think she'll come out of this quite well and she and Darwin were able to settle to his satisfaction."

"How much did he milk her for?" Bridget asked, leaning her head against her hand.

Jeneva rolled her eyes. "I swear, Roshawn!"

The woman flicked her tongue out. "Don't pretend like you didn't want to know."

Bridget laughed. "I'm not at liberty to disclose any specific details but let's just say there will be a number of students for the next few years who'll be able to pay their way through culinary school courtesy of the Darwin Tolliver Scholarship fund. And the tabloids have officially settled, as well."

"Was it millions?" Roshawn queried.

"Well, let's just say if I keep on winning cases like this one, the law offices of Bridget H. Tolliver will be one of the most sought-after firms in the state."

"That's what I'm talking about!"

Jeneva laughed as they changed the subject. "Are you and Darwin planning to take a honeymoon?" she asked.

Bridget nodded. "He wants to go home to Shreveport for a few days, then we're going to take a cruise."

"Very nice."

"Uh, you always know you can come to Phoenix, don't you?" Roshawn asked.

Bridget wrapped an arm around her friend's shoulder. "You really miss me, don't you?"

"Don't let it go to your head," Roshawn said with a deep laugh.

A commotion in the other room pulled at Bridget's attention. She came to her feet and moved to see what was going on. Darwin was stretched out on the sofa, baby Belinda resting against his chest. Dario and Alexa were playing a game of tag around the sofa. Bridget stood in the doorway, her arms crossed over her chest as she watched them.

Darwin grinned as he met her gaze, acknowledging her with a slight nod of his head. She smiled back. Before she could say anything Mama Frances came rushing into the room.

"Lord, have mercy! You babies get out in that yard with that running. You know better. Alexa, Dario, you two come on with Mama Frances and let Uncle Darwin get some rest. Uncle Jake is gone take you babies to get some ice cream. Jake!"

Bridget and Darwin both laughed.

Mama Frances shook her index finger at one and then the other. "You two don't need to be letting these children run wild in the house. Don't be starting no bad habits they gone take home. I'm the only one allowed to do that," she said as she reached down and took the baby out of Darwin's arms. "Bridget, go put your husband to bed before we have to take him back to that hospital. I'm not in any mood to be spending no more time in that hospital."

Bridget nodded. "Yes, ma'am."

They watched as she made her way back outside. As

his mother closed the door firmly behind her, Darwin's eyes moved back to his wife's face. His heartbeat seemed to race as he sat up in his seat, staring at her. Everything about the woman warmed his soul.

She'd been an exquisite bride, a breathtaking beauty, as she'd come walking down the aisle in his direction. Her dress had been off-white, a calf-length design, sleeveless with a simple V-neck. It had been beautiful against her rich complexion and she had been prettier than any picture imaginable. But it had been the look of excited anticipation that had hit him like a sledgehammer. Her eyes had locked with his and in that instant he swore he could read every thought, wish and want that dressed her spirit. The longing shimmered in her dark eyes and she glowed with pure joy. In that moment, he had felt his heart beating in his chest, an unadulterated syncopation that he was certain was beating in unison with hers.

After the shooting Bridget had refused to leave his side. Even during his surgery there had been an acute awareness of her presence and her prayers. The sense that she was near and concerned. It was many days later when he'd learned just how frightened she had been. He'd awakened to find her sleeping upright in a chair beside his bed and only when he spoke her name and had made a joke about missing his birthday and leaving her waiting at the altar did he see a visible blanket of relief wash over her.

He had no doubts about her love for him. Every ounce of her emotion was visible in the way she looked at him and the tone of her words. Bridget loved him beyond reason and he loved her just as much and more.

As he sat staring at her a sudden wave of heat rushed

from the top of his head down to his toes. An electrical current of energy seemed to surge with full force, igniting every fiber of his being. His eyes suddenly widened, sheer delight blessing his expression, and he found himself laughing out loud, his enthusiasm punctuating the quiet in the room.

"Are you all right?" Bridget asked, eyeing him curiously. "What's so funny?"

Darwin nodded enthusiastically. "Oh, baby! I'm better than all right," he exclaimed gleefully.

He pushed himself up with his good arm, moving onto his feet. Crossing the room, he kissed her mouth, still chuckling excitedly.

"Darwin, what's going on?" Bridget asked, amusement painting her expression.

Darwin ignored her question, peeking over her shoulder into the kitchen. "Ladies, I need to steal my wife away for a few minutes, please," he said, tossing Roshawn and Jeneva a wink.

"Keep her!" Roshawn chimed.

"We'll hold the fort," Jeneva responded.

He grabbed Bridget's hand and pulled her along behind him. At that moment Mecan and Mama Frances came through the patio door.

"What are you doing up?" Mama Frances scolded. "You're supposed to be resting!"

Darwin grinned. "I know, Mama. I'm going up to bed right now. Bridget's going to tuck me in."

"It's about time," his mother said, reaching to kiss his cheek. "Bridget, baby, you stay with him till he falls asleep, please. Otherwise, he'll be right back down here getting into trouble."

"She will, Mama," Darwin said, answering for her. "I'm not letting her leave me. In fact, you folks stay as long as you want and lock the doors on your way out. We will see you tomorrow sometime."

"Okay, baby," Mama Frances said. She leaned to give Bridget a kiss and hug, as well.

Mecan met his brother's eye. "If you need anything just let us know. Okay, little brother?"

Darwin's grin widened. "I've got this handled, big brother," he said. "You folks have a safe trip home," he said hurriedly as he headed for the stairs.

In the privacy of the bedroom, Darwin closed and locked the door. Bridget moved across the room and pulled back the bedspread. She looked toward Darwin, who was still standing in the center of the room, his mile-wide smile beaming at her.

"What's going on with you?" she asked again, her hands moving to her hips. "Why do I get the feeling you're up to something?"

Darwin laughed. "Oh, baby, baby. I'm definitely up!"

"What are you talking about?" Bridget asked curiously. "You're not making any sense."

"Come here," Darwin said, beckoning with his index finger.

She moved to his side. "Do you need help?"

He nodded, reaching for her hand. "I need you," he said suggestively, his voice deepening an octave as he pressed her palm to the front of his slacks. He stared into her eyes, his face shimmering with excitement.

Bridget's eyes widened as her fingers wrapped around pulsating steel. "Does this mean…" She stared, suddenly giggling with him.

"I think my problem done fixed itself," Darwin said, moving closer against her. He closed his eyes, his head falling back against his shoulders as Bridget stroked the length of a very heavy erection.

"Oh, yes," he moaned, pleasure searing through his nerve endings. "I am definitely fixed."

Bridget wrapped her arms around his neck and kissed him hungrily, her tongue snaking its way past the line of his teeth to dance against his. Darwin felt himself harden even more, every muscle quivering with anticipation. He pulled his mouth from hers.

"I need a hand out of these clothes," he whispered huskily, pulling at his belt buckle.

"But what about your bandages," Bridget said hesitantly, a wave of concern crossing her face. "Maybe we should wait until after you go back to see the doctor."

Darwin pressed his pelvis back against her. "Woman, if you don't make love to me right this minute, I will probably pass out from cardiac arrest. Don't you make me call my mother up here, 'cause I will tell on you. What kind of wife will leave a man hanging on his wedding night?"

Bridget laughed. "Somehow, I don't think your mother would be too unhappy with me. You are supposed to be resting, or did you forget?"

Darwin laughed with her. He dropped his belt to the floor, pulling at his zipper. "Bridget, don't tease me. I want you so badly I'm about to explode right here. Baby, I'm hurting!"

Bridget grinned, reaching for the buttons on his dress shirt. "Well, I guess we're going to have to do something about your pain then," she said coyly. She planted a damp kiss against his neck, drawing a slow trail up to his earlobes, across his cheeks and back to his mouth.

Darwin moaned again, wanting blowing past his parted lips.

"Does it hurt?" Bridget whispered.

He nodded. "Oh, yes! Make it feel better," he said, his eyes still closed as he moved against the edge of the bed to sit down.

Bridget cupped his cheeks between her palms and kissed his mouth again. "Does that feel better?" she asked.

"It still hurts," Darwin muttered as he lay back against the mattress.

She kissed and licked one nipple and then the other. "How about now?"

He shook his head. "Still hurts."

Bridget dipped her tongue into the crevice of his belly button. Darwin inhaled swiftly.

"Oh, oh, oh! That's good medicine," he whispered back.

Bridget giggled as she pulled away from him.

Darwin opened his eyes, staring up at her. "Don't stop," he said, his eyes pleading. "Why are you stopping?"

Bridget laughed, waving her head from side to side. "Too much medicine is not good for you either, Darwin."

He sat up on his good elbow, his mouth hanging open. Bridget's face was buoyant, laughter spilling past her eyes. She reached for the waistband of his slacks, mischief shining in her expression.

"Lay back," she commanded, easing him back to the bed. Slowly and deliberately, she pulled at the zipper to her dress. Darwin watched as she let the garment fall into a puddle on the floor. She stood in matching bra and panties, silk and lace meant to be tempting. Her fingers rested against the lean line of her hips as she gently eased her body over his.

"Now," she said sternly. "I will only do this if you promise that you will tell me if we start bothering any of your injuries. I'm not taking you back to the hospital to have to tell them you were reinjured trying to make love to your wife."

"I promise," Darwin said eagerly.

Bridget smiled, easing her hands back into his pants. "Good, then it's my turn to take you to heaven, Mr. Tolliver."

Rhonda poked her head into the office. "Mr. Tolliver, is everything okay?"

"Rhonda, girl, we're cooking with grease now! Life doesn't get any better than this."

"We're really glad to have you back, sir," the young woman said as she moved into the room. She ventured to speak for all the staff. "Everyone missed you."

"I missed you all, as well," the man answered.

"And he missed being able to cook," Bridget said from her seat on the sofa. "The minute he started to complain about my cooking I knew he was getting better and it was time to send him back to work."

"Don't believe her," Darwin chuckled. "I have never complained about her cooking."

Bridget nodded her head vigorously. "Oh, yes, he did," she mouthed to Rhonda.

Rhonda laughed.

Darwin dropped down to the seat beside his wife and gave her a quick tickle. Bridget laughed as she wiggled out of his reach. "Stop! You play too much." She giggled, jumping to her feet.

Darwin crossed both arms over his chest and pretended to pout. "I swear. A man doesn't stand a chance with you women. This has to be abuse," he said as he stood back up.

Bridget rolled her eyes. "I have to go to work. I'm due in court at ten-thirty." She wrapped her arms around his waist and kissed his cheek. "I will see you later."

"Good luck today," Darwin said, hugging her back.

Bridget tossed Rhonda a quick wave. "Call me if he starts acting up," she said teasingly.

Rhonda waved back. "I will. Bye, Mrs. Tolliver."

She and Darwin both watched as Bridget made her way out of their sight before resuming their conversation.

"So, did you enjoy your cruise?" Rhonda asked, moving to collect a stack of files from Darwin's desk.

He grinned. "We had a great time. Perfect weather, great company and incredible food. As soon as Bridget prints out the photos from the digital camera I'll make sure to bring them for you to see. So, what's on my schedule?" Darwin asked, changing the subject.

"The set director wants you to inspect the new kitchen and give it your okay. I need this week's food lists and recipes for the Web site administrator by tomorrow. You have a two o'clock meeting with the producers, and—"

"I get it!" Darwin exclaimed, interrupting. "I've got a full day."

"Yes, sir, you do," the woman said with a shy smile. She moved back toward the door, pausing in the entrance. She motioned as if to speak, then hesitated.

Darwin nodded his head as if reading her mind. "Somewhere in that schedule, Rhonda, pencil in an hour for us to do some cooking. In fact, that's the best way for me to evaluate the new kitchen. I do have a cookbook to finish, remember?"

Rhonda beamed. "Yes, sir, Mr. Tolliver," she said, closing the door behind her as she exited the room.

Back behind his desk, Darwin reached into his brief-case and pulled a framed wedding photo of him and Bridget into his hands. Staring down at the image, he found himself grinning from ear to ear, joy like he'd never known before washing over his spirit. He placed the picture on his desktop, still admiring the reflection staring back at him. As he took a look around the office, the ice-blue room suddenly felt exactly like home.

He smiled, reaching for his cell phone, hoping he could catch Bridget before she reached the courthouse. She answered on the second ring.

"Everything okay?" she asked.

"I was just missing you," Darwin answered, crossing his right arm over his left. He could feel her smile flowing over the telephone line.

"I miss you, too, honey."

"I just wanted to tell you I love you," he said, conviction punctuating each word.

"Are you sure about that?" Bridget teased. "You might change your mind."

Darwin chuckled. "Never. Woman, I will love you always."

On the other end, Bridget nodded. "I'll take always," she said.

Darwin chuckled. "You do know that always means forever, don't you?"

"That's the only way I'll take it."

Without another word, Bridget disconnected the line. Darwin leaned back in his chair, his hands clasped behind his head as he pulled his feet up on the desktop and settled in, a wide grin flooding warmth throughout the room.

His TEMPEST

Favorite author

Candice Poarch

To gain her birthright, Noelle Greenwood assumes
a false identity and plays a risky game of seduction
with Colin Mayes. But when her feelings become
too real, the affair spirals out of control.
Then Colin discovers the truth....

*Available the first week of June
wherever books are sold.*

www.kimanipress.com

KPCP0200607

Can she handle the risk...?

daring
devotion

ELAINE OVERTON

Author of FEVER

Andrea Chenault has always believed she could live
with the fear every firefighter's wife knows. But as her
wedding to Calvin Brown approaches, she's tormented
by doubts as several deadly fires seem to be targeting
the man she loves.

*Available the first week of June
wherever books are sold.*

KIMANI
ROMANCE
™

www.kimanipress.com

KPE0220607

Love is always better...

The Second Time Around

Angie Daniels

Visiting her hometown, Brenna Gathers runs into
Jabarie Beaumont, the man who jilted her at the altar
years ago. Convinced by his father Brenna was a
gold digger, Jabarie never got her out of his system.
Now he's on a mission to win Brenna's heart
a second time.

*Available the first week of June
wherever books are sold.*

KIMANI
ROMANCE™

KPAD0100607

From five of today's hottest names
in women's fiction...

CREEPiN'

Superlative stories of paranormal romance.

MONICA JACKSON
& FRIENDS

Alpha males, sultry beauties and lusty creatures confront
betrayal and find passion in these super sexy tales of the
paranormal with an African-American flavor.

**Featuring new stories by
L.A. Banks, Donna Hill, J.M. Jeffries,
Janice Sims and Monica Jackson.**

Coming the first week of June
wherever books are sold.

KIMANI PRESS™

www.kimanipress.com   KPMJ0600607

Acclaimed author

Adrianne Byrd

BlueSkies

Part of Arabesque's At Your Service military miniseries.

Fighter pilot Sydney Garret was born to fly.
No other thrill came close—until Captain James Colton
ignited in her a reckless passion that led to their short-
lived marriage. When they parted, Sydney knew fate
would somehow reunite them. But no one imagined it
would be a matter of life or death....

"Byrd proves once again that she's
a wonderful storyteller."
—*Romantic Times BOOKreviews* on
THE BEAUTIFUL ONES

Coming the first week of June
wherever books are sold.

ARABESQUE®

www.kimanipress.com

KPAB0120607